THE DUKE SHE MARRIED

JESSIE CLEVER

SOMEDAY LADY PUBLISHING, LLC.

THE DUKE SHE MARRIED

Published by Someday Lady Publishing, LLC

Copyright © 2022 by Jessica McQuaid

ISBN-13: 979-8-9852018-6-4

Edited by Judy Roth

For all those who love the smell of a new book

CHAPTER 1

*S*he knew what she was supposed to fear.

But as she huddled inside the carriage, rocked by the ferocious storm that had set upon them some miles back, she knew she didn't fear what everyone might assume.

She didn't fear the rumors about her soon-to-be husband, the ones that called him the Ghoul of Greyfair.

It was marriage itself she feared because the neglect and criticism she had faced in her childhood had taught her that relationships of any kind were not safe, and she was about to enter into the most perilous one of all.

Marriage.

She had left her family's home in Mayfair three days previously, knowing she must journey to the outermost reaches of Kent, but never suspecting the weather would turn so foul so near her journey's end as if sensing her fear and attempting to compound it.

Now as the carriage rattled with achingly slow progress over the uneven roads, rutted now as everything turned to mud in the deluge, she tried to recall the feel of each of her sisters' hugs. Their sturdy arms wrapped around her, their familiar scents. The feel of Alice's spectacles pressed against her cheek. The crackle of Adaline's braid along her ear.

She kept her eyes shut, recalling the moment with painful clarity so she could never forget why she was doing this. She had to save her sisters and poor Uncle Herman.

Her eyes popped open at the thought of her uncle, the poor man upon whom so much had fallen in the past several days. When their father had been lost at sea in his final attempt to acquire funds to save the family and free Amelia from the marriage contract that was their only hope, Uncle Herman had unexpectedly become the fifth Earl of Biggleswade and the Atwood sisters' new guardian.

The bumbling, forgetful bear of a man had taken to his duty with stunning fierceness, and closing her eyes once more, Amelia could feel the bristle of his whiskers against her forehead as he bent to kiss her goodbye.

She swallowed and threw out her hands to catch herself as the carriage rocked ominously. Fear and apprehension roared up inside of her, but she only tightened her grip on the bench beneath her and stared purposefully out the window.

But even as she was consumed by fear, she felt the lick of something else, something secret and forbidden deep inside of her. It happened every time something changed in her life. This little spark of something that scared her even more than anything else ever had. The hope that things might change. Even now, knowing the grim rumors that surrounded her future husband, knowing the danger such an attachment involved, she felt it. The hope that perhaps finally she would be enough.

She couldn't help but think of the rumors then, sorting through the stories for the facts on which they were based. They *were* rumors after all. At the heart of it was a man who had suffered great tragedy. The Greyfair title's country seat,

Lagameer Hall, had burned to ashes, and the duke's wife had perished in the fire. The rumors, however, suggested it was the Duke of Greyfair himself who had set fire to his estate in a jealous rage, killing his wife. Only in his wrath, he'd been unable to escape, and the fire had left him horribly disfigured.

Somehow the idea that she might be marrying a wife-killer was less terrifying than the idea of marrying at all.

It was at that moment that the carriage came to a spectacular, crashing halt, tossing Amelia against the opposite bench as though she were weightless. The storm pounded against the carriage, and for a moment, her ears rang with it, drowning out the sound of her own heartbeat. She struggled to right herself, but the carriage had tipped to an extreme angle, and it was all she could do to wedge herself in one corner, giving herself time to regain her senses.

Her hands went to the door automatically, scrambling to get the thing open, but her efforts were useless. The handle wouldn't turn. She threw herself against the door, but the way the carriage listed to that side, her efforts were futile. Again, the door did nothing more than rattle at her impact.

In the near blackness, she tried to make out the shape of the opposite door, but it floated somewhere above her, far too high for her to even hope of reaching it.

She was trapped.

She swallowed down her panic. This was not the time to let her imagination wander. There had simply been some trouble. Surely the coachman would come to her aid.

Unless he had been injured in the wreck.

The panic was real now, gripping her lungs as if to keep her from breathing. Her chest heaved, and she closed her eyes.

What would Adaline do?

She would tell Amelia to remain calm and wait for help.

It was then she noticed the wetness that grew along her back. Fumbling in the dark, her fingers encountered a thick, gritty substance spread over the length of her already sodden cloak. She pulled her fingers away and studied them in the darkness, but all she could see was a viscous substance dripping from her fingers. Cautiously she held her hand up to her nose, inhaling the unmistakable odor of wet earth with a salty tang she thought might be the ocean.

She jerked away from the corner, trying to pivot to see behind her. A flash of lightning lit the small space as if knowing her intention, and there it was.

The carriage had tipped entirely on its side, and mud seeped through the spaces around the door. Another flash of light. There was nothing visible through the window except the shifting earth below them and water.

Water everywhere, pouring through the cracks of the door and around the windowpane.

Dear God, the whole cabin would fill and drown her.

Panic turned to resolution.

She fumbled in the darkness, her hands searching the tufted ceiling. She found the leather strap used to help ladies gain the carriage. She slipped onto her backside, raising her leg. It took all her effort to lift it, dredging it from the folds of her ruined cloak, her wet skirts. Finally she managed to slip her foot inside of it. She tested it with her weight, feeling a spike of hope when it held.

She reached above her, her fingers finding purchase in the seam of the bench. She worked her fingers into the cushions until they collided with the wooden framework beneath. She was glad for her gloves, no matter how soaked they had become, because the wood below the bench was rough, and splinters tore at the cotton.

She started to move.

Inch by painful inch, she climbed the wooden framework

of the bench like a ladder, but the slim frame only allowed her fingertips to gain a hold, and soon her hands throbbed with the effort.

She was nearly to the top when her foot slipped in the harness. She made a valiant leap, reaching blindly for the strap on the ceiling on the opposite side of the carriage. If only she could catch it, she could haul herself up to the other door.

Her fingers only met air. She was suspended for but an instant, her body hanging, her fingers outstretched for one last hope. Her breath caught and with it the knowledge that she would soon fall, trapped in the bottom of the overturned carriage.

And then someone grabbed her arm.

The scream of surprise stuck in her throat as her gaze flew upward trying to see who had caught her hand. Again it was as though Mother Nature sensed her intent, and the sky lit with an unearthly brilliance.

Her rescuer was illuminated for only a second, but she caught the unmistakable outline of a man she somehow knew was not the coachman. Wide shoulders. The upturned collar of a greatcoat. The circle of the brim of a hat. But his face was left in total darkness.

He didn't speak, but she wouldn't have heard anything he said anyway, the roar of the storm having grown to deafening levels with the open door. He latched on to her arm with his other hand and lifted her directly upward, and again, she felt the sensation of being weightless.

Her skirts tangled about her legs as she tried to find something off of which to leverage herself and help her rescuer, but it seemed help was not needed. In seconds she was free of the carriage and in the thick of the storm.

Rain pelted her, slashing sideways with a biting wind. Her hood would be useless, but she snatched at it anyway as soon as her rescuer set her on the side of the carriage and released her hands. She watched him walk to the edge of the over-turned carriage and disappear over its side. The wind thundered in her ears, and she witnessed everything as though without its true sound.

She had thought him gone, and for a moment, terror seized her. Would he leave her here on the overturned carriage to wait out the storm? But then her eyes adjusted to the new landscape, and she realized he had dropped onto a waiting horse. He had a hand held out, reaching toward her.

She scrambled to her knees, her skirts catching in the wooden scrollwork of the carriage. Something tore, and the heels of her hands slipped along the surface, but she made progress, crawling in the direction of his outstretched hand.

It seemed an eternity, but she felt his hand close over hers once more, and then just as before, she moved without effort as he lifted her onto the horse. The animal pranced under the new weight but seemed to quickly find its balance, striking into the earth and then they were lurching forward.

She became aware of several things at once.

The most important of which was that Dinsmore Castle lay not twenty yards in front of them. She knew it to be the castle for the utter blackness around them was interrupted by dots of warm, beckoning light. Light that must have shone from the castle's windows. Everything else was an impene-trable black, and she knew from what little she had learned of Dinsmore Castle from her father that it was so black because having been built on island in the estuary, the castle was surrounded by the sea. Instantly her mind filled with the image of the water rushing into the carriage, and she swal-lowed the fear that made a lump in her throat.

It hadn't been the rain that was seeping in. The carriage must have overturned on the causeway leading to the castle.

The realization had her clutching at her rescuer's arms,

now folded snuggly around her as he moved the horse forward through the storm. It was then she became aware of the second thing.

Her rescuer was bigger than she had first imagined. She had thought the storm had quieted, but in reality, she had fallen into the cocoon of the man's body. He was sheltering her with those broad shoulders she had seen outlined by the flash of lightning, and his strong arms were unforgiving as they wrapped around her.

Something primal raced through her at the idea of a man protecting her, and she swallowed convulsively. Only moments before she had expected to die, and the flash of appeal that raced through her was so unexpected as to halt her breath in her throat.

Amelia rather liked the feel of the man's hard chest holding her up, of his muscled arms wrapped so snuggly about her. Muscled, she knew, because she could feel the contour of his forearms through the grip she had on him. Something strange and foreign rushed through her then, and even with so much plying at her nerves, she felt an utter sense of calm.

No one had ever touched her like this.

It was ridiculous. He was only touching her because the act of rescue required it, but for a moment, she held the feeling, trying to memorize it, knowing all too soon she would be lost again.

The horse seemed to know its way in the dark and pushed forward, the man doing very little to guide the animal. The lights grew brighter, and soon she could make out the faint suggestion of stonework. They passed some sort of wall, but it was hard to discern what it might be.

Through the spitting rain and the howl of wind, another sound emerged, a distinct ringing, and she understood the horse had moved onto a drive reinforced with some kind of stone, and its shoes were ringing against the hard surface. The sound buoyed her hope, and she knew they would reach shelter soon.

As soon as the thought formed in her mind, the horse slowed and turned at the slightest movement of the man's hand. She tightened her grip, suddenly reluctant to leave the shelter of her rescuer's arms.

Because as soon as she arrived at the castle, she was to wed the man her father had promised her to, and for just one more blissful second, she wanted to believe in the magic of falling in love with a complete stranger. She wanted to believe for one moment that this man held her so tightly because he wished to, because she was worthy of such closeness.

But this was not a novel and ladies like Amelia were not destined for love matches. So when the horse stopped, and hands reached up to her, pulling her to the ground, she let them take her.

She was aided in her drop to the ground by at least three manservants. She couldn't make them out in the darkness and rain, but their tall and broad statures suggested as much. Even as these strangers grabbed hold of her, it was only one man's touch she registered. One man's touch that she memorized so she could hold on to it forever.

The way her rescuer's grip on her lingered just a little longer than it needed to as she was passed safely into the hands of the servants on the ground, and just for a moment, she let herself believe that he had enjoyed touching her and was reluctant to let her go.

From there it was a blur.

She was rushed through a stone archway, hung with the intimidating slab of a wide oak door, and candlelight stung her eyes, blinding her momentarily.

She had thought they would take her to the castle proper,

but the room she stood in was much too small. She blinked, taking in the rough wooden benches, the dark wet stone.

This was a chapel.

Reality crashed into her with a sickening blow, and she struggled to gain a breath.

"Oh my dear lady, you've had such a fright."

The voice was warm, beckoning, and Amelia latched on to it.

"Come, child. The quicker we see this done the faster I can get you into a warm bath."

Yes, a warm bath. A warm bath would be lovely.

The owner of the voice appeared out of the shadows. Taking in the woman's starched apron and prim white hat, Amelia thought she might be a housekeeper.

She blinked, trying to center herself in the chapel when her eyes fell on the man at the altar. Her heart stopped, the enormity of what she was about to do engulfing her. Even in the candlelight she could make out the man's sheepish smile, the way he bent his head and pulled at the crown of his felt hat, ducking his gaze away from hers.

It struck her then that perhaps her groom was as nervous as she was.

But then the man shuffled his feet, as he backed away, making space at the altar for one more. She swallowed, and the very real fear that her heart was going to beat straight out of her chest consumed her.

The housekeeper's hand was on her shoulder then, pushing her forward. She caught sight of a man in robes, his shoulders hunched, his fingers flexing against the worn covers of the Bible he held between both hands. He smiled, but it didn't quite meet his eyes.

A great boom sounded through the small chapel, and a rush of wind sent her skirts and hair into a whirl. She jumped at the noise, pushing her hair from her face to look back the way she had come because someone had come through that great oak door.

She tried to see through the darkness, but the chapel only held a few lit candles, and most of the space remained shrouded in shadows. But then he stepped forward, and the light shone behind him, and there it was.

The outline that was imprinted on her memory.

The upturned collar, the broad shoulders, and the brim of a hat.

Her rescuer stopped beside her, rain dripping from his coat and hat, the hat that hid his face from her, but it needn't matter. She already knew who he was.

Her groom had arrived.

* * *

SHE HAD BEEN TRYING to get out.

Without aid.

She had nearly managed it too by the time he ripped the carriage door open.

If he let it, the frantic pounding at the vestibule door still echoed in his ears, how it rang through the cavernous space as though the storm itself were trying to break through the castle's defenses. He had heard it even in his tower, and just as he rounded the second landing of the staircase in the front hall, Albert had tumbled inside, more of a puddle than a man, and Mrs. Fairfax had stood transfixed at the sight of the poor coachman, drenched and lying on the floor.

He had known then something had gone wrong, and the realization that so much careful planning would end in a disaster over which he had no control rippled through him with cruel intensity.

But then the truth had overcome him.

A woman was trapped in that carriage.

He watched her now, reluctant to hand her down to the stable lads, wanting to see her safely inside the chapel.

Stephen was in there and Mrs. Fairfax, and she would be all right.

Until he came to wed her.

Emotion gripped his throat, an emotion so complex he wasn't sure he would ever untangle it.

He shivered, recalling the moment he had left the security of the outer walls, Hercules, his horse, picking his way along the battered causeway.

It had been too late to send word to his bride, to stop her journey to Dinsmore Castle. The storm had come upon them with a lethal suddenness, stealing the last rays of an otherwise glorious spring sunset. But as the weather often did there along the varied coastline, it whipped into a frenzy before anything could be done. He knew it would be safer to bring the carriage into Dinsmore than to have them turn around.

But as he had made his way along the causeway, Hercules seeming to sense his way in the near darkness, dread had pooled in his stomach.

She was his last hope.

If she died, it would mean the end for so much.

The Earl of Biggleswade had been desperate, and Lucas had paid a handsome sum for the Atwood girl. He needed a wife, and it was not as if they were thick on the ground. Not for him anyway. It didn't matter that he was rich or a duke. The rumors were enough to have any marrying mama rushing to keep her daughters away from him...and safe.

He had gritted his teeth, unconsciously tugging down the brim of his hat to shield his face, even now when there was only relentless rain to see him for what he was. But though he knew she was safe he could still see it. The carriage. Sitting on its side as it had spilled off the causeway.

It had been no small feat to climb the broken axle, wrench open the door against the exploits of the ravaging weather. But when he had pulled up the door, he hadn't expected a hand to be reaching for him. Instinctively he had reached out, his hand closing over the much smaller one flailing in the air as though searching for a hold. It had been even darker in the carriage, but as he had firmed his grip on the slight hand, the rest of the tableau had come into focus.

The woman, his bride, the Atwood daughter, hanging absurdly from his hand.

She had been trying to climb out.

The realization had rocketed through him, and for a moment, it had sent him off balance. He had been expecting the daughter of an earl, a spoiled debutante, a naive girl fresh out of the schoolroom. He had not been expecting this. A woman so self-possessed, so brave, so—

Beautiful.

Lightning had split the sky at exactly that moment, illuminating the face of the woman he held in his grip, and even in the second he had taken in her features, he understood she was beautiful. It was something not known but rather felt. He had felt her beauty in a way his eyes could never relay to him, and panic rushed through his veins in a dizzying flood.

Her lips were parted, her eyes round and wide, her chin perfectly curved, her cheekbones high, her expression open and searching. Together it painted a picture so compelling his throat closed.

A beautiful bride had not been a part of his plan, but what had he been thinking? It was not as if he could ask Biggleswade if his daughter was plain. If the man had had any decency in his body, he would have called off the marriage contract negotiations at once, and Lucas would have been without hope.

But now...

Only the need to return to the castle, to get her somewhere safe, had propelled him forward then. He could still feel the imprint of her in his hands, against his chest. It had been so long since he'd touched another person, since another person had touched him.

The darkness swam up, the darkness that had plagued him since the night of the fire, the night that had changed everything.

A woman as beautiful as the one who sat in his arms deserved someone with a whole face. Not a monster like him.

But she had held him so tightly, as if he had the power to save her.

The lie had torn through him, and he had felt like an impostor.

Why then had it been so hard to hand her down to the waiting stable lads? Why had he lingered so long to ensure Mrs. Fairfax had seen her inside the safety of the chapel?

He waved off Barnes's attempts to take Hercules for him and walked the animal to the stable himself, dismounting inside the structure's sturdy walls. Silence roared in his ears after the onslaught of the storm, but he soon realized the stables were anything but quiet. The lads worked to calm the horses, and two more rushed to him to take Hercules's reins.

"I want him properly dried," he called to Barnes, though he needn't have. The man knew what he was doing, but like anything in his care, Lucas felt the need to dictate his wishes to see the job done properly.

Barnes gave a knowing smile and a nod. "Right sure, Your Grace. A bundle of carrots too, I presume?"

"As many as the beast wants," he said, patting Hercules's flank as the lads led the animal away.

He didn't wait to see that his orders were carried out. Both because it wasn't necessary—his servants were perilously loyal—and because the drive to see himself wed pushed him on. He darted across the few paces of yard that separated the stables from the old chapel and pushed his way inside.

Perhaps it wasn't as bad as he had believed. It was probably just a trick of the moment, the pulsing adrenaline, the rush of excitement, and the threat of danger. She couldn't possibly be that beautiful.

It needn't matter anyway. He only needed a wife for one reason.

To give him an heir.

Instead of removing his hat as he entered the sacred space, he pulled it lower, throwing the entirety of his face in shadow.

Mrs. Fairfax had only lit the number of candles needed for the ceremony and nothing more, and the chapel lay in an incomplete darkness as he preferred. He made out his cousin, Stephen, standing awkwardly to the side, his hand braced against a pew, ready to act the witness to this charade. Mrs. Fairfax stood opposite, her hands pressed against her apron, unmoving, the second witness required of the ceremony.

But then his bride turned, and what little light there was shifted across her face, and he could see every inch of her clearly in the candlelight.

The breath froze in his lungs as his eyes devoured the sight of her, his body starved for the beauty of her face, his soul hungering for the connection one could only find in a lover. In that single moment, his entire person yearned toward her.

He blinked, and the moment shattered, and he remembered why he was there. Hurrying to marry this woman he had never met in the dark of a stormy night in a moldering stone chapel.

He tugged at the brim of his hat, bringing it even lower on the right side of his face, as the old rage simmered just below the surface. When he stepped up next to his bride, he couldn't look at her, he couldn't see her face, because just then he was seeing another wedding, another bride, the one he had thought he loved.

But she hadn't loved him. She had hated him.

She had made him the monster he was, and he wasn't thinking of only his ravaged face.

He spoke the words he was instructed to speak and placed the ring on her finger over her gloves, not giving her time to remove them and risk having to touch her bare skin. It was over in a matter of minutes, and he heard the words he had been dreading.

"You may kiss your bride, Your Grace."

As if the heavens understood the perilousness of his situation, a thunderous boom rent the air, and the candles flickered in the sudden draft until sputtering out, plunging them all into darkness.

He didn't hesitate. Bolstered by the comforting darkness, he grabbed his bride, his hand going into her mane of thick dark hair, wrapping about her head to tilt her back, to open her to him, and he kissed her.

He kissed her with the soul of a man dying for a woman's touch. He kissed her like he had once dreamed of kissing someone else, someone who had made him into a bastard who stole kisses from innocent women in the dark.

He ripped his mouth away, and in the impenetrable blackness, he strode to the door, leaving his wife lost in the inky dark because that was the kind of monster he had become.

CHAPTER 2

*S*he hadn't remembered the requirement of a kiss.

Her mind had been so full with the enormity of what she was about to do that she'd forgotten the details of it. The fact that tradition would dictate he kiss her at the wedding ceremony had been lost in her trepidation of the marriage act itself and the consummation of it. Yet it was this small detail that wrecked her.

Because while she had forgotten it, she had never known how much she would enjoy it.

Him kissing her that was.

In all the rumors she had heard circulated about the Ghoul of Greyfair, none of them had mentioned how expertly he could kiss. Unfamiliar as she was with the act, she wondered if she were giving him too much credit, but then wasn't kissing subjective in the first instance? Need it matter if she were inexperienced if the solitary kiss she had had was extraordinary?

And it had been. Quite extraordinary.

From the moment he grabbed her, she was hurtled back to the rush of pleasure she had felt nestled in the cocoon of his arms, and she was startled anew by the force of her response to him. And yet she still hadn't seen his face. A face told so much about a person, but her body seemed to know him without such knowledge.

This kiss was more than just a meeting of lips. He had used his entire body to seduce her with that single kiss, and he had been exceedingly thorough. She tingled from where his lips had caressed hers to the place at the base of her skull where his fingers had massaged the ache there to the imprint he had left at the small of her back as he had swept her into his arms and held her so tightly.

She stood, thankful the darkness hid her as she tried to catch her breath. She thought she might be swaying on her feet, but that might have been a trick of her mind as her eyes were unreliable in the blackness that engulfed them. She heard the rustle of skirts, the scurry of feet as someone rushed to relight the candles, but it wasn't those sounds that caught her attention.

It was the heavy booted feet that stalked away from her, resolutely and unhesitatingly in the direction of the door.

The familiar crushing sensation of rejection sliced through her, and she pressed her lips together to hold her breath steady, to not let on how much it hurt to hear her husband leave her there on the altar.

She was being ridiculous. He didn't even know her. How could he find fault with her already? But her mother's cruelty came rushing back to her as evidence that criticism didn't require a cause.

The flare of light from a match scorched her eyes with sudden brightness, and she closed them instinctually. She opened them as soon as possible but the outer door had already slammed shut, the whisper of a dying wind the only sound that remained in the chapel to suggest her husband had been there at all.

She turned to see the woman she thought to be the housekeeper placing the match to a wick and then another before picking up the iron candelabra that had sat on the altar through their brief and solemn wedding ceremony.

The minister had scuttled off in the dark as well it would seem, although she hadn't heard the outer door close. Blinking again, she realized the other gentleman had vanished as well. She peered around her, noticing for the first time the corridor that led off the back of the chapel.

"Come now, Your Grace." The woman placed a warm arm around Amelia's shoulders.

She couldn't help but jump at the sudden contact, and the woman made a soft shushing noise.

"Oh, I'm sorry, Your Grace. You must be in quite a bit of shock. Were you hurt in the accident then?" The woman's voice was soft and melodic, almost as though she were trying very hard not to sing. The wondrous tone was in such disparity to the cold, unfamiliar surroundings that Amelia found herself drawn to it.

"I don't believe I am hurt," she said, her voice soft as her thoughts remained distracted.

The woman held the candelabra aloft, and Amelia blinked against the direct light.

"You look as though you've been tousled but good," the woman said. "Bless your heart. You'll need a proper bath and some food if I've anything to say of it. Come along now."

She put her hand to Amelia's shoulder once more as if to steer her from the chapel, but Amelia froze.

"If you don't mind," she interrupted, waiting for the woman to look back at her before saying, "But who are you?"

The woman's face was soft and rounded in the candle-light, but it was hard to distinguish the whole of it. Her smile, though, came through as she said, "I'm sorry, Your Grace. I've forgotten my manners. It was just such a fright when Albert came banging on the door, you see. We thought it was far worse."

Albert? Was he the coachman?

And who was included in the woman's statement? Surely Amelia's now husband hadn't worried for her. No one had ever worried about her.

"I'm Mrs. Fairfax, Your Grace. The housekeeper here at Dinsmore Castle." She made a shooing motion now. "Come along then. You'll need food and a hot bath."

Amelia wasn't sure she'd ever eat again, but the idea of a hot bath sounded like the most precious thing just then.

Mrs. Fairfax led her to the corridor off the back of the altar, but Amelia couldn't help one last look at the outer door, wondering what was so terrible about her as to cause her husband to run back out into that storm.

At first, she thought the candle wasn't enough to penetrate the darkness around them, but then she realized it wasn't darkness at all, but rather heavy stone, black with age, that pressed in on all sides of the impossibly small corridor. She hesitated, her feet scraping against the stones, and for a breath, she wondered if this was what it felt like to be buried alive.

Mrs. Fairfax paused, holding the candle higher. "Are you all right, Your Grace? Have you been hurt after all?"

Amelia shook her head before she realized Mrs. Fairfax might not be able to see the gesture. "No, I'm quite all right, Mrs. Fairfax. It's just…" But she didn't know how to finish the sentence.

She couldn't put it into words how she felt. For a brief moment in time she had allowed herself to indulge in the proximity of her rescuer, in the romance of what had happened, in his daring and courage, in the wistful idea there could be more. And now she was married to him, this man who had sparked emotions in her she hadn't known existed.

But then the sound of his retreating footsteps brought her crashing back to the truth, and too easily her fear came bubbling to the surface. At least she knew from the beginning how she was to be received here, just as her mother had dismissed her offer of help at her sick bed. It was better to know one's place than to be left with hope of more.

Amelia truly needed to learn. She always did this. She always believed that this time things would be different. That someone would notice her, that someone would want her, only to be reminded of the truth. Amelia Atwood remained utterly forgettable and unwanted.

Still, she would always have that kiss.

"I know, dearie." Mrs. Fairfax reached back a hand to pat Amelia's arm reassuringly, and in the small space, Amelia feared the woman would upset the candelabra and plunge them once more into darkness. "Dinsmore can seem a bit much when one first meets it, but I assure you you'll fall in love with the place just like we all do."

Amelia couldn't help raising an eyebrow at this, but like everything else, the gesture was lost in the dark. Mrs. Fairfax turned back to the corridor in front of them and pressed on. Amelia tugged her cloak closer about her as if to shield herself from the dark but soon realized the soaked garment only caused a thorough shiver to start coursing through her body.

With trembling, cold hands, she reached up and struggled with the ties at her throat that had become stuck in the chilling wet. By the time she had wrenched the last of the ties free, they had reached another oak door, old and weighty, with brackets of iron piecing it together. Mrs. Fairfax reached up, and with one hand clenched about an iron ring, pulled the door forward with a screeching groan.

Amelia didn't realize she had braced herself, her mind

flooded with images of ghosts and specters that might haunt an old castle, until the door fully opened, and she saw…

A welcoming hearth complete with rug and sleeping dog.

The sight was so jarring after the sinister images she had conjured in her mind that she stood transfixed in the doorway.

The dog lifted its head at their arrival, one bushy eyebrow tweaking as if it were trying to shed the last of sleep's cobwebs.

He whined and laboriously got to his feet, and Amelia swallowed and backed into the doorframe.

The dog was a beast.

Rangy and wiry, the canine must come up to her chest, but she didn't wish to get close enough to find out. She hovered in the doorway, reaching instinctively once more for her cloak before realizing her mistake and releasing her grip on the soggy cloth.

"Oh, he's nothing but a harmless pup," Mrs. Fairfax said, and Amelia slid her gaze to the side to see the housekeeper exchanging the candelabra for a lantern left on a great wooden and iron table that took up much of the center of the room. "Looks scary as any evil creature, but he'll roll over and give you his belly for nothing but a smile from you, I promise."

Amelia did not believe the woman, but then the dog began to move, lumbering on its spindly legs over to her before he did that very thing, rolling to the stone floor, feet in the air, belly exposed.

She laughed. She couldn't help it. The beast of a dog was rendered innocent and nearly cuddly in but one simple movement, and her heart squeezed at the purity of it. Just a dog coming to find some comfort.

She knelt and tentatively stroked a hand across the lighter gray fur of his belly. He made a noise then, and she jerked her hand back before realizing the noise was something close to a purr.

She laughed again. "Does this wee beast have a name?"

She looked up when Mrs. Fairfax didn't respond to find the servant watching her carefully, a questioning look in her eye. Amelia felt a flicker of apprehension, but the housekeeper quickly shook her head, and the look was gone.

"His name is Argus. I'm afraid you might have made a friend for life." Mrs. Fairfax picked up the lantern and blew out the candelabra in one motion. "I do hope you like dogs, dearie. You'll never be rid of this one now."

It was the second time the housekeeper had used an endearment, and Amelia felt a shifting within her. She wasn't sure what she had expected as the duchess to a castle such as Dinsmore, but hearing the housekeeper's informal address of her new mistress, and some would say improper endearment, had the tension about her shoulders loosening for the first time in weeks.

She looked down and realized Argus had bent his head to look at her while she scratched his belly, and it almost appeared as though he were smiling.

"I like dogs," she heard herself say, although she had had no reason to wonder if she did before that very moment. Her mother and father had never liked animals, and until that very moment, Amelia had never had the opportunity to know whether she liked them or not.

She gave the dog one last pat before straightening.

"Come along now, Argus. The poor girl needs to get out of those wet things and warm up." Mrs. Fairfax didn't wait for a response, and with the lantern held aloft, moved away into the shadows.

The light from the fire only traveled so far, but Amelia got the sense they were in some sort of hall. It was too small to be the great hall of a castle like Dinsmore, but perhaps a solar or gathering space meant for family.

She followed Mrs. Fairfax, careful to keep her eyes straight ahead of her, afraid to peer too closely into the shadows that loomed up on either side. As the housekeeper had predicted, Argus trotted after them, and as he drew along beside her, she realized he did come up to her chest. She had only to reach out to scratch the wiry mane that stuck up along his floppy ears. But whereas before, the great dog had struck a note of caution in her, he was now a comforting presence, trotting along beside her, his toenails ringing against the stones of the floor.

They were several paces down the corridor before she got the nerve to peer into the shadows around them. She couldn't make out much though, just the looming sense of stone arches and scattered furniture. In her mind she painted cobwebs and dust across the face of it, spotting the darkest corners where ghosts could hide.

She wasn't sure how far they walked before the stones under her feet disappeared, only to be replaced by wide wooden planks. They stepped free of the corridor moments later, and Amelia realized they had entered a different part of Dinsmore Castle, likely a later edition to the original stone structure.

She struggled to take it in as the wall sconces were not lit, leaving the space in shadows much like the rest of the castle. For a moment she indulged in the fear the rumors were likely meant to conjure. What was the Ghoul of Greyfair hiding in the dark of his castle? For surely the sconces would be lit if the Ghoul had nothing to hide.

Such childish notions were baseless, and she let them vanish like the smoke disappearing from the globe of Mrs. Fairfax's lantern. The man who had kissed her so passionately minutes ago was no ghoul. Of that she was certain now.

But that did not mean the man didn't have something to hide.

She was so lost in her thoughts she didn't notice Mrs. Fairfax had left her, and she looked about, finding the woman perched on a staircase to her left.

Amelia followed, lifting her sodden skirts with one hand to keep from tripping. She absently reached for the railing with her other, her fingers brushing cold metal unexpectedly, and she snatched back her hand, cradling it against her chest. In the dim light cast by Mrs. Fairfax's lantern, she could just discern the shape of a roaring lion's head etched into the iron spindles, its fangs distinct even in shadow. The etching was far more sinister than anything her mind had conjured thus far, and her heart beat a little faster.

More carefully she placed her hand on the railing, reminding herself once more that she had to be strong. For Adaline and Alice and Uncle Herman.

They climbed, and when she thought the staircase should end it kept going. They rounded another landing and now they swept up the outer wall of the space they were in, and she discerned it must have been a double revolution staircase. Such a beautiful and intimidating thing to consider in a space she couldn't see, and suddenly she wished for daylight so perhaps she could make it out.

It was an odd sense, that lick of anticipation. She hadn't had much to look forward to in the last several months, and to think Dinsmore Castle had given her reason was if not concerning at least warranting her consideration.

When they reached the upper level, Mrs. Fairfax turned, and Amelia and Argus followed dutifully. When the housekeeper opened a door at the end of the hallway, Amelia expected to see the duchess's rooms, but instead she faced a stone staircase, climbing up in a perilous spiral into complete darkness.

"The duchess's room is in the east tower," Mrs. Fairfax explained.

Amelia swallowed, willing her heart to slow.

Again, they climbed, more slowly now, as the stone was uneven, worn from years of heavy boots. Amelia tried to find support by fitting her fingers into the stones making up the outer walls of the tower, but her fingers slipped, too icy and numb to gain a proper hold.

Argus had disappeared somewhere above them, seeming to have no issue with the treacherous stairs.

Finally they gained a landing, and Mrs. Fairfax wasted no time in throwing open the door opposite them.

Amelia braced herself, prepared for a room made entirely of cold, unforgiving stone, one she might not be able to even see for the lack of light. Her sense of hearing seemed to grow tenfold, and she swore she could discern the whisper of spirits about her.

But once again, she was met with a sight so completely unexpected it was a moment before she could move. She stepped into the room behind the housekeeper, and at once, she felt an odd stirring sense, as if she had been there before.

The tower room was fitted in lush tapestries that blocked the worst of the chilling drafts, and Amelia felt the room was warmer than any other part of the castle she'd been in so far. The resplendent bed before her was thick with quilts and pillows and adorned with copious hangings to keep out the night air should she grow cold. She couldn't quite make out all the colors in the weavings, but golds and reds flashed in the light of the roaring fire in the hearth.

Simple, elegant pieces of furniture dotted the exterior. A dressing table, a wardrobe, and a set of chairs by the fire.

Argus had already claimed a spot there, curling along the floor as if he had done so for years, and once more, Amelia was overcome with a sense of completeness.

The chairs that flanked the fireplace were accompanied by a small table already laden with a tray of food. Amelia's stomach clenched in response, but then her eyes settled on the copper hip bath set to the side, steam rising from it in beckoning swirls.

"Move quickly, dearie," Mrs. Fairfax said. "We've had the water at the ready for some time. In with you now."

It was a moment before Amelia realized Mrs. Fairfax had already turned to the door, lantern still in hand. For one moment, Amelia felt the stomach-dropping sensation of fear as if Mrs. Fairfax were leaving her forever.

She made to say something, but Mrs. Fairfax cut her off with a knowing smile.

"Have a nice bath and some good supper, dearie. I'll send a maid up to see to you in the morning. You'll want for nothing while you're here, I promise." She turned to leave but something drew her back. "Your Grace, if I may. I know you must be feeling lost tonight. I see now you're quite a young thing, and I know you've just lost your mother, and such a loss is the most terrible thing a child can know. But—" The housekeeper paused, her teeth worrying her lower lip as she considered her next words. "His Grace, the duke, he's got a good heart no matter what is said of him. I meant it when I said you'll want for nothing while you're here, and I promise you he'll keep you safe." She smiled as if this were to reassure Amelia, but when the housekeeper finally closed the door behind her, Amelia couldn't help but wonder.

Who would keep her safe from the duke?

* * *

LUCAS CAME through the door with enough bluster to rival the raging wind, and it drew the attention of the cluster of men speaking in solemn tones in the center corridor of the stables.

He stopped so swiftly his greatcoat swirled around him as his cousin, Stephen, tumbled in behind him and pulled his felt hat from his head, wringing the water from it.

"Shouldn't you be with your bride?" Stephen asked, shaking water from his coat.

"Mrs. Fairfax will see her to her room," Lucas said, moving in the direction of the stalls.

He felt Stephen and Barnes watch his progress down the corridor, but he didn't stop. His eyes scanned the stalls until he found what he was looking for. The matched pair that had pulled the carriage were already being seen to, stable lads darting in and out of their pens with blankets and towels, bags of oats.

"Are they hurt?" He didn't turn around, knowing Barnes would have followed him.

"The gray has a cut on her flank from the broken pole, but it's nothing she won't recover from with a bit of salve and a few apples." Barnes's tone was light, and Lucas knew it was the man's way of masking his concern for the horses.

Lucas nodded and finally turned, searching out Stephen from the smattering of stable lads that had gathered at the commotion.

"Did you send someone out to the causeway?"

Stephen shook his head. "They made it as far as the outer wall, but the wind's picked up. I didn't think it was safe for the lads."

Lucas knew him to be right, and it gave him a sense of comfort that he had his cousin to rely on when everything else around him seemed to be spinning out of control.

His bride was not at all what he had expected.

When Biggleswade had approached him with the offer, Lucas had assumed the girl to be a wallflower of some kind.

Either mousy and quiet, or better for him, lacking in looks. For why else would an earl be willing to pawn the girl off? He knew of the title's financial straits, but surely they couldn't be so bad as to sell one's daughter in marriage. But his wife was none of those things he had assumed. In the short time he had known her, he had found her brave and strong and worst of all, quietly beautiful.

It was a beautiful face that had tricked him before.

Bile rose in his throat, and he swallowed it, hard, willing the ghosts of memories to stay at bay. He had to think objectively about this. It had taken him nearly two years to gather the courage to seek a bride to give him an heir, and he would not waste any more time. The sooner the deed was done the better. He knew only too well the fragility of life, and it had gnawed at him since that day. More than ever the need for an heir burned through him. They were so close to making the estate the bountiful place it had once been. He wasn't sure when this relentless need to produce an heir had begun to plague him. It was all so much a blur those first few months when Stephen had finally prodded him from his sick bed, and Lucas had seen just what was waiting outside the castle walls.

A purpose.

A purpose to get out of bed, a purpose to see him through when everything had changed. It had worked for a while, but soon his endeavors felt flat and pointless. For what did it matter if he did not have an heir? Someone to carry on his work when he was gone?

He knew he could not go about the matter the conventional way. Only an arranged marriage would work. Except his plan seemed so much easier when his bride was a mere faceless idea and not the warm, strong woman he had held in his arms.

He clenched his hands into fists and studied the men

going about their work. "We'll go out at first light then," he said to Stephen now. "We'll need to examine the damage to the causeway and see if the carriage can be saved."

Stephen scratched at his forehead. "I'm sure we'll be able to rescue the carriage, especially if the tide lifts it in the morning and frees it from the mud. But Lucas..."

Lucas met his cousin's eye, the tone in his voice one he had heard so many times before, one of caution and concern.

"The causeway." Stephen licked his lips, his eyes never leaving the gray horse as a stable lad administered a sticky salve to her flank. "If the causeway is crumbling, it will be mighty expensive to repair." He shifted his eyes to Lucas then, and Lucas saw in them a measure of worry.

But he only clasped his hand on Stephen's shoulder. "We'll figure it out, cousin. We always do." A sense of certainty passed over him. While Stephen worried about the funds, Lucas worried about the tradesmen who would soon finish repairing the castle's outer wall. They would need a new task soon, and a causeway would fit the bill. "We'll head out at first light and assess the damage."

Once more Stephen's face reflected his inner feelings as his eyes searched Lucas's face. He seemed to sort through several thoughts before settling on what he obviously deemed the most important.

"I think you'll be rather occupied this night, cousin. Perhaps I should go out with a group of lads in the morning while you..." He let the sentence trail off, his lips remaining parted in question.

"While I—" But Lucas had filled in the remainder of the sentence in his mind by then.

He turned away and bit back a curse word.

Stephen touched his arm to draw his attention back. "Lucas, I know tonight might be causing you some concern." He gestured to the two horses. "But look at what she's endured this night, and from what I saw, she did not melt into a puddle of hysterics. She seemed like quite a brave lady. You can't assume she'll balk at the sight of your scars."

Lucas reached up, adjusted the brim of his hat unconsciously as his cousin spoke. "She can't know about…" But he couldn't speak the words. Even the mere mention of it was too much, and the past threatened at the edge of his mind, pushing to be let in, to force him to relive the horror of that night.

"No one knows, Lucas. You made sure of that. The few people who do will never tell." Stephen's voice was steady and calm, and Lucas felt the past recede. For now. Stephen clapped a strong hand to his shoulder. "Go now. Your bride is waiting for you." He dropped his voice and leaned in so only Lucas could hear him. "You've come too far to not see the marriage consummated."

The truth of his cousin's words pierced him like a white-hot dagger, and he bit down to keep the fear at bay.

The fear that his bride would find him repulsive and reject him, and once more he would be left without an heir.

"Go," Stephen prodded. "Before you lose your nerve." His tone turned humorous and cajoling, and Lucas met his cousin's playful gaze.

But that was just the problem. Lucas hadn't summoned the nerve to begin with. He had kissed his bride in the dark, stealing her touch like a beggar stole a loaf of bread, gathering fistfuls of her as if he were a starving man who wanted more than was his right.

He nodded and swallowed, not trusting himself to speak. He was nearly to the door when he turned back. "You'll come find me if anything should happen in the night." It wasn't a question, but Stephen nodded anyway, raising a hand in acknowledgment.

Lucas cast one more glance at the horses before heading back out into the storm.

He was drenched once more by the time he reached the heavy oak doors of the castle. He pushed his way inside, and it wasn't until he was met with absolute quiet that he realized he had been bracing himself.

Did he expect to find his wife lingering in the foyer? In the dark no less.

He was being a ridiculous fool. A coward, really. She was his wife now, and he had every right to take her. He flexed his hands into fists, his stomach turning at the lecherous thought. He would never force a woman, wife or no.

He looked up, his gaze traveling through the iron railings of the staircase only visible as dim shapes in the near black. But he didn't need light to know what lay above. He could see it all too clearly in his mind, so used to the dark had he become.

But now, in the layout of the castle he conjured in his mind, something was different. His wife lay waiting for him in the duchess's room.

He knew Mrs. Fairfax had ordered a bath. Was she still in it? Lathering her naked body with soap? Caressing her skin in the warm water until it turned pink?

And her hair. That thick mane he had plunged his hands into—did it hang heavy around her shoulders now? Was it fragrant with the sweet-smelling soap? God, he couldn't wait to bury his face in it.

He froze, one hand on the stair railing, his feet frozen to the floor.

He hadn't been with a woman since…

He couldn't remember.

Intimate relations with a woman were so far beyond his reach that it hadn't even entered his mind in years. It hadn't even been a consideration for the year of his recovery after the fire, and then…well, his mind had been lost elsewhere.

But now his wife was waiting for him.

At just the thought, parts of him awoke he had thought long dead. His body tightened, coiling as if in anticipation of what lay ahead. He could lose himself in her, his beautiful wife. He could drown out the things that haunted him, and there would be only her.

He took the steps two at a time, never hesitating even though the stairs were little more than a hazy outline. He knew his way, never stopping until he reached the upper floor. He turned in the direction of the tower, the path familiar, and he gained the tower stairs within seconds.

It wasn't until he reached the landing where the duchess's room was that he stopped.

There was a light under the door.

He waited, watching the light, hoping for a sign of movement. Anything to give him a clue as to what might be inside.

But the light never wavered.

He heard Stephen's voice in his head, propelling him forward, and finally he moved, striding the last few paces to the door. He knocked softly and opened the door before anything else could stop him.

But he only made it two steps inside before he stopped, utterly suspended by what he saw.

She was asleep.

She lay tucked up in the bed he had had specially made when he signed the marriage contract with Biggleswade. He had wanted his bride to be comfortable at Dinsmore, and he could only think to replace the rotting monstrosity that had been the duchess's bed before. This bed seemed too generous now as it engulfed her curled form, but her face was relaxed in sleep, and he could do nothing more than study her.

In the flash of lightning he had made out her wide eyes,

rounded cheeks, and pale, unblemished skin. But now he saw all of the pieces at once, and the picture they formed took his breath away.

He envied her the peace that radiated from her just then, and he hated himself for it.

Movement at the corner of his eye drew his attention to the fire. Argus lifted his head from where he had been resting it on his lanky, wiry paws. He tilted his head as though in question, and Lucas nodded in response.

"Keep her safe tonight, old boy," he whispered and backed out of the door, closing it softly behind him.

CHAPTER 3

*T*he first thing she noted upon waking was sunshine. Buckets of it poured into the room. She glanced to the side, noting the heavy shutters that were now thrown wide from a generous, single window set into the curved wall of the tower room. The light was such a blinding contrast to the darkness of the night before, she forgot where she was for a moment.

Then the memories came rushing back to her. She sat up in bed so quickly the room swam, and she gripped the bedclothes, willing the space around her to come into focus. If the shutters were open, that meant someone had to open them. She blinked, trying to bring things into some kind of order, but she'd slept so heavily it took several precious seconds to bring the room to rights. She pressed a hand to her head, a throbbing brewing behind her ears, and she tried to recall the previous night.

The storm. The carriage accident. The stone corridor closing in around her.

Her husband.

Leaving her at the altar. Leaving her after thoroughly kissing her.

She peered down at her left hand where the smooth gold band shone in the sunlight. She had placed it on her index finger after removing her gloves for it was too big for the proper ring finger. She feared it would slip off if left there. The nightdress she had found waiting for her on the duchess's bed was also too large, and she wondered if the duke hadn't been sure what kind of wife he was getting and had sized up to be safe.

The thought left her cold, but she still couldn't help the sense of regret that her husband had not put the ring on her bare finger himself or that it fit properly. It was silly, she knew. To think there would be kindness in his actions. He didn't even know her.

She blinked, looking up, a curious mixture of tension and hope spilling through her. Was it her husband who had opened the shutters? Was he here now?

The room was still and quiet around her, and the sunlight had grown warm on her cheeks. It was all so very tranquil, and once more she felt the confusing sense of home even though she had never been in this room before last night.

When the head popped up on the other side of the chair in front of the fire, she choked on a scream.

"Good morning, Your Grace," said the young girl, her smile bright and her eyes brighter.

"Good morning," Amelia stammered as she tried to take in the girl, not missing how her shoulders relaxed when she realized it wasn't her husband.

She knew husbands were meant to visit their wives on their wedding night. The fact that hers hadn't bothered didn't surprise her in the least.

The young woman stood by the fireplace, a small brush in one hand, a dustpan in the other. "I trust you slept well. After that horrible night you had." She shook her head, making a tsking noise. "You poor thing. You'll be feeling right as the weather once you've had some of Mrs. Fairfax's bread and apple butter. Isn't nothing like it, I tell you."

The girl hung the brush and dustpan on a pin in the wall by the fireplace.

"Thank you," Amelia said, although her voice was weak. She was momentarily confused by the young woman's presence and the mention of Mrs. Fairfax's apple butter until she remembered Mrs. Fairfax had said she would send up a maid. "I do beg your pardon, but what is your name?"

The girl's smile was quick again, but now that she was standing, Amelia was able to take in other, distressing details. Her simple gown was ragged in places, and there was evidence someone had tried to hide the tears with careful stitching. The girl's face and hands were clean but red and chapped as though she bathed in cold water with cheap soap, and her blond hair was flat with grease, but she had neatly pinned it back in a chignon. It hurt to look at the poor girl as it was quite obvious she had tried particularly hard not to show her difficult circumstances.

But seeing the young woman, the ravages of a hard life clear in her appearance, reminded Amelia why she was there, and she felt a quiet sense of determination. She was doing this for Alice, Adaline, and Uncle Herman.

"My name's Ethel, Your Grace." She gave a small curtsy. "I shall be looking after you until Mrs. Fairfax can find you a proper lady's maid."

The girl, although young, was certainly of an age to be a lady's maid herself, and her statement left Amelia questioning. "A lady's maid? Well, I should think you're up to the task, Ethel."

The girl turned red at Amelia's words, and Amelia wondered if she'd ever suffered praise before in her life.

"Oh, that's right kind of you, Your Grace, but Mrs. Fairfax thinks it's best if you have a lady what's stays here at night."

Amelia sat up straighter in the bed. "Stays here at night?"

The girl nodded and bent, fussing with a tray on the table where dinner had been placed the previous night. "Oh, yes. It would be best. I can't stay here, you see. Someone must watch after me mum now as she's sick and all." She straightened, wiping her hands on her apron with a shake of her head. "Her cough's worse at night, you see. It's better if I'm there to fetch her some tea if it gets real bad. The poor thing won't get any sleep otherwise."

Amelia put out a hand against the mattress as if it would help the sudden swirling of her thoughts. In such a simple sentence, the girl had revealed a difficult truth and set Amelia's own plight into better clarity. The worst thing she faced was being a duchess whereas this poor girl was obviously working as best she could to take care of her ailing mother.

Amelia pushed back the covers and stood, the voluminous nightdress cascading around her legs. She pulled the material into one hand and marched around the edge of the bed.

"I'll inform Mrs. Fairfax that I shall have you as my lady's maid," she said, peering about the room. "I shan't have need of you in the evenings, I don't think. I've never had a lady's maid before, you see, and I'm quite capable of preparing myself for bed. You may return to your mother so you can care for her." She looked about them. "Do you know if my trunks were brought up?"

Ethel stood with her eyes wide and her lips parted. She seemed to gather herself and said, "Mr. Marley's gone out with some men this morning to try to retrieve them from the carriage, Your Grace."

"Mr. Marley?" Amelia asked, suddenly realizing there was

likely a host of servants of whom she would need to learn their names. But would the butler have gone out to fetch her trunks?

Ethel nodded. "Mr. Marley is His Grace's cousin. He helps with managing the estate and such."

Amelia nodded, absorbing the information. Was he the other gentleman in the chapel the previous night? It wasn't unusual for someone to find residence with a more well-to-do member of one's family, but it was yet another piece of information that did not fit with the rumors about the Ghoul of Greyfair.

She turned to the window. "Can I see the causeway from here?" she asked.

When she reached the window, she was forced to shield her eyes from the sun, but as she blinked the world outside into focus, the breath froze in her lungs.

She had arrived in the dark, the world turned hazy by the storm, but now she could see rather clearly the place she was to call home, and it was nothing like what she expected as Alice regaled her with the gruesome tales of the ghoul and his lair.

Mrs. Fairfax had said this was the east tower of the castle, and Amelia took a moment to gather her bearings. The sun rose behind them, enough to flood the room with sunshine, but it was obviously still quite early, and it bathed the mainland with warm yellow light, sparking off the cobalt waters of the estuary that separated the castle from the land proper. What had been the night before a real cause for terror, was now calm and inviting, and she wondered if anyone ever swam in it.

But her eyes moved farther down, taking in the yard below. The first thing she noted was how green everything was, that unnatural bright green of early spring. The yard was much larger than she had imagined, and in the far corner trees were neatly spaced in rigid lines. An orchard. Right there within the safety of the castle walls. Was this where Mrs. Fairfax got the apples for her apple butter? The trees held precious tiny buds, the grass shone with a newness and vitality that alluded to the promise of summer, and—

The yard was filled with men and women moving about, hustling with pails and sacks and scurrying with carts and mules.

"What is going on?" she asked, her eyes roving over the bustle below.

Ethel came to stand beside her at the window. "They're repairing the wall, Your Grace. They've been working on it for some time now. Those old stones are quite heavy, you know. It takes a lot of care and skill to see them fixed."

Amelia reached out a hand to brace herself against the opened shutter of the window so she could lean farther out to take in more, and her fingers touched etched iron. She snatched her hand back, remembering the roaring lion of the night before, but when she looked to where her hand had been, her eyes were met with something else.

The impression of a woman, her silhouette lovingly molded into the iron of the shutter's knob.

"Ah, I see you've met our lady," Ethel breathed with reverence.

Amelia looked swiftly at the maid. "Our lady?"

Ethel nodded and moved away, gathering up the bedclothes as she set the bed to rights. "The lady of the castle." Ethel lifted her chin as if to take in the whole of the edifice. "He built this for her. That would be the current duke's grandfather. They were sweethearts, you see. They fell in love at a tender age, and he promised to wait for her. He spent three years building this castle in anticipation of the day she would come of age, and they could wed." Ethel tucked the covers under the pillows, fluffing them as she went. "But she never got to see it." Ethel shook her head forlornly.

"Why didn't she get to see it?" Amelia was transfixed, hypnotized by the lilt and pleasant cadence of Ethel's voice.

Ethel straightened, her expression one of heartbreak and loss. "She died. On the way to the wedding." She shook her head and smoothed the quilts one more time. "The duke was a broken man, and he had this castle." She straightened, gesturing around her with her palm up. "It's like a love letter, don't you think? To the woman who held his heart." She dropped her hands and shook her head. "Became a constant reminder of all he had lost."

Amelia swallowed the sudden lump in her throat, her eyes sliding nervously to the window. She had almost died on the way to her wedding. Was this castle cursed? Were the brides of the dukes of Greyfair doomed to meet unholy fates? What if there was something to those dark rumors?

"I like to think of the castle more for the show of unending love like it was meant to be," Ethel said then, and Amelia looked back to find the maid peering about the room, warm appreciation lining her features. "Even though they could never wed, the duke had proclaimed his love in the most public of ways. This castle stands as a testament."

The girl turned and picked up a garment that had been lain over one of the chairs. It was Amelia's gown from the night before appearing freshly pressed and pristine.

"Mrs. Fairfax thought you might need this at least until they are able to retrieve your trunks. Shall I help you dress?"

Amelia's mind was cluttered with the dichotomy of the moment. The young, work-worn girl speaking of love and labor in the same breath. It was all terribly confusing and not in the least what Amelia had expected to find at Dinsmore Castle. Her heart warmed at the idea of what else she might find.

It was odd, that anticipation that thrummed through her once more. She hadn't expected to find reason to feel hopeful when she reached her new home. Of course, there was always the lingering wish for things to be different, but Ethel and Mrs. Fairfax were kind, and her husband seemed keen on ignoring her. Perhaps this would work out in her favor.

She glanced back at the bed, the skin prickling along her neck as she knew her husband wouldn't leave her alone forever. In fact, she knew she must seek him out that very morning. There were duties expected of a duchess, and she would need her husband's counsel on what it was she was to do at Dinsmore. She felt the familiar stabbing of uneasiness at the thought of engaging with another person, but speaking of her duchess duties seemed harmless enough.

"Yes, of course. That was quite thoughtful of Mrs. Fairfax."

Ethel shrugged. "She's quite a thoughtful lady, she is. It was she who thought to have Mrs. Mitchum look after me mum so I could work here."

Amelia stilled. "Mrs. Mitchum?" There were just so many names. How could she remember them all?

Ethel nodded and laid the gown on the bed before reaching behind her for what looked like Amelia's chemise and corset, also appearing as though they hadn't taken a dip in the estuary the previous night.

"Mrs. Mitchum looks after people in the village. She gives them tinctures and tonics and such when they tell her what's ailing them. She's a right smart one, she is. Although some people don't think so." A shadow crossed over the maid's face then, and it was so unlike her effervescent personality that Amelia started at the expression.

"What do other people think of her?"

Ethel looked up, her gaze direct and unflinching. "Other people call her a witch."

41

* * *

HE WAS certain they were only able to get the carriage free with the help of the incoming tide, which loosened the mud's hold on the vehicle.

In the starkness of daylight, he couldn't stop his stomach from churning at the sight of it.

It was far worse than he had realized. The carriage was completely on its side, implanted in the muddy bank of the causeway. He thanked God the pole had snapped as the carriage toppled over or the horses might have been injured, or worse, killed. He eyed the twisted wheels and snapped axel at the front of the conveyance and unconsciously tugged on the brim of his hat, pulling it farther down on the right side.

He'd given Albert the day off and an extra week of wages. How the man had managed to jump clear of the wreck to seek help, Lucas would never know, but the coachman had performed an incredible feat that night. Had he not reached the castle in time, Lucas's bride might have drowned.

Amelia.

For what felt like the hundredth time in the past quarter hour, his gaze unerringly found the window in the east tower, and again, for the hundredth time he wondered if she were awake yet.

He could too easily recall the image of her engulfed by the enormous bed, her hair loose and dark against the white linen of the pillows, and he obviously wished to torment himself by bringing the image to the fore again and again.

Why hadn't he gone to her? She had likely been exhausted from the events of the day, and perhaps she would have...

What?

Let him maul her?

He swallowed the bile that rose in his throat and turned

back to the operation at hand. He wasn't surprised when he had stepped into the castle yard that morning to find two of his tenants, their draft horses in hand, waiting to assist with the recovery of the carriage. News such as this spread quickly across the estate, and he couldn't help but be warmed by the generosity of his tenants. It spoke to the attitude he had tried to cultivate on the estate since arriving there to make it his full-time residence almost two years ago after Lagameer Hall had been destroyed, and it was reassuring to see his efforts bearing fruit.

Stephen shuffled over to his side then, backing out of the way of one of the draft horses as it tossed its mane in preparation of pulling yet again.

"The poor beasts are having a tough go of it," Stephen muttered as the horses gave another lunge, pulling the chains that attached them to the carriage taut, clinking and snapping into place as the carriage heaved upright, the mud making a sucking sound as it finally relinquished its prize.

Lucas stepped back, Stephen following close behind. Water poured from the vehicle as mud oozed from the cracks along the door. He eyed it critically, tallying in his mind the funds it would take to buy a new carriage, funds he could have used elsewhere on the estate to help his tenants.

"I've asked Donaldson to have a look at it," Stephen said then, his voice flat, and Lucas turned to see his cousin just as carefully studying the condition of the vehicle.

Donaldson was the village blacksmith, but he had a reputation for tinkering and an unmatched level of skill at detail work. If anyone could save the carriage, it would be him.

Lucas nodded and said, "Thank you."

Stephen only nodded in return and moved to direct the men to pull the carriage about. They had borrowed a cart from the mill, and the next feat would be getting the damaged conveyance loaded onto it to be hauled into the village for repair. More draft horses had been commandeered for the task, and they stomped their feet impatiently, itching to get to work.

While the carriage was now on the causeway, it became apparent rather quickly that getting it onto the cart with a broken axel would be near impossible. He shucked his greatcoat, rolling back his sleeves as he bent to work with the other men, using brute force to get the damned thing up onto the cart. They slipped in the muddy ruts the storm had caused, and several of them narrowly escaped getting crushed by the carriage as it tilted and skidded in the shifting ground.

He was caked in mud, soaked through to the bone with icy estuary water and his own hard-earned sweat by the time the carriage was loaded. Stephen stood next to him, his brow glistening with sweat, his chest heaving as he tried to even his breathing, and Lucas couldn't help a wary perusal of his cousin.

"I'm not going to drop over dead from a little exertion," Stephen muttered, but Lucas felt no shame at having been caught assessing his cousin.

He turned his back to the carriage as the men strapped it down to secure it for transport. "It's not that so much as I don't want to carry your dead arse back to the castle."

Stephen laughed. "You wound me, cousin. After all, I did carry your arse once." The playful note in Stephen's voice had vanished by the end of his sentence, and when Lucas turned to meet his eye, he found a thoughtful expression on his cousin's face.

He clamped a hand on the man's shoulder. "And it will never be forgotten."

The moment was shattered at a loud cry from the men as the last of the restraints were secured. He raised a hand to the man on the bench before the driver turned and sent the horses into motion. The cart lurched forward and stalled, stuck again in the mud, but the mighty horses dug in, their enormous knees bending into the load. All at once the cart sprang forward, and the horses moved as though they carried nothing at all.

"I'll see to having the causeway graded once some of it has dried, and then we can see to the damage that's been done," Stephen spoke quietly as the two men watched the ruts grow deeper in the road as the cart struggled forward.

"Your Grace."

The voice was unfamiliar, and Lucas turned without thinking, only to swing back, surprise and shock gripping him.

His wife. What was she doing out here at such an early hour?

He fumbled to retrieve his greatcoat from where he had cast it aside. It was thoroughly coated in mud, but he hardly noticed as he shrugged into it. The rolled sleeves of his shirt caught on the stiff fabric though, and momentarily he became trapped. He pictured himself as she must have seen him. A grown man struggling to get his coat on. He didn't miss Stephen's snicker of laughter either.

"Your Grace!" Stephen finally called back, and Lucas heard him shift, stepping between Lucas and his bride.

She should be in the castle resting. She'd been through a perilous ordeal the night before, and he wasn't speaking of her marriage to him. Surely she needed to recuperate. But from the quick glimpse he'd seen of her, she'd appeared as though she'd been through nothing more than an exhilarating shopping excursion on Bond Street in London.

"Your Grace, allow me to introduce myself. I'm Stephen Marley, cousin to the current Duke of Greyfair."

Lucas heard some scrapping and assumed Stephen had bowed to the new Duchess of Greyfair.

God, when he thought of her like that, it seemed all too terrifyingly real.

Finally his arm popped free of the sleeve, and he was able to reach up, flicking up the collar of the coat until its stiff corners prodded both of his cheeks uncomfortably. He gave one final tug to the brim of his hat, tipping it so far to the right it nearly fell off his head. He righted it, assuring it was firmly in place before he half turned, keeping himself at an angle to his wife.

He caught her in a curtsy, and even as she sank down, her eyes traveled up and met his as though she could sense him watching her.

"Mr. Marley." Her voice was soft yet firm, and he was coming to realize her beautiful exterior was no match for her quiet strength. "It's a pleasure to make your acquaintance. I understand I have you to thank for retrieving my trunks." She gestured behind her. "I encountered the men bringing them to the castle just as I stepped outside."

Stephen seemed to warm under the woman's attention, and Lucas felt a surge of jealousy course through him. How absurd. What had he to be jealous of? It wasn't as though he had married his wife for love. This thought sent a spike of pain through him so acutely he coughed and turned away to gather himself.

He would never do anything for love ever again. Let Stephen have the duchess's affections.

But when he turned back and found his wife showering Stephen with a smile so brilliant it caused a tightening in his chest, he suddenly felt like a boy again ready to wrestle Stephen for the best piece of Cook's lemon cake.

"Anything I can do for you, Your Grace, you must only ask."

"Please call me Amelia. I'm afraid being a duchess will

take some getting used to, and it would be nice to hear my own name now and then."

Was Stephen blushing? Blast the man.

"Of course...Amelia." He gave her another bow. "If you'll excuse me, I'd like to see the carriage makes it to the village for repairs."

Lucas stiffened. "You're going to the village? Surely you'll take one of the horses."

It was only when his back was turned to Amelia that Stephen rolled his eyes. "Thank you for your concern, Your Grace." He spoke Lucas's address with heavy sarcasm. "But I find myself in want of some exercise."

Lucas watched him go, unable to stop the protective instinct that simmered inside of him as his cousin ambled his way down the causeway toward the retreating cart and carriage.

He didn't realize his wife had stepped up beside him until she spoke. "What..." Her voice trailed away, and he looked down. Her face was in profile, but she was so close to him now he could see the deep brown pool of her eyes. Suddenly he wanted to get lost in them, in the peace and comfort that exuded from them.

He hadn't expected this. When he had sought a bride, the idea was sterile and flat. But now his wife was here, next to him, and she was anything but. She was sights and sounds and—oh God, did she smell of lavender?

He wrenched himself away from the sight of her and turned his attention back to his cousin. "He was born with a twisted foot. He's walked with a crutch his whole life." It was at that moment said crutch became so ensnared in the mud, Stephen stopped and used both hands to wrench it free. As the crutch suddenly gave, his cousin stumbled backward, neatly catching himself and the crutch and moving on as if nothing had happened, but they weren't so far away as to miss the sound of his muttered cursing. "It doesn't seem to stop him though."

"You're lucky to have him."

He looked down swiftly at her words. No one had ever said thus to him. Most lamented Lucas's situation, calling Stephen a burden and worse, a parasite.

She must have felt him studying her again because once more her gaze traveled up to his, and he hoped the collar of his greatcoat and the brim of his hat provided enough shadows to hide the details of his face.

"Family is so important. You're fortunate to have someone to rely on."

Something warm and molten flowed through him then, and the ground shifted beneath his feet, but he knew it had nothing to do with the mud of the causeway.

"Yes, I am," he said softly.

She nodded, her chin firm as she seemed to come to a conclusion. "I was hoping you'd care to break your fast with me this morning. We didn't exactly have time to speak to one another last night, and I should like to understand from you what you expect from me as your duchess."

That image of her tucked into bed sprang into his mind, and he had to look away, words stumbling uselessly against his suddenly numb lips.

"Your role?" he managed after several tries.

He made to turn back to the castle, but it would have put her on his right side. He pivoted, nearly falling in the mud as he did so, but finally she was to the left of him again, and he strode forward, stupidly thinking he would outpace her and her dangerous invitation to breakfast.

But much like everything about her, she surprised him by taking two quick steps to every one of his, keeping pace with him along the causeway.

"Yes, I should very much like to help you in managing the

estate in any way that I can. I know my father's holdings were not as vast as yours likely are, but I've had all the proper schooling. I can assure you—"

He stopped abruptly, turning just enough to meet her gaze. "Your father's holdings *were?*"

She stopped, her eyes wide, and she'd never been more beautiful to him than in that moment, early spring sunshine cascading all around her, and he realized she wore no hat like a lady should. Her hair was plaited back and coiled, and her gown was of a simple, serviceable design. It must have been for her to keep up with him the way she had.

Her lips parted, no sound emerging, and he thought her eyes turned watery. After a moment, she said, "I beg your pardon. I thought my father's solicitors would have sent word. My father is dead."

CHAPTER 4

*S*he was not going to cry.

It was the first time she had spoken the words aloud. It was the first time she had spoken about her father's death at all to someone who was not her sisters, Uncle Herman, or her father's solicitors.

Although her father had largely ignored her, he was still her father, and at the mere suggestion of his death, her chest constricted to where she thought she would never breathe again. Her heart hammered, and tears sprang to her eyes so forcefully it was as though she had stubbed her toe on the sharp corner of a table leg.

She couldn't let the duke see her weakness, and through sheer force of will, she held the tears at bay and raised her chin, biting the inside of her cheek when her lips trembled.

She fixed a soft smile to her lips, hoping to appear docile and encouraging. "I'm terribly sorry about this. I had thought my father's solicitors had notified you of the occurrence."

She couldn't see his face clearly the way it was hidden in shadow from the upturned collar of his greatcoat and the low brim of his hat, but she could feel him studying her.

The moment of silence gave her time to reflect on the oddity of his appearance. The spring sunshine was warm on her shoulders, and she'd forgone a bonnet when she'd seen the beauty of the day, thinking the relaxed rules of the country would save her from any impropriety. And yet he was bundled as though he expected another storm like the one from the previous night.

Had the fire that killed his wife truly disfigured him? How hideous were the scars if he chose to hide himself like this? She felt a stab of sympathy, both for the physical pain and the mental torment such scars might cause.

But he hadn't been so concealed when she'd first arrived on the causeway to see the men at work removing the fallen carriage from the bank. He hadn't been wearing a coat at all then, and she'd seen with surprising detail the curving muscles of his back rippling under the thin linen of his shirt as he worked. She'd been unable to keep her eyes from the corded muscles silhouetted along his forearms and the impossible breadth of his shoulders.

She knew what it felt like to have such power and strength pressed against her body. She'd felt it the night before, and seeing it now in broad daylight sent a thrill racing through her. It startled her, and her feet had refused to move farther down the causeway once her mind became mired in the collision of memory and reality.

And then, unbidden, she had recalled the kiss, stolen under the cover of darkness. She had felt him then too. All of him, held against the length of her.

Everything in her past had told her relationships were only avenues of criticism and disapproval. From the moment her father had announced she would wed, she had been filled with dread at the idea that another person might now find her to be not enough. But this. This startling and unexpected attraction was not something she could have imagined, and it frightened her even more.

However, another curious matter distracted her. She had the distinct feeling the duke was avoiding her. He hadn't come to her bed the previous night, and then there was his reaction to her approach just moments ago. She had seen the way he whirled away from her the moment he registered who addressed him. He'd donned the greatcoat and hat then, and the theatrics he went through to keep her at a certain distance was obvious and alarming. Had the duke decided to discard her already?

She blinked now, remembering the way he had run away in the dark after kissing her, into a storm no less.

Suddenly it wasn't so difficult to hold her chin steady. Still, in the back of her mind lurked the very real issue of the uncertainty of their marriage. Why hadn't he consummated it last night? What was holding him at bay? Was he unsure of his decision? Would he take back the funds he had given to procure her?

The thought left a sour taste in her mouth, thinking of herself as something to be bartered, but she tried to remember worse had happened to other women in society. She was grateful she had been given a warm bed, food, and a bath. She even had Ethel. Her lot could be far worse, but the question of the legality of her marriage haunted her.

She swallowed compulsively. Would she be required to seduce the Ghoul of Greyfair? She hadn't wanted the marriage, and now would she be required to throw herself into it to ensure the safety of her sisters?

She didn't know the first thing about seduction, but even at the thought, her body flushed with the memory of his kiss. It was then that her brain simply shut down. She knew she was staring now, but somehow she couldn't force herself to blink, let alone look away.

But then the duke clamped a hand to her shoulder, the force of it jostling her. "I'm very sorry for your loss," he said and stomped away.

He was several yards down the causeway before she realized he was walking away from her.

Again.

She picked up her skirts and went after him. It was slow progress as the muddy road clung to her boots, but she caught up to him at the castle's outer wall that ran along the perimeter of the island on which the castle had been built.

"Your Grace!" she called, but he didn't slow. "Your Grace, I can assure you the marriage contract will go through as it was intended—"

He stopped so abruptly she nearly collided with him.

"I know as much. You're here, aren't you?" His tone was flat, his words short. She was so used to being scolded, her shoulders had tightened in expectation of it, but she realized his tone did not hold a reprimand. She wondered for a moment if that was just how he spoke, in short, clipped words.

"Yes, of course. And I wish to thank you for sending your carriage to fetch me," she added hastily, gesturing to the causeway behind them. "I'm just so very sorry about what happened. I hope it can be repaired."

He had a curious way of looking at her. He kept his body turned away from her and only peered at her with a sidelong glance. It almost made her wonder if she had missed a step in dressing that morning. It was true the task had been made more difficult as her trunks hadn't been rescued yet, but she felt sure Ethel had done a fine job of it. Still, she raised a hand to her hair, smoothing it back into its coiled braids.

"Yes, I'm sure the carriage shall be fine." Again he walked away from her.

She followed. "I had hoped we could discuss—"

"Mrs. Fairfax can help you with anything you should need," he called back over his shoulder and then he was gone completely, slipping through the maze of men working on repairing the outer stone wall.

She stopped, her feet kicking up dust in the castle yard, and she jumped back as men struggled to move a cart heavy with gravel and debris from one side of the yard to the other. By the time the path had cleared, she'd lost sight of her husband entirely.

She wasn't sure how long she stood there, blinking at the spot where he had disappeared, a tumble of emotions cascading through her. Doubt. Confusion. And worst of all, fear.

She had to make this right. She had to make a success of it. Marrying the duke had been one thing, but she felt suddenly that she must succeed at being his duchess if she were to keep him satisfied with the terms of the contract. What if he demanded his funds be returned if he were not?

She stood in the yard, the sun beating down on her, the workmen bustling around her, and unbidden, her gaze was drawn to the castle.

She could see it clearly now in the daylight, and she was struck by the grandness of it. She had been correct the night before in thinking there were two parts to it, one older and fashioned of stone, the other newer and built from wood.

Stone towers bracketed either end of the main structure composed of a towering rectangle of stone and an equally elegant structure rendered from wood and brick. It was obvious the castle had been neglected for some time, but it was seeing the attention it rightly needed now.

Besides the outer wall, a crew worked fastidiously repairing the cement balustrades of the main staircase leading to a set of wide oak doors. Another crew crawled along scaffolding that covered the front, their tools set to repairing the windows and patching the masonry.

It was a sight to see, and she couldn't help but feel lost in the middle of it. She rubbed at her arms, suddenly chilled even in the sunlight. She shook her head as if to clear her troubling thoughts. She didn't wish for this marriage, and she knew the dangers that may lie in it, but she had to keep her sisters safe. She slipped inside in search of Mrs. Fairfax.

After a few wrong turns and with a little guidance from a footman, she found her way to the breakfast room. Once more the light of day gave her a different perspective of the castle, and she was coming to understand what Ethel had meant about it being a testament to a man's love for a woman.

There were surprising details at every turn. The flowers carved into the door headers at intervals or the swirling plaster medallions in the ceiling framing a mural or an intricately carved scene. But she most delighted to find the lady of the castle, or at least her silhouette rendered in iron, in small details about the castle. In the iron knobs of the window shutters and the brass plates along the doorknobs. She wished she had more time to linger, but she must speak with Mrs. Fairfax.

When she reached the breakfast room, the sideboard was laden with platters, and Amelia recalled what Ethel had said about Mrs. Fairfax's apple butter, and her stomach growled. She had just filled her plate when the housekeeper entered, a steaming urn in her hands.

"Good morning, Your Grace. I trust you slept well."

Amelia set down her plate and faced the housekeeper. She had meant to dive right into her questions, but she froze at the sight of the woman. In the dim light of the previous night, she had taken the housekeeper for an older woman. Now she was surprised to find herself facing a woman that could be no more than fifteen years her senior. She was soft about the edges, her face doughy, except not with age. But it seemed...happiness?

She recalled Stephen's laughter, Ethel's bright smile, and now Mrs. Fairfax's glow of happiness. It was rather a stark contrast to the doom the rumors of the ghoul suggested.

Amelia drew a breath and dove in. "I don't wish to over-step, but I should very much like Ethel for my lady's maid. I understand she does not stay at the castle at night, but I assure you I shall be fine on my own in the evening hours."

Mrs. Fairfax's expression became almost alarmed. "But Your Grace, Ethel—"

"Is a competent young woman who is facing some diffi-culties. Should that preclude her from advancing in life?" She tried to keep her features neutral and yet give no room for argument.

"You are absolutely correct, Your Grace," she said after a quick search of Amelia's face. She wondered briefly what the housekeeper had seen there to cause such a swift response.

Amelia went on before she could lose her nerve. "I should also like a tour of the household. Would you have time today to accompany me? I can only imagine the work that must go into running a household such as this, and I shan't wish to take you away from any pressing duties."

Mrs. Fairfax's expression opened then, her eyes lighting once more. "Of course I shall have the time, Your Grace. When would you like to begin?"

"Immediately after breakfast if you are able." She picked up a piece of bread. "But first I must try this apple butter I keep hearing about."

The housekeeper nearly bubbled over with embarrassed pride, her hands pressing nervously to her cheeks.

Amelia took the woman's momentary befuddlement to

ask a more delicate question. "Mrs. Fairfax, have you been in service to the duke for a considerable time?"

Mrs. Fairfax wrapped both hands around the tea urn, her expression becoming pensive. "Yes, Your Grace. I have."

Amelia noted the use of her title rather than the endearment the woman had used the night before. She set down her fork and knife, folding her hands in her lap to meet Mrs. Fairfax's gaze directly.

"I don't wish to pry," she said. "I'm very well aware of the rumors circulating in society about my husband. It's only I wonder if there's anything I should know that could help me."

Mrs. Fairfax set down the tea urn, and in a surprising move, she eased herself into a chair opposite Amelia. She sat, her eyes wide as though she were so taken in by Amelia's statement she wasn't really thinking about the impropriety of the situation.

"Help you with what, dearie?"

Amelia's courage was bolstered by the use of the endearment. "It just seems as though my husband runs away from me a great deal."

She was not expecting the housekeeper to divulge her husband's secrets. After all, such a thing would be the mark of a poor servant. But she didn't miss the look of complete sadness that skated across Mrs. Fairfax's features before she could school her expression against Amelia's words.

The housekeeper leaned forward, her hands folded on the table before her.

"Your Grace, if I may speak bluntly?" Amelia nodded, but Mrs. Fairfax had already continued. "His Grace has suffered. Far more than any of the rumors can suggest. I can only tell you that it will take time and a great deal of patience to help the duke now."

"Help him?" Amelia sat up straighter at the words,

curiosity and not a little apprehension thrumming down her spine.

Mrs. Fairfax pursed her lips before continuing, but her eyes had shifted as though she were seeing another place. "He will need to be shown that the past will not always repeat itself, and that can only be revealed in time."

The housekeeper stood and floated from the room before Amelia could even decipher what the woman had said.

The past will not repeat itself?

The rumors about the Ghoul of Greyfair all painted the duke's first wife as the victim of tragedy. But Mrs. Fairfax's words made it sound as though it were the duke who was the victim instead.

Amelia picked up her bread now smeared with apple butter and took an overlarge bite, hoping the sweetness might clear her confusion.

* * *

She was in Mrs. Fairfax's office in less than an hour. Once more she had gotten lost in the twisting labyrinth of Dinsmore's corridors, but she found a most helpful scullery maid carrying a bucket of cold ashes down to the kitchens who helped her find her way.

Mrs. Fairfax was seated behind a scarred desk far too large for the tiny room in which it was located off of the kitchen. The housekeeper was addressing a maid when Amelia entered, and she stopped midsentence, standing swiftly. Only the desk was crammed into the corner so smartly Mrs. Fairfax had to twist herself to stand at all.

"Your Grace," Mrs. Fairfax said, her face a painting of surprise. "You finished your breakfast already? I shouldn't wish to rush you."

Amelia smiled. "It was most enjoyable. I assure you. Ethel was right about your apple butter."

Twin spots of color rose to Mrs. Fairfax's cheeks as she ducked her head. "It's my mother's recipe. I can only take the credit for replicating it."

"The credit is well earned," Amelia said. "I do hope you have time to take me around the castle today, Mrs. Fairfax. I assume without a duchess in residence in some time, the castle's stores have not been properly cataloged recently."

Mrs. Fairfax blinked. "Well, yes, ma'am, but shouldn't you like to rest after your arduous day yesterday?"

Amelia shook her head and stepped up to Mrs. Fairfax's desk. "Not at all. I should like to begin in the rooms you feel require the most attention." She looked about, suddenly unsure. "And perhaps you might have some sleeve aprons I could borrow?" She pressed her hands to her stomach to smooth her gown. "I only have a few gowns, you see, and I'd hate to make more work for Ethel." She stopped and reconsidered. "I suppose I shall call her Jones now that she's a lady's maid." She shook her head. "There's quite a bit to get used to I'm afraid. I cannot tell you how much I appreciate your support, Mrs. Fairfax."

Mrs. Fairfax lowered her gaze to Amelia's gown, and it was not the first time Amelia felt embarrassed by the state of her apparel. It had been ages since the Atwoods had been able to afford a new set of gowns for her or her sisters, and the gowns she had left that were wearable showed obvious signs of mending.

"Of course," Mrs. Fairfax said, her tone neutral, but Amelia didn't miss that questioning look that skittered across the housekeeper's features. It was the same one Amelia had caught on the woman's face the previous night, as if she were assessing Amelia and finding something unexpected. She wasn't sure if it were a good thing or not, but

Amelia couldn't help but find censure in it. She swallowed, pushing down the feelings of inadequacy. It was only a gown after all.

Mrs. Fairfax dismissed the maid and rummaged in her desk before extracting a pair of sleeve aprons. She handed them to Amelia.

"It's not really my place, Your Grace, but there's a fine modiste in the village. If you should like to have a new wardrobe made up. There will be certain social demands on your time now as Duchess of Greyfair, and your wardrobe would be affected by them."

Amelia blinked, taking in the way the housekeeper folded her hands nervously in front of her. For the little time Amelia had known Mrs. Fairfax, she had determined the housekeeper had no qualms with stating her mind, but it seemed as though even she were reluctant to comment on Amelia's appearance. The feelings of inadequacy surged.

But still, the housekeeper was right. Amelia would need a new wardrobe. She couldn't possibly present herself the way she was. The shame it would bring on the Greyfair name. She felt something shift inside of her then. The past twelve hours had proven to be unexpected. She would never have imagined the loyalty she felt to the Greyfair title nor that it would come so swiftly, but then, she hadn't expected to feel so much hope in her new home.

She swallowed. "Speaking of appearances, I should like to thank you for your kindness in thinking to provide a night-dress for me on my arrival. It was quite unexpected."

Mrs. Fairfax blinked, her lips forming a soft O. "Your gratitude is misplaced, Your Grace. It was the duke who thought to ensure you were provided for upon your arrival."

Amelia stilled, one arm halfway through an apron sleeve. "The duke?"

Mrs. Fairfax nodded. "He ordered the new furnishings for

the duchess's room as soon as the marriage contract was signed. The other things he fretted over for weeks before you arrived. I must say I'm sorry for the size of the nightdress in particular." Mrs. Fairfax pressed her lips together, and color came to her cheeks. "His Grace only thought of it the day before yesterday and was quite adamant we procure it before you arrived. It was all the modiste had ready in such short notice." The housekeeper's gaze traveled up and down Amelia's person. "I take it the garment was rather overlarge?"

One thought after another whirled through Amelia's mind. No one had ever done such nice things for her, and her chest tightened with the unfamiliarity of it. But she had to remember, before yesterday, she was only part of a contract to the duke. He didn't know of her shortcomings.

It was several seconds before she could clear her mind to answer Mrs. Fairfax. "Yes, it was quite overlarge, but still much appreciated."

She paused, thinking how to ask her next question. Like much of everything she had anticipated about her marriage, her thoughts about the previous duchess had been marred by the rumors swirling about the duke. But now, hearing Mrs. Fairfax speak of the trappings the previous duchess might have used, suddenly made the woman real instead of a character in the grim stories of the duke's past. But more, it suddenly occurred to Amelia that her husband had been married before, to this woman who had died tragically.

Had he loved her? Did he pine for her? She couldn't help it as her eyes drifted about the room, remembering what Jones had said about the castle being an ode to a lost love.

"Did the previous duchess choose the decor for the duchess's room?" It sounded so innocuous when said like that, but suddenly Amelia needed to know. Had the duke replaced the furnishings in the room because he couldn't bear to look at them? Did they remind him of his first wife?

Mrs. Fairfax's expression went blank for an instant, and Amelia's stomach clenched. But then she shook her head. "No, ma'am. The previous duchess had no interest in such things, and further, she was never in residence here at Dinsmore. The duke only made this his primary residence after —" Mrs. Fairfax stopped speaking so abruptly it was as if she had simply run out of air. "This is the primary residence of the Duke of Greyfair now and has been for only the past couple of years," she said then, her words vague.

A new sense of apprehension descended on Amelia then that had nothing to do with the dark rumors about the duke. Mrs. Fairfax had chosen her words carefully; that much was clear. So what was she hiding?

Even as these cautious thoughts tripped through her mind, Amelia couldn't help but recognize the fact that the housekeeper was protecting the duke. Was it merely out of concern for her position, or did her loyalty run deeper than that?

"I see," Amelia said. "So the duke shouldn't be concerned if I choose to change some of the decor to be more suitable for a ducal household?"

Mrs. Fairfax was quick to shake her head. "I don't believe so, Your Grace."

Amelia smiled, hoping to set the housekeeper at ease. "Splendid. Where would you like to begin our tour?"

Mrs. Fairfax squeezed her way around the desk. "It's probably best to begin on the upper floors. The rooms there have never been used, and I'm afraid most have given way to storing things."

Amelia moved out into the corridor as Mrs. Fairfax bustled along, reaching for a ring of keys clanking at her waist.

"Was there much to be stored then?"

Mrs. Fairfax gave her a sidelong glance, and Amelia

couldn't help but think the housekeeper was deciding how much or what to say.

"I assume you know of the circumstances that brought the duke to Dinsmore." The housekeeper studied her, but Amelia kept her gaze resolutely forward, her fingers clenched on her apron sleeves, wondering what the woman would say. "What could be salvaged as far as furnishings and heirlooms from the duke's previous home were brought here." Another sidelong glance. Amelia kept her expression neutral even as her heart pounded, the sound echoing in her ears. "The duke's attention was drawn to more immediate matters when we arrived here, and I'm afraid the items have been left to gather dust in the upper floors. I suppose it is time to see to it."

She said nothing more as they climbed the servants' stairs to the upper floor. The kitchen and the basement rooms appeared to be housed in the newer part of the castle, and Amelia ran her hand along the polished banister of the stairs. The storm and darkness of the night before had allowed her mind to conjure all kinds of beasts and misgivings about the castle, but as she drew her hand away, she noted how clean it all was, even here in the servants' area.

She followed Mrs. Fairfax, winding their way back through the twisting corridors until they arrived in the vestibule with the wide wooden plank flooring. It was late morning now, and the space was flooded with light. Amelia stopped, suddenly stricken by the sight of it.

What had been a dark, cavernous void the night before was in actuality a resplendent and grand entryway. A double revolution staircase rose up directly in front of the great oak doors that led into the castle yard. The landing of the staircase was flanked by a row of stained-glass windows, their panes sending a rainbow of colors against the dark wood that made up the paneled walls of the space.

She stilled, drinking in the tableau rendered in the stained glass. It was a knight, resplendent in full armor atop a muscled steed, his sword drawn and at the ready as though he were headed into battle. The sight was arresting, and a sense of comfort fell over her. The castle had its own knight, always at the ready.

She remembered suddenly the lion she had accidentally touched the night before, and she stepped closer to the staircase, bending forward to exam the wrought iron spindles. She could feel Mrs. Fairfax watching her, but she didn't care. Now that she knew of the castle's history, she felt an odd need to take in all its details.

She found the lion's head, perfectly etched into the iron at the top of the spindle, its mouth open, its fangs neatly outlined in the metal.

"Why the lion's head when the other etchings are of the lady?" Amelia asked without looking up.

Mrs. Fairfax shifted behind her. "It was a good luck charm of sorts," she said, and now Amelia did straighten and met the housekeeper's gaze as she continued. "The duke meant them to ward off evil spirits."

Amelia swallowed and said nothing else.

They continued their trek up the staircase and down the corridor to another flight of stairs, this one curling around an open gallery that led to the upper floors. Amelia's head swam with the finery of the wood paneling, the intricately woven carpets that covered the wide plank floors, the gilded frames of portraits, the exquisitely rendered sconces in brass, and the occasional chandelier of fine crystal.

What had been like a nightmare only hours before was now revealed for the majesty it was, and Amelia couldn't help but notice the sense of home deepening within her. When they reached the final landing, she paused, her fingers trailing over the balustrade as she allowed her senses to fill with the sights, sounds, and even the smells of the space around her. It was as though at any moment the ghost of the lady for whom the castle was built would appear.

Would she give Amelia her blessing in taking over the management of the castle? Or would she try to frighten her away?

It was several seconds before she realized Mrs. Fairfax had disappeared into one of the rooms off the corridor. Amelia followed, adjusting her apron sleeves as she prepared to get to work.

Only when she stepped into the room behind Mrs. Fairfax did she freeze, a needle of dread dragging along her spine like a single fingernail.

The room was cluttered, crammed with what appeared to be furniture draped in dust cloths, boxes and crates stacked haphazardly about the room. While the rest of the castle had been pristine, these rooms were obviously left alone.

Was it by order of the duke or were the servants simply reluctant to come in here?

For just inside the door, peeking out from a dust cloth gone askew was a delicate wooden cradle, its gentle renderings blackened by soot.

Amelia stared, trying to force herself to blink, to look away, to even draw a breath.

The rumors had never mentioned a child. Had the duke lost a babe in the fire?

While the dread and despair at the sight of the cradle overwhelmed, something else grew far stronger, roaring inside of her until she was forced to ask, "Did a child perish in the fire as well?"

Mrs. Fairfax had avoided mention of the fire directly, but Amelia would not skirt the issue. The housekeeper had been adjusting crates along the wall to make room for them to enter, and her hands stilled at Amelia's words.

"No," the housekeeper finally said after a noticeable hesitation. "There was no child."

While the answer should have been comforting, Amelia couldn't help but notice the way Mrs. Fairfax avoided her gaze when she gave it.

CHAPTER 5

*H*e was hiding. In his own room. In his own damned castle.

He had thought he was acquiring a timid, meek debutante for a bride when he'd made the deal with Biggleswade. He couldn't have known the Atwood daughter would be so terrifyingly strong, resilient, and...likable. Worst of all, he didn't know he would feel such an inexplicable attraction to her.

He sat in his tower room, reclining in the chair behind the pitted wooden table he used as a desk, his booted feet propped atop it, and pretended as though there wasn't a pressing need to be somewhere else.

He couldn't wait any longer. He'd worked too damned hard to secure a wife to give him an heir. Why was he stalling now? He had to address the issue tonight. But if he only waited a few minutes more, the duchess's room would be that much darker.

He scratched at the place where the collar of his greatcoat rubbed against his cheek. He'd been unable to relinquish the garment upon returning to the castle that evening, and he sat there like the utter fool he was, dressed as though he might leave at any moment, hat firmly affixed to his head. But there was something about knowing she was within the castle walls now that made him reluctant to give up the items he had begun to think of as his armor.

What if she saw him? All of him?

In his mind, he kept picturing her as he had first discovered her, that one hand reaching through the dark. How could he have guessed then what she would do to him, the reaction she would stir inside of him?

He shuddered and pulled his coat tighter around him. No one had seen the true state of his face except Stephen and Mrs. Fairfax. He himself had studied the totality of the damage in a mirror only once. Now when he attended to his toilette, he was careful to keep the better part of the right side of his face out of the mirror's circumference.

But how was he to make love to his wife without her seeing his face?

Would it be awkward to keep his hat on?

He dropped his feet to the floor and stood. There was no sense in sitting there ruminating. He was married now, and this was for the rest of his life. He might as well get on with it.

But he couldn't stop the lick of apprehension that curled through him as he left his room, winding down the spiral stone staircase in the near dark with utter ease.

His own demons he could battle. He had for more than two years now. But this new one, this unexpected attraction, how could he keep it at bay where it could do him no harm?

Much as he had the night before, he paused in front of her door, studying the line of light that ran under it. Like the night before it remained unmoving, a steady beam giving no clues as to the occupants inside.

Occupants he knew because Argus had been strangely

absent for most of the day. The wolfhound was usually his shadow, traipsing after him in his business about the estate, but since his wife's arrival, the wolfhound had found a new person to shadow.

The idea did something odd to Lucas's chest, and he decided to ignore it.

This time he knocked more loudly, hoping to wake her if she had fallen asleep. It was time to get on with this business.

"Come in."

He snatched his hand back as if the oak door had scalded him. He hadn't been expecting a response, and the sound of her voice had sent a momentary spike of terror through him. He swallowed and pushed open the door.

He reared back immediately upon entering, throwing up a hand to shield his face. The room was flooded with light. Light everywhere. From the candles on the dressing table to the roaring fire to the candelabra glowing in the corner. He backed up until he ran into the door, unable to go any farther without leaving the room.

"Your Grace?" came his wife's concerned inquiry.

He peered around the edge of his hand still blocking his face. "That's a great deal of light," he muttered, realizing he made very little sense.

There was a scuffling noise and Argus's distinct whine before the light in the room dimmed a degree.

"I'm terribly sorry. Is that better?"

He moved his hand an inch and saw she had extinguished the candelabra. He eyed the now smoking fixture, guilt flooding through him. She had responded to his strange statement without hesitation. She hadn't even asked for an explanation. Now what did she think of him? Likely that the rumors of the Ghoul of Greyfair were true, that he indeed preferred the dark.

He knew of the rumors, of course. He had worked very hard to nurture them after all.

He dropped his hand completely but kept his back against the door.

"Yes, that's much better. It's just…" He let his voice trail away because what was the explanation? That he didn't wish for her to see his face? That would hardly make things better.

It was then that she came into focus, and his heart simply stopped beating in his chest.

She wore a dressing gown of such a soft, ethereal blue it made her appear like something angelic, which only made it seem worse that he should think he could touch her. That gorgeous thick dark hair lay in a loose braid over one shoulder, and she stood calmly, her hands folded in front of her, her eyes wide and expectant as though she were waiting for him to do something.

He realized she would be inexperienced at this, but it had not truly registered with him how innocent. He would be required to lead her through all of what was about to happen, and yet he could not move away from the door.

He wasn't sure how long they stood like that, each studying the other, until finally she blinked and looked away, moving to a tray that had been left on the table by the fire.

"I had Mrs. Fairfax bring up a tray. I didn't see you at supper, and I was concerned you hadn't eaten."

She hadn't seen him at supper or luncheon or tea for that matter. He had done his best to avoid her, and now he felt a stab of guilt at her thoughtful gesture.

"Thank you, but I'm not hungry." His stomach was far too twisted into knots at the moment to think about food.

Her eyes flashed to his, and an expression passed over her face so quickly he couldn't quite name it. He had the horrible sense it was disappointment, and worse it wasn't in him but rather in herself.

He pushed away from the door. "It was very thoughtful of you to think of me." The words came out stilted, and he cursed himself. He was perfectly capable of speech. Why should he get tongue-tied around her?

When she turned those soft, wide eyes on him, he knew perfectly well why.

A smile came haltingly to her lips, and her eyes moved about the room as if searching for the next topic of conversation.

Feeling his guilt increase as she clearly struggled to amuse him, he said, "I trust you're settling in well."

God, he sounded like a blathering idiot.

But her smile was firmer now as she turned back to him. "Oh yes, everything is quite lovely. Mrs. Fairfax showed me around the castle today. It was most helpful."

Something dark stirred within him. "Showed you around the castle?"

Her smile remained steady. "Oh yes, it's such a lovely estate. I understand your grandfather built it."

The thing inside of him settled, convinced her exploration of the castle was innocent and she did not wish to seek out his secrets.

He went to scratch his forehead before remembering he had pulled his hat ridiculously low. "Yes, my grandfather built it," he muttered.

She took a small, curious step toward him, and he would have stepped back had the door allowed him to.

"I understand he built it for his betrothed. It's rather a sad story but also painfully lovely."

He blinked. "It's a lie," he said before he could think better of it. He closed his eyes, hating himself.

Hadn't he once been considered the most eligible bachelor of the *ton*? Hadn't he once wooed women with mere words?

71

When he opened his eyes, he saw her expression had fallen, and he hated himself.

"Oh," she whispered.

"My grandfather swindled the estate from a rival in a hand of cards. It was only the stone structure then. My grandfather built the rest of it as a grand snub to said rival."

Her eyes widened, and her lips parted soundlessly, and he wondered why he couldn't just shut his mouth.

"I see," she said, and she looked about her as though she were lost. "So it's not a love letter to one's betrothed?"

He snorted. "Hardly. It's a brazen show of wealth and excess. My grandfather could be a bastard when he chose to be."

Dear Lord, he should throw himself from the tower. What an imbecile he had become.

Perhaps Stephen was right when he insisted Lucas needed to take a more active part in estate business. Isolating himself from others was clearly causing him to lose all social graces.

But then she smiled. It was just for an instant and clearly done reluctantly, but something warm and solid pulsed within him at the sight of it.

He had made her smile.

A flash of memory coursed through him then, and he forced his eyes toward the fire. Her small hand reaching up, searching for help in the dark. What if she had been hurt? What if she had died?

As soon as the thought entered his mind, everything else seemed to vanish. His ability to breathe, his heart's ability to pump blood, everything. He stood, suspended in the moment as the horrors of his past assaulted him.

Once more he was back in the fire, searching through the flames even though he knew it was hopeless.

It was because he was lost in his own torment that she

was able to do it. She reached up, her fingers clasping around the brim of his hat before he realized what she was about.

"Please, let me help you out of your things so you're more comfortable."

The hat left his head before he could stop her, but as the light hit him full in the face, he reacted more out of instinct, one hand going up to snatch the wrist that held his hat, his eyes darting to her face as reality crashed around him, as the sickening sense of dread pooled in his stomach until he thought he might be sick.

But worst of all, he watched her face, waited for her reaction when she saw him. For he had been too late. The hat was gone, and the warmth of the fire burned across his skin.

Her eyes widened, her lips parted, a gasp escaping them, and then—

Her free hand flew to his face, cupping his scarred cheek.

"Oh God," she said, snatching her hand back. But then reached forward again, the hand hanging suspended between them, but his mind had turned to mush at her first touch, and he couldn't figure out what the hell was going on. "Oh God," she said again. "Did I hurt you?"

Her hand. That same hand that had been reaching out of the darkness moved again, and once more she laid it against the ravaged side of his face, softly, carefully. Her touch was cool and distracting, and he wanted to cry at the joy of being touched by another person. It had been so long since anyone had touched him.

Her eyes roved over his face, her lips still parted in question, but he couldn't speak.

"It's only…when we were children, Nanny always pressed her hand to whatever injury we might incur in our play, and it always made me feel better, and it was just…well, it was instinct. I'm sorry. I hope I didn't…does it hurt?"

Her words were a jumbled mess, but he hadn't heard anything more beautiful in all of his life.

He shook his head. He felt himself do it, and yet it was as though he were no longer in his body but rather standing outside of it, looking in, somehow longing to be the one to be touched by this beautiful creature who seemed unafraid of his ugly scars.

He still held her wrist in his grip, his hat hanging seemingly forgotten from her fingertips. He suddenly didn't care about his hat. He only wished she would keep touching him.

And she did, only now her hand was moving, tracing the rutted contours of his face, traveling higher, around his ear to where his hair no longer grew, his skin nothing more than pebbled scars. When she reached the deep trough above his ear, he couldn't stop the flinch as her fingers glided over the sensitive skin, and he hated himself the moment she pulled her hand away.

"It does hurt. I'm sorry. I'm didn't mean—"

She took a step back, and panic gripped him. He let go of her wrist and without thinking set his hands to her hips as if to hold her in place, to keep her with him.

"No, it doesn't hurt. It…" He stumbled over the words as she continued to watch him, her concerned eyes only making him fumble more.

He closed his eyes, willing himself to remain coherent. He had never described what his scars felt like before, and both not knowing how to word it and having her look at him like that—God, she looked at him like he was worth saving—nothing had ever been more difficult than finding a way to tell her how it felt. "They are sensitive and…itchy."

He felt the rush of shame that had grown so familiar in the past two years as soon as the words left his lips, and he hated himself anew. He had all but compared himself to a dog with mange, but when he opened his eyes, his racing thoughts and self-recriminations vanished at the sight of her face.

The look of concern had been replaced by one of determination, and it sent a lick of fiery anticipation through him.

She pressed a hand to his chest, and he wondered if she would slay him with just her touch.

"Sit," she said.

He did as she told him to, unhesitatingly, but not without letting his hands drift unnecessarily over the curve of her hips. Was he always destined to steal intimacies from her?

But then she walked away from him.

"What are you doing?" His gaze followed her across the room, hungry to watch her easy movements as she walked, the way her hips swayed and her long legs caught against the telling fabric of the dressing gown.

She bent, rummaging in a trunk tucked along the foot of the bed. He was surprised when she lifted not one but two stacks of books from the trunk before returning to it once more. He indulged himself however, getting his fill of her rounded bottom. When she emerged, she held a small ceramic pot aloft in one hand as if she were presenting him with a rare jewel.

"What is that?" He eyed the pot, but the look of triumph on her face was irresistible.

"Relief," she said and advanced toward him.

It wasn't the kind of relief he had in mind, but he sat back in his chair, for the first time in a long while not thinking about anything else but that very moment.

* * *

His face.

All at once she felt what it must have been like, whatever it was that had caused it, and it was like a blow to her stomach. But even as the specter of pain sliced through her another sense came roaring behind it, a stronger one, an instinctual one.

The need to protect him.

The urge was startling, and her fingers trembled on the ceramic pot in her hands. She knew this man was dangerous, and any kind of relationship she formed with him would be perilous, but this...these emotions he pulled out of her were so unexpected. She wondered what else she should fear from him.

The scars traveled across the right side of his face, spreading along the ear and into the hairline. A thicker ridge spread just behind the ear, and the hair there grew in spots, leaving the angry, red welts bare.

Those scars were reminders of what had happened. She was coming to understand the rumors about the Ghoul of Greyfair were not fact but rather founded in some kind of truth, and she feared what really had happened was far darker.

Her own pain lessened when she had touched him, the ghosts retreating once more to the shadows. But then the touch became different, more, and she'd wanted to explore him.

But then he had touched her. His grip on her hips had sent a spike of pure pleasure through her, and behind it, the guilt of selfishness. She had exposed his secret, and here she was taking pleasure from him. But worst of all, she didn't wish to feel it. The pleasure he drove in her. It was too dangerous.

She understood the hat and greatcoat now, the darkness and secrecy. Only she had taken away his choice to tell her, and even through the wave of guilt, she wanted him to touch her again.

She pushed the selfish feelings aside as she pried the cork

from the small ceramic pot and set both on the table by the chair, shoving the untouched tray of food to one side.

"My sister once burned herself quite badly, and she said this helped a great deal once the scar had healed over." She scooped some of the salve onto her fingers. "I think the witch hazel has something to do with it. It's said to help with irritation." She stopped in front of him, holding the hand cupping the salve in the palm of the other. "May I?"

He looked at her directly now and not with a sidelong glance, and the effect was powerful. But more, she saw his eyes were the color of a summer sky. If anyone had witnessed them, they would know he was no ghoul. No one with eyes like that could be. His hair was long where it grew and uneven as though he trimmed it himself, but it framed a face of strong features that mesmerized her. She swallowed, willing her stomach to settle.

"Your sister?" he asked as she bent to examine the pebbled skin of his right cheek.

"My youngest sister, Alice. She's rather prone to such mishaps."

"Is she clumsy then?" His tone was curious rather than accusing, and she couldn't help a smile.

"No, actually. Adaline—that's my older sister—started calling her the dangerous daughter when we were still quite young. Alice has a hazardous interest in science, I'm afraid."

She started at a deep fold just in front of his ear, whispering her fingers across his skin to prevent further irritation as she applied the salve.

"Science?" Now his voice was incredulous, and she found her smile grew firmer.

"Yes. She was attempting to replicate a voltaic pile." She dipped her fingers in the ceramic pot again, and when she turned back found he had raised a single eyebrow. "A battery. She was attempting to prove something about chemical reactivity versus metal reactivity. She's lucky she was only left with a small scar on her wrist."

"Has she had any formal schooling?"

She was concentrating on applying the salve to the ridge along the back of his ear but moved her gaze to his at this. He raised both eyebrows and slid his eyes away from hers as though embarrassed, which only made her feel guilty for speaking of her sister in the first instance.

"Your family didn't have the funds for formal schooling, I take it."

She straightened, massaging the remnants of the salve into her hands. "We did once, but after my mother took ill, paying for her care absorbed most of it."

She made to cork the ceramic pot, but he caught her wrist. She looked up quickly and found his gaze intent on her.

"I'm truly sorry for what you've lost, Lady Amelia. I can't imagine losing your parents in such close proximity like that."

Several emotions climbed up her throat at the exact moment, and she found all she could say was, "Amelia." She swallowed and tried again. "You must call me Amelia."

His lips softened as he spoke her name, as though he were trying it out and found it to his liking. "Amelia then. And you must call me Lucas."

She nodded and turned back to the ceramic pot, happy to have something with which to busy herself.

"Amelia Atwood," he murmured. "That's a lot of As."

"My mother thought it cute."

"What do you think of it?"

She shrugged. "I'm no longer an Atwood, so it hardly matters."

"I suppose that's true," he said, and she wasn't sure, but it was as though something crackled between them.

She wiped her hands on one of the linen napkins on the tray of food. "Do you have any siblings, Your Grace?"

"Lucas." Again his tone was distracted as though he were lost in something she had said.

"Lucas," she said just as quietly.

It was a beat before he answered her, and when he did his voice was low as though he were thinking of something else. "No siblings. It's just been Stephen and I since childhood."

She felt her feet shift as though she were disappearing, evaporating little by little, in the intensity of his gaze, but even as she felt herself fade, she became acutely aware of pieces of herself. How long had her heart been beating like that? Were her hands shaking from effort or from something else?

Lucas stood abruptly, and she backed up, rubbing her hands together to stop them from trembling.

"Amelia." He spoke her name as though he were swallowing a particularly sour piece of fruit. "I have come here tonight because we must consummate the marriage. I trust your sister—was it Adalyn?"

"Adaline," she provided, dropping her hands to her sides.

"Yes, Adaline. I trust she told you what to expect."

"Yes, I'm quite prepared," she lied and nodded firmly as if to solidify the untruth.

She wasn't prepared for this at all, but she was mildly relieved that she mustn't seduce him. But the relief lasted only a second as she thought about what was to happen. He was going to touch her, all of her. What would happen? Would her body respond to his the way it had so far? Could she risk allowing her attraction to him grow like that?

Relief flooded his features, and his shoulders slumped.

She didn't know why, but it hurt, seeing his reaction to her words. Was consummating their marriage such a burden to him then? Or was it worse than that?

Strangely, Mrs. Fairfax's words from earlier came back to her then, and she wondered not for the first time if something darker haunted the duke.

Lucas.

He had asked her to call him Lucas.

It suddenly made him seem real, thinking of him by his given name, and she wondered again if he mourned for his first wife. The image of the blackened cradle flashed in her mind, and it was all she could do to keep her breathing even.

She studied him now as he looked about the room as if trying to decide what to do next.

Was it lonely to be him? One would never question if the Ghoul of Greyfair was lonely, but it wasn't the ghoul she studied now. It was Lucas, her husband, and he seemed…

Just as lost as she sometimes felt.

She licked her lips and fingered the knot of her dressing gown's belt. Her heart began to race anew, but it was different now. This wasn't tension she was feeling. It was anticipation, as though her mind were three steps ahead, a decision already made, a decision so unlike herself it would change everything.

"Good," he said then, looking anywhere but at her. He shuffled his feet backward until the chair he had been sitting in stood between them. He placed both hands atop it, rubbing his palms across the fabric, and still he stalled. Until finally, "I can give you some time to—"

"I liked it when you kissed me." The words were out like a gunshot, and her hand flew to her heart as it threatened to tumble from her chest in shock.

Had she really just said that?

Her mother was always quick to remind her that her feelings didn't matter, and this coupled with being lost between her sisters, Amelia had never voiced her feelings like that.

There was no place for them, and now she'd gone and done...that?

Her statement was little more than dipping her toe into the ocean, and yet it felt as though she had plunged into the icy estuary headfirst. The shock of it took her breath away, and ridiculously, that was all she said.

That she had liked it when he kissed her.

In those flashes of hope before her arrival at Dinsmore Castle, when she believed that here things might be different, that here she might be enough, this was not what she had imagined.

Humiliating herself in front of her new husband.

Why couldn't she be elegant and graceful like Adaline?

Why couldn't she be intelligent and witty like Alice?

Instead, she was just Amelia, and she had a terrible talent for speaking what was on her mind when she really should have kept her mouth shut.

She was staring at him, unable to look away, her heart pounding in her temples as she waited for his reaction.

"I liked it when I kissed you too." The words were whispered, and she thought she had misheard him.

He moved, sliding to the edge of the chair as though he might step back around it, but then he stopped as if changing his mind.

"We could try doing it again." Again the words tumbled from her lips.

His lips parted, and she realized he had a nice face. She wondered if he had been quite handsome once. He was several inches taller than she, and he had the steely leanness born of hard work. She pictured him as she had come upon him that morning on the causeway, remembered the feel of his strong arms around her the night before, and suddenly heat was climbing up her neck.

She tugged at the folds of her dressing gown, trying to get air against her skin.

"I don't wish to make you uncomfortable, Your Grace. I know what is required of us in the marriage act, but I don't want you to think—"

He moved so quickly there was no more time for words.

Those strong arms she remembered—*longed for*—were suddenly around her again, and he was kissing her. She made a noise of surprise that melted into a groan as he pressed against her, his hands fisting into the back of her dressing gown as though he couldn't hold on to her tight enough.

He devoured her, and she let him, reveling in the way he consumed her. His kiss was powerful and hot, taking from her at the same time he gave. But while his lips tormented hers, his hands roamed over her body, sliding along her hips, digging into her back, cupping her buttocks.

She wanted to cry from the intensity of it. Never before had someone touched her like this, and she suddenly realized how terribly lonely she was.

She wanted more.

She wanted all of it.

With him.

The realization shocked her, but instead of easing back, her fingers curled into his shoulders, lifting herself against him. He made a sound then of such sheer pleasure, a thrill shot through her.

She had done that. Kissing her had done that to him.

His hands moved deliberately now, and she stilled, waiting, anticipating. His clever fingers found the belt of her gown, undoing the knot as though it were nothing at all, and then his hands slipped beneath the folds of fabric.

Only to immediately pull them back out, snatch at the opening of her gown, and press the sides back together.

He tore his mouth from hers, his eyes wide, startled.

"You're naked." His words were ragged, his breath uneven.

"Yes," she managed, blinking as though it would help gather her scattered senses. "I thought it would be easier."

"Easier?" He spoke the word as if he'd never heard it before.

She nodded. "Easier for when we..." She slid her eyes toward the bed, unsure of how to say it. "Consummate the marriage."

He followed her gaze to the bed, his expression opening as though he hadn't realized it was there. "Right. Yes. Well." He stopped then, stringing only the three words together like an aborted trail of breadcrumbs. Then he met her gaze again and said, "Shall we?"

And she couldn't help but think it sounded more as though he were inviting her to promenade instead of make love.

She felt a stab of something then as though she had unconsciously been hoping for more. But what had she been expecting? Love?

The familiar pain coursed through her, but she ignored it. As ever, her feelings didn't matter. She stepped back and pushed the dressing gown from her shoulders.

CHAPTER 6

*S*he was naked.

His fingertips had stolen the barest of touches, but it was enough. He knew now how smooth her skin was, how supple. How very warm she was. He wondered if she were warm enough to reach the coldest parts of him.

She had enjoyed his kiss.

Even now when she knew the truth about his face, she had admitted as much.

But she still hadn't seen the rest of him. The thought served as an icy shock, and the nerves that had plagued him all day came roaring back, stronger now.

Somehow he felt as though he were lying to her by not saying anything about the rest of his scars. The ones that traveled down his right shoulder, over his back. It was like he had lulled her into submission by not telling her the full extent of the damage that had been done to him.

But she had touched him, unhesitatingly, almost instinctually, and that must have counted for something.

But then she had pushed the dressing gown from her shoulders.

It lay in a pool at her feet, the firelight licking her naked body. His tongue lodged in his mouth as if it had grown three sizes, and his heart pounded so furiously he could hear it in his ears.

He swallowed. "Amelia." He spoke her name like an oath or maybe it was a prayer. A prayer for what? Salvation? For this not to be a dream?

He wanted to tell her how beautiful she was. With her pert breasts, the gentle swell of her belly, the achingly perfect curve of her hips, her pale sturdy thighs. But he couldn't make his tongue move, his lips to work.

When his eyes reached her legs, his mind instantly flooded with images and sensations, picturing perfectly what it would both look and feel like to have those legs wrapped around him as he tortured her into exquisite ecstasy.

He stood there, fully clothed, completely hard, aching and confused.

He had thought this part of him dead. He had believed begetting an heir would be a heartless transaction. But this was anything but that.

Too many things swarmed through him to even understand what it was he should do next. He should touch her. He knew that much, but at the same time he knew it, he feared it.

It had been so long since he'd been with a woman, and now, to be with one so beautiful she rendered him senseless was the ultimate torture.

But then his life had been nothing but obstacles, and it hadn't broken him yet, though it might try.

He suddenly felt every layer of clothing on him as though it weighed a thousand stone more than it really did. He shucked his greatcoat, his eyes never leaving her face. But then once more he was left standing there.

"Is there something I'm supposed to do?" Her voice

faltered, only a little, but it was enough to have him feeling like an ass.

"No." The word came out too quickly, too pronounced, as though he were scolding her for asking a question. "No, it's not that. It's…"

But what was it?

What was holding him back?

His scars. The answer came instantly to his mind, but even he knew that wasn't the truth. There was something else, something he couldn't name standing between them as if it were a real obstacle.

He prodded at it, this sense of immobility.

A beautiful woman stood in front of him. She was completely naked, willing him to take her, and she was his *wife*.

Silence engulfed them. Argus's snores and the intermittent crackle of the fire the only sound in the room.

That was when the most awful thing happened. He let the silence grow. He let the moment expand until it took over, and what little courage he had summoned had vanished.

"Perhaps if we were to snuff out the lights."

It took a moment for him to figure out what she had said. She didn't wish to see him then. All of him.

But then she continued, "You seem most at ease in the dark, and I only wish to make you more comfortable."

Comfortable.

She was concerned for his comfort? As he stood there and ogled her while she was naked?

He'd had enough. Of himself.

He closed the distance between them, pulling her into his arms before he could let himself rethink it.

"I don't want darkness," he nearly growled. "I want to see every part of you."

He saw her eyes widen right before he captured her

mouth in a searing, hot kiss. Years of loneliness and anguish poured out of him with that kiss, and yet it wasn't enough. He couldn't get enough of her.

His hands swarmed down her back, cupped her buttocks, pressed her against him. He nibbled kisses along her jawline, pressed his lips to that spot behind her ear, plunged his hands into her thick mane of hair, destroying the loose braid.

It wasn't enough.

He was devouring her like a starved man at a feast, and yet it wasn't helping. He was still starved. He was still crazed with hunger for her.

He hadn't even realized he craved the company of a woman. Not like this. Not like now.

But he knew that wasn't the truth. It wasn't any woman who would do this to him. It was her. This creature who had reached out of the dark to him. This woman who continued to defy all of his expectations for her.

He wrenched himself away from her, his breathing ragged, his hands trembling even as he held her at arm's length.

"Amelia," he said again, surer this time. "I want to make love to you. I very much want..."

He had let his eyes drop. It hadn't been on purpose, but it had happened, and he caught sight of her nipples, pebbled and pert. The sight of them rendered him incapable of finishing his sentence for they were a clear indication of her arousal.

She was responding to him.

He knew a woman could pretend. A woman could fake enjoyment, pleasure. But this...this wasn't faked.

Before he knew what he was doing, he reached out a hand, caressed one breast with two fingers. She sucked in a breath. He both felt and heard it, and he wanted to look at her face, to study her expression, to know what she was thinking, feeling, but he couldn't look away from her body. He couldn't look away as he trailed those two fingers over her breast, circling her nipple, watching it tighten.

"Lucas."

His eyes shot up. Her eyelids were half shut, her lips parted on a soft moan.

He pulled the hand from her breast to bury it in her hair, pull her close. Her eyes flew open, and he held her there, capturing her attention.

"Amelia, the rest of me. The rest of me is scarred like my face, and—"

"I don't care about the rest of it as long as you kiss me again."

The words went straight to his heart, and he did as she bid, his mouth plundering, taking and giving until she was limp in his embrace.

Only then did he carry her to the bed, picking her up and holding her against his body like he had done the night before. But now there was no sense of danger, no threatening storm, and he allowed his body to relax, to take in the feel of her, the way muscle gave way to curve, the way her arms reached for him, held him that much closer.

They tumbled to the bed together, each unwilling to let the other go, and he spun them until she was above him. She was propped on her elbows, and he took advantage of it, pulling her up until he licked one nipple into his mouth, sucking the hardened tip until she moaned, her fingers spiking through his hair. It was too much and yet not enough.

He rolled again, pinning her to the mattress, lapping his tongue over her nipple before moving to the other one and repeating the torture. His hands skimmed down her sides, memorizing every curve, discovering every valley.

He pressed his lips to the space between her breasts,

traced the contour of her breastbone, finding his way to her collarbones and higher. He drank her in at the same time he teased, driving her pleasure higher.

When he placed his lips against the juncture of her neck and jaw, just below her ear, she came up off the mattress, her fingers digging into his back, and it was as though life itself shot straight through him.

"Lucas." His name was a plea now, raw and gasping, and like she had cast a spell over him, the rest of the world fell away.

He sat up, and with one hand, reached over his head and tugged his shirt from his body in a single, fluid motion. He was back in her arms before he could draw another breath but now his chest was pressed against her, skin to skin, and nothing had been more exquisite in his life.

"Oh Jesus," he moaned against her lips, his hands curling into fists, driving into the mattress as he tried to calm himself, to not take her so quickly.

It didn't work.

She wrapped one leg around him, opening herself to him, and he couldn't help but flex his hips, pressing his hard shaft into her.

He had to get his trousers off.

He sprang from the bed, tearing at fastenings at the same time he tried to toe off his boots. Something tore. He stumbled removing the second boot. He fell back on the bed, slipping between her legs as he cradled her in his arms.

He had to go slow. No matter how much he repeated it, no matter how much he told himself that this was her first time, that he had to be gentle, his body ignored it. The fire of lust and sheer pleasure roared through him, obliterating everything else.

"Lucas," she mumbled against his kiss. "Lucas, I feel... something. I need..."

"I know," he said against her lips. "I know."

His hand swept down her side, traced the curve of her thigh, found the soft flesh at her hip.

He hesitated, his fingers caressing her skin, back and forth, as if to savor it. This moment before he touched her, before he touched her *there*, in her most intimate place. He wanted to enjoy it, to understand it, to mark it. This time before and after.

He felt the weight of what he was about to do. He didn't know how. He hadn't expected it. He hadn't expected *her*. But he knew they couldn't ignore whatever it was that burned between them.

Finally he touched her, slipping his fingers between her folds, finding her hot center. Pleasure shot through him, and his hips moved involuntarily against her. She moaned, her head going back, that gorgeous spray of dark hair falling across the pillows.

It was too much. It was too much to see, too much to taste, too much to feel.

He slipped a finger inside of her, and she bucked, her hand flying to his wrist, pinning his hand between them. She opened her eyes, met his gaze. He could see the fire there, the one he felt too, and suddenly he wasn't alone.

"Lucas," she breathed. "Lucas, what…"

He stroked her, crooking his finger in a come-hither motion. She bucked again, her head going back, her eyes sliding shut as her lips parted, as he could see her pleasure radiate from her.

He couldn't wait. He wanted to give her her pleasure first, but he throbbed now, and he knew he wouldn't be able to stand it much longer.

He shifted, his finger moving to her sensitive nub even as he pressed at her opening, just a little, feeling her expand. He slid deeper, the sensation too much, and he shut his eyes against it.

God, he wasn't going to last.

It had been too long. He wasn't used to this.

But those were just excuses. He knew that. Somehow deep within him he knew.

It didn't matter how long it had been. It didn't matter because what he found with her was unlike anything he had found before. It was hot and carnal, but it was pure and perfect too. And he simply wasn't strong enough to resist it.

He slid the rest of the way into her, his finger stroking furiously at her nub. God, he had to give her pleasure. He was desperate for it. But his body was already tightening, coiling, and he knew—

She sat up, her fingers digging into his shoulders as she arched, her breasts pressing into his chest. A scream tore from her lips, and the sight of her, the taste of her, the sound of her was too much.

Something happened then. Something so unexpected, he forgot for a moment where he was, who he was with.

The past came roaring out of the darkness like an arrow, its lethal tip ablaze in memories, threatening to engulf him.

He began to thrust, no longer feeling her beneath him, no longer understanding what he was doing. The need to finish overpowered him, and he forgot all else.

But the past was stronger, and suddenly he wasn't seeing Amelia. He wasn't *feeling* her.

Instead he saw Lila, standing before him, the flames of the fire blazing behind her. She smiled, that terrible, sickly sweet, knowing smile, the one that had taunted him for more than two years. Since the moment she had told him of what she'd done, the pleasure it had given her to admit her betrayal. The flames grew, all but engulfing him, and at the last possible moment, she turned, the rounded swell of her pregnant belly silhouetted by the bright flash of flames.

He jerked free, emptying his seed against the softness of Amelia's belly. Disgust and terror coursed through him, and he rolled to the side of the bed. He forced his eyes open, focusing on the hazy outline of the shuttered windows, anything to distract himself from the painful, tormenting thoughts that ricocheted through his mind, tearing at him.

He was going to be sick. His stomach churned, and he swallowed hard, sucking in air to clear his senses. It was only then that he realized he was shaking. He sat on the edge of the bed, unsure if he could get his feet under him, when he felt the twitch of his arms. He stood, striding away from the bed.

"Lucas."

Her voice stopped him. All at once everything inside of him was rendered quiet, still. He peered back over his shoulder where he had left her, and suddenly the past was gone, vanished like smoke.

He blinked, looked around him.

What had happened? What *was* happening?

Amelia lifted her head from the pillows, her eyes wide with concern. Oh God. He had…they were…

He moved swiftly, going to the ewer on the stand in the corner, pouring fresh water into the bowl. He soaked a length of flannel and came back to the bed.

His seed was still there, mocking him, and he wiped it away, his heart thundering in his chest. He didn't speak and thankfully neither did she. He only hoped she didn't understand what had just happened.

He set aside the flannel and slipped back into bed, pulling her against him. She was still warm and loose from their lovemaking, and he held her against him, hoping her warmth could break the icy grip his memories had on him.

As he expected, she fell asleep quickly, her breathing evening out, her arms falling away from where she had held him.

Only then did he slip from the bed. He didn't bother dressing. He simply gathered his clothes and boots in a ball, snuffing out candles as he went about the room. Argus didn't even stir as Lucas crept out into the dark, leaving his wife alone.

* * *

SHE LAY in the dark unmoving, listening to the sounds of her husband running away from her.

Again.

But this time it was far worse, her thoughts circling around a single understanding. She had seen his scars now, all of them, and she had witnessed her own treacherous reaction to him. But that wasn't the worst of it.

Her husband had scars that were invisible to the eye, and those were the ones she feared she could never heal.

She had seen the moment he left her, long before he had slinked away in the dark. It was like he was there and gone all at the same time. His body had stiffened in her arms, his muscles tightening.

And then after...after...

She had felt the bed shake slightly from the tremors that raked his body as he had perched on the edge of the bed after the act. Had seen the way he rose, walking on uncertain legs, his movements sharp and mechanical.

She had called out to him, the only thing she could think to do to bring him back to her.

For one splintering second, she had believed it to be her. That something about her had disgusted him, but then rational thought had taken over, and she knew it was something else that plagued him.

She let her hands drift down her body until they encountered the stickiness he had left against the softness of her belly. He had made some attempt to clean her, but somehow she knew something wasn't right.

She had believed he felt the same thing she did. This unexpected and surprising connection between them that sparked every time they touched. She had never thought she would find such a connection, even though she had secretly longed for such. Maybe she had been wrong though.

Something had pained him, so much so that he'd run away into the dark again. Did his first wife still haunt him? Or worse, was he haunted by what he had done to her?

A chill passed through her, and she shoved the bedclothes aside. She went directly to the fire, filling the scoop with coal from the bucket beside it and tossing it on the embers in the hearth. It sparked and lit immediately, sending light and heat into the room. Argus hardly lifted his head, and she scratched the place between his ears, finding comfort when she didn't expect it.

She studied the hound's eyes in the firelight, finding depth and warmth and kindness. Her heart constricted. She'd never had a dog and hadn't known a simple look from one could be such comfort.

"Go back to sleep, old boy," she whispered. "All is well."

She found she meant the words, a sense of inevitability settling within her. She stood and went to the ewer on the dressing table, finding the water Lucas had poured earlier in the bowl. She found a clean flannel and clean towel and used them to properly clean herself before finding the voluminous nightdress she'd worn the night before.

She had her own things now. Ethel had put them away that afternoon, but now that she knew the origin of the nightdress, she couldn't think to sleep in anything else. Kindnesses such as the nightdress were so rare to her that it didn't matter if the garment fit.

Within minutes, she was padding back to the bed only to stop, her bare toes curling into the thick carpet beneath her feet. She eyed the bed, suddenly feeling a swell of emotions that warred with one another until her head pounded. She tugged a quilt free from the many on the bed and turned back to the fire. She chose the chair closest to Argus and curled into it, tucking her feet under her and wrapping the quilt snuggly about her.

She thought she wouldn't sleep, her mind presenting a kaleidoscope of images with which to torment her, but her body must have been exhausted beyond anything her brain could conjure, and soon a restless sleep gripped her.

She woke when someone touched her shoulder, and she jerked upright, dropping the quilt on an unsuspecting Argus, who rolled, lifting his belly upward as if sensing someone was near enough to give it a rub.

She blinked until she brought Jones into focus, the young woman's brow wrinkled in concern.

"Your Grace," she spoke softly. "Are you all right? Would you like me to fetch Mrs. Fairfax?"

It was a beat before Amelia realized where she was, and the events of the previous night came cascading back to her until her heart sped up and her lungs thirsted for air. She swallowed and pushed her hair out of her face, forcing a smile.

"No, that's all right." She reached out and blindly patted Jones's arm. "I'm quite fine really. Just some terrible dreams. You know how that can be, I'm sure."

Jones eyed her as if she didn't believe her for a moment.

Amelia felt a pang of guilt and smiled harder. "I hope I didn't frighten you. It was just so pleasant to sleep by the fire." She yawned and stretched, hoping to convey a sense of normalcy, but Jones's suspicious gaze never faltered.

As if the young woman came to some kind of conclusion, she made a noise of acknowledgment and turned away.

Amelia got to her feet, returning the quilt to the bed as Jones pushed open the shutters on the window.

"Ethel, I wasn't able to find a moment to speak with you yesterday."

The maid paused, her arms still outstretched as she maneuvered the heavy shutters aside, her eyes riveted with concern on Amelia's face.

She smiled, hoping to ease the young woman's concern. "I spoke to Mrs. Fairfax yesterday, and she was agreeable to the idea of you being my lady's maid. Should you like the position?"

The young maid turned from the window fully, sunshine illuminating her from behind, so she looked something like an angel. "But Your Grace—"

Amelia held up a hand. "I won't hear any objections to it. Mrs. Fairfax agreed that you are well suited to the role."

The woman's eyes widened, her lips parting without words coming forth, and Amelia realized her eyes were a beautiful deep brown. Ethel Jones was likely quite pretty and might have been called a beauty if life hadn't already worn her down at such a tender age.

"Yes, of course, Your Grace. It's only..." Jones's voice drifted away.

"It's only what?"

The woman moved earnestly about the bed until she stood in front of Amelia. "Do you think I'm experienced enough for the position, Your Grace? I'm not ashamed of where I've come from. It's only that I haven't been employed here very long, and I should very much like to be a proper lady's maid and see my work completed to your satisfaction is all."

Amelia smiled more easily now and reached out, taking the maid's hands into hers. "It's your motivation more than anything that tells me you're right for this job, Jones. Besides, I've never had a lady's maid. I should think we'll both discover what the position entails together. How does that sound to you?"

Jones's smile was quick, and Amelia was surprised to see how it made her appear more youthful.

"I should like that very much, Your Grace." The maid squeezed her hands and released them, moving to the hearth to see to the fire.

Amelia's eyes fell on the tray Jones had likely brought with her and left on the table between the chairs. Her stomach growled at the sight, and she put a hand to her stomach. She wasn't usually quite so famished in the morning. She drew a steadying breath, knowing what was different that morning.

The suspicion that had haunted her the night before, that the deed had not been done properly, came wiggling back, and she moved to the tray to busy her hands while her thoughts began to tumble.

"Jones," she said as she picked up the steaming teapot and poured herself a cup. "This Mrs. Mitchum you mentioned yesterday. The woman who stays with your mother. You said she helps people."

Jones stood and brushed off her hands on her apron. "Oh yes, Mrs. Mitchum is always helping people. She's rather brilliant, she is," Jones said with a serious shake of her head. "I don't know how she knows so much, but she can always mix a cuppa that will heal any ailment."

Amelia sifted through this statement and realized Mrs. Mitchum must have a way with herbs and plants to help people with certain conditions. It wasn't unheard of, and Amelia's own nanny had known what kind of tea was good for a certain situation. But Amelia could also see how such a woman could easily be labeled a witch.

Amelia sipped at her tea as Jones went to make up the bed. "Does Mrs. Mitchum ever accept visitors?"

Jones turned, her expression clouded. "There isn't something ailing you, is there, Your Grace?"

Amelia shook her head quickly. "No, it's nothing like that." She spoke the words in a rush as she tried to assemble a reasonable explanation that didn't reveal too much. The sudden sense that she might inadvertently betray a confidence passed over her like an icy shiver, and she took another swallow of tea.

"I would like to begin visiting some of the tenants today," she said, strengthening her voice. "Does Mrs. Mitchum live on one of the parcels?"

Jones's expression brightened again, and Amelia felt a relief as her half-truth had clearly been enough. "Mrs. Mitchum lives in the village I'm afraid. She rents a cottage off the main thoroughfare. But I should be happy to take you to her at any time."

Amelia yearned toward the idea. She wished she had someone to speak to that had more experience with marital matters than she did. She was feeling overwhelmed with all she didn't know, and in the midst of her unsteadiness, she remembered the soot-covered cradle. She took another swallow of tea.

"That would be quite lovely. Thank you, Jones," she said after a space. "Is my green gown ready for today?"

Jones had just reached the other side of the bed, bending to tuck the quilt back in when she paused, her teeth worrying her lower lip as if considering Amelia's question.

"Jones?" Amelia prodded.

The maid straightened. "I spoke with Mrs. Fairfax this morning when I came in, Your Grace. I know it wasn't my place at the time, but I was concerned, you see."

Amelia stilled. "Concerned about what?"

Jones held a sheet between both hands, the fabric taut. "I was putting your things away yesterday when they brought your trunks up, and I noticed...well, I noticed a few of your items are rather worn. Not at all what's expected of a duchess, and I just thought—" The rest of the words came out in a rush, ending abruptly in stunned silence as though Jones couldn't believe she had said that much.

"And what did you speak to Mrs. Fairfax about?"

Jones looked down at the sheet in her hands. "I asked her how it was I could arrange an appointment for you with the seamstress in the village."

Amelia wasn't used to people taking care of her, and to see Jones struggling to learn her position at Dinsmore Castle and help her warmed her like nothing ever had. Was it only the day before that she had suspected Mrs. Fairfax of finding her attire unpleasant? It seemed she would need to keep an open mind about her interactions with the people of Dinsmore, even if it were so terribly difficult to drown out the sound of her mother's criticisms. These people were trying to help her, and she needed to accept that. She set her teacup aside.

"And? What did Mrs. Fairfax say?"

Jones looked up tentatively. "She said she'd arrange it straightaway."

Amelia pressed her hands together and stood. "Excellent. I should very much like a few new things. You'll come with me, of course. You're more familiar with the happenings at Dinsmore and can tell me anything else I should need."

Jones's face flushed, her lips parting once, twice, before

she finally spoke. "Thank you, Your Grace. I should be honored."

Amelia couldn't help but think of her husband slinking off in the dark as she studied Jones's exuberant expression. It was as though she had been right in her suspicions about marriage. It was fraught with danger, times when she would be reminded she was not enough, but at least she had Jones and Mrs. Fairfax to make it seem not quite so terrible.

CHAPTER 7

He left his tower room as soon as the sky lightened, signaling the approach of dawn. He saddled Hercules himself, not wishing to disturb the stable lads and grooms, although some had begun to filter in by the time he left.

He let the animal set their pace. They had been paired for long enough now that it was as if the animal could sense his master's mood and ambled in the direction of the causeway, allowing the rider to observe that around him.

The work on the outer wall was progressing swiftly, and he thought they may have it done by the end of the month. If that were the case, he would need to find work for the tradesmen by then. It would cost a tradesman dearly if he must travel between jobs. A day he didn't work was a day without coin with which to feed his family. Lucas couldn't allow that to happen.

He could admit the thought wouldn't have crossed his mind before he arrived at Dinsmore nearly two years previously. But now these were the notions that haunted him, that pressed in on him as time sped by him. After his life had fallen to ash, he'd been left to consider the remnants. When there was nothing else left in a person's life, the important things became starkly clear, and for him, coming to Dinsmore, seeing the castle, the land, and the tenants, it had become clear all too quickly.

He had to save this spot of the world, and he had to make it right to pass it on to the next Greyfair duke.

Except he needed an heir for that.

He inadvertently squeezed Hercules with his knees, and the horse jerked back in protest before carrying on at his own pace. Lucas patted the horse's neck and moved his thoughts to more practical matters.

Since he'd arrived at Dinsmore, much-needed repair work had been completed on the estate. The castle was a minor holding in the Greyfair title and had been neglected by past dukes in favor of Lagameer Hall, and it had sadly shown its neglect.

He picked his way over the yard, and Hercules found his footing at the causeway, leading horse and rider out of the castle proper. He wasn't surprised to find the causeway had already been graded and graveled. It appeared as though nothing at all had happened there, but even then, his stomach clenched in memory.

But the pain of remembrance was more acute now after the events of the previous night. Thought after thought tumbled inside of him, each warring for position. Her lack of inhibition, her hand closing over his scars as though she could help ease his pain from wounds made so long ago. The way she had stood before him, only firelight on her body.

I liked it when you kissed me.

Something tightened in his chest as he recalled her words, said so simply, so easily. She shouldn't have. She shouldn't have liked anything about him, and yet she had.

And it still wasn't enough.

He swallowed and pushed the horse on. When they reached the mainland, Hercules instinctively turned right, heading up the plateau that led away from the estuary. It was a path they had taken often, and the horse clearly knew the way as Lucas's hands remained loose on the reins.

The sun was just beginning to rise behind him then, and he felt the warmth of the early morning rays. Within moments, he heard the first scattered notes of birdsong, and he stilled Hercules with a simple movement of his knees. He turned in the saddle, giving himself just enough time to peer over his shoulder as the sun finally crested, appearing full in the sky just over the line of the horizon. It was at that moment the birds burst into song, the sound almost deafening as they greeted the new day.

The sun dappled the surface of the estuary with oranges, reds, and golds, and he could smell the tang of the salt as the wind came in from the ocean. It was a moment he had experienced many times since coming to Dinsmore, and it always had the power to calm his soul.

But not that morning.

That morning he only felt the continued twist of failure.

He hadn't been able to do it.

He had endured everything. The marriage contract negotiations, the price for a respectable bride. God's teeth, he'd even had to rescue the woman when the world itself had tried to kill her. And still.

He hadn't been able to give her his seed.

It had taken courage and not a modicum of desperation to seek out the arrangement with the Earl of Biggleswade for the hand of one of his daughters. It had taken sheer fortitude to go into her room last night, and now...

He was still without the chance of an heir.

He had to try again. The thought was not an entirely unpleasant one. In fact, it was rather appealing, and his hands clenched around the reins, remembering the softness of her skin, the curves that fit perfectly in his palms.

But even as he recognized the attraction, something great, something dark cast a shadow over it, and he feared he would never be successful.

He would never be able to produce an heir.

His stomach clenched at the thought that all his efforts to this point might have been futile, and he turned away from the promise of the sun, heading into the forest that lined the ridge.

The trees were dense along the path, and the forest served as a natural windbreak from the sometimes fierce ocean winds. The village lay on the other side of it, tucked into a valley along the coast. But he wasn't going to the village that day, and Hercules seemed to know it.

He turned off the main path several yards in and headed northwest, moving along the line of the ridge. They traveled nearly two miles before turning more directly west, heading inland.

It was nearly a half hour before they broke through the trees, and he was met with a familiar scene.

This part of the valley still lay in shadow, the sun not yet high enough for its rays to reach this far. But Lucas could make out the features he sought. It was a landscape he had studied so often in the past two years that he thought he could traverse it on a moonless night.

There was a break in the hills just at the western most part of the ridge, and the valley swept down to the southeast, creating a natural, flat trough.

An ideal place to build a railroad.

The valley led directly to the village, and from the village to his tenants' farmland beyond. He had spent more than a year lobbying the local railway agent to consider the route for a spur line off the South Eastern Railway at Gravesend. A spur line would allow his tenants to get their goods to market faster and more cheaply. There had only been one problem.

The valley below him did not belong to the Greyfair title, and the marquess who did lay claim to it did not want a railway running through his estate.

Dobson Riggs, the Marquess of Aylesford, would die a stuffy, old aristocrat, so help him God. Much like many gentlemen of his ilk, he abhorred railroads and thought telegrams to be the work of the devil.

But it also meant the region along the River Medway lagged behind the economic development of its neighbors and pushed Lucas's tenants into an unfavorable position. It cost more and was more difficult to get their crops to market and left the London market completely out of their reach. The solution of a spur line had seemed simple enough until his first encounter with the marquess.

Or rather Stephen's encounter as Lucas avoided meeting with the marquess.

The spur line wasn't projected to be lucrative enough for the railway to offer the marquess an exorbitant sum to purchase the land outright and was only interested in an easement on the property for an annual percentage. Both terms had sent the marquess into a fit of apoplexy. To think a gentleman such as he should engage in something so close to trade.

Lucas had spent the past year trying to appeal to the man's generous side, but he appeared not to have one. After such attempts proved fruitless, Lucas now simply hoped the man would die. The marquess's son was known in these parts for the rogue and rapscallion that he was. He hardly frequented the estate along the Medway, preferring to spend his time at the parties and jubilee of London. Lucas was certain it would be a lark to convince the man to allow the railway an easement.

He was so lost in his thoughts Stephen was nearly upon him by the time he realized his cousin was there.

"Running away before the sun has even risen?" Stephen said by way of greeting. "I take it the events of last eve did not go well. Was it your ugly mug then that she couldn't stand?"

Lucas slid him a glance. "I'm afraid it's far worse than that."

Stephen settled his gray mare next to Lucas's steed. "I'm sorry then, cousin. She seemed like a generous and kind girl."

Lucas looked at him sharply. "She was not disgusted at the sight of my scars."

Stephen raised an eyebrow but didn't speak. Lucas shifted uncomfortably in the saddle, wanting to look away at the same time his pride wouldn't let him.

"She applied a salve to them, in fact." He'd hardly whispered the words, but in the quiet of the dawn, he may as well have yelled them.

Stephen's lips parted as his eyes widened, but still he didn't speak.

Finally Lucas felt compelled to break the silence. "It was a rather nice salve. It feels not quite as tight this morning." He raised a hand to the right side of his face where the scars were a patchwork of ruts and divots across the skin. They did feel better this morning. Perhaps Mrs. Fairfax could learn how to make the stuff.

Or he could ask his wife to apply it once again.

He swallowed, the memories of the previous night flooding back to him. Her gentle touch, the way she smelled of clean soap and fresh air, the hint of lavender, how she didn't flinch when her fingers touched the ruts along his cheek.

"Did you tell her what happened then?"

Lucas shook his head quickly. "Of course, I didn't. The truth would send her fleeing."

Lucas clenched his hands at the mention of the past. Hercules tossed his head in rebuke, and Lucas loosened his grip.

"I think you may just be surprised by the lady. She's been a surprise since she arrived, hasn't she?"

Stephen's words could not be truer, but Lucas felt the truth of what had happened in the fire, and then even before that, like a brick in his stomach. It lurked in the shadows, and he lived in fear that one day it would come out. But the only people who knew the truth were Stephen and Mrs. Fairfax, and he trusted both implicitly. He had a suspicion Barnes knew some of it, but the stable master was not one to mince words.

No, Lucas was sure his new wife would never find out.

"Stephen," Lucas began tentatively. "I couldn't...that is I could, but then, I couldn't..." His lips wouldn't form the words, but Stephen seemed to understand.

"You couldn't finish the deed then."

When he said it like that, it sounded as though Lucas was incapable of killing the fox at the end of a hunt.

"Something like that," he muttered.

"But wasn't that the whole point of this? You wanted an heir to carry on the work you've started here. Has that changed?"

"No, that hasn't bloody well changed. It's only..." But he couldn't make the words come.

"It's only your wife is a sight comelier than you had planned? It's only that your bride is a brave lady who is not afraid of the beast you think you are?"

Once more Lucas looked sharply at his cousin. "I don't think I'm a beast."

"Och, and he lies to me," Stephen murmured with a shake of his head. "You've been hiding in the tower of that castle since you arrived here. Do you think I don't know why? Do you think I don't understand why you've sent me, your twisted foot of a cousin to do your bidding with the Marquess of Aylesford? And this." He gestured to Lucas's garb. "Are you supposed to be some kind of marauder? Will you be rescuing any damsels later? I should like to be there."

Lucas tugged on his greatcoat. "You've never commented on my dress before."

"You've never had a beautiful wife before." He pointed over his shoulder in the direction of the castle. "A wife who is waking alone in her bed. More's the pity."

"Perhaps you should have married her."

Both of Stephen's eyebrows went up at this. "Och, I would have had I known. You're lucky I didn't see her first." His face sobered then, and Lucas braced himself for what was to come next for Stephen was not one to skirt the truth. "Lucas, cousin, you need to remember something. Amelia is not Lila. You cannot lay blame for the sins of another at her feet."

"It's not Lila that haunts me," Lucas said quietly.

As if sensing Lucas's torture, Stephen waited before saying, "Is it the babe then?"

Lucas's pride finally gave up, and he didn't meet Stephen's eye as he asked, "What if I lose another one?"

When Stephen touched his shoulder, he jumped, not expecting the contact. When he turned his gaze on his cousin, he found an unexpected, tortured compassion there.

"You can't live your life asking questions like that, cousin. It would mean you've lost all faith."

Looking back over the valley, Lucas couldn't help but wonder if his cousin was right. Maybe it was too late for Lucas.

"We should get back. The finishing stones should be delivered this morning."

"I've already asked Barnes to look out for the delivery," Stephen said, even as he turned his horse toward Dinsmore. "Lucas?" he said after they had entered the trees. "You said you couldn't finish the deed. Does that mean you started it?"

Lucas only grunted in reply.

Stephen's laugh was lost in the trees. "You haven't gotten rusty in your old age, have you, cousin?"

Lucas stopped Hercules to peer back at his cousin. "Rusty?"

Stephen's face was full of mischief. "You haven't forgotten how to pleasure a woman, have you?"

Lucas rubbed his chin with one hand even as he heard the echoes of Amelia's cries of pleasure. He decided against saying too much and instead said, "How could I possibly pleasure a woman looking like this?"

Stephen nudged his mare around Lucas and as he passed his cousin, he said, "The last I checked it's not the face that does the pleasuring."

Lucas could only watch his cousin amble away.

Though her family had run out of money, it was clear Amelia's life in London had been nearly luxurious compared to the lives the Greyfair tenants led. By the third tenant she visited, Amelia knew this with uncomfortable certainty.

The Greyfair tenants were poor, terrifyingly so, and Amelia was filled with an overwhelming need to help them all at once.

But what could she possibly do?

Appeal to the husband who continued to run away from her?

Give them her own coin of which she had none?

She sat in the front room of the Wilsons' cottage while Mrs. Wilson poured tea from a cracked teapot painted in faded daffodils. It may have been lovely once, but Amelia feared the handle would break clean off at any moment, scalding Mrs. Wilson terribly.

Amelia sat on the edge of her chair, its worn and flattened cushion providing very little comfort, watching Mrs. Wilson carefully, ready to spring into action should the woman suffer a horrible fate.

Only when the woman set down the teapot did Amelia allow her shoulders to relax.

"We hadn't heard the duke wed," Mrs. Wilson said now in a tone that was somewhat nasally yet kind. "I'm so honored that you should think to visit us, Your Grace."

Mrs. Wilson had the unfortunate circumstance of time-lessness caused by hard work and blistering poverty about her. She may have been twenty or she may have been thirty years of age, Amelia could not to tell. The apron pinned to her frock was neatly pressed but stained. Her hair was neatly plaited but greasy and pale. Her hands were red from scrubbing yet there was dirt still under her nails.

Amelia swallowed as her chest tightened. She realized she hadn't been prepared for this. She hadn't been prepared to see her tenants suffering and knowing she could do very little about it.

And yet Mrs. Wilson seemed unfazed by her own dire circumstances.

"Of course, Mrs. Wilson," Amelia said, accepting a steaming teacup from the woman. "I thank you for taking the time to see me." She tentatively took a sip of the tea and found the taste worn as though the tea leaves had been used more than once.

"Ach, of course, Your Grace. It's rather nice actually. It's not every day I haves the time to sit with a cuppa and a fine lady like yourself." She gestured behind her at the wall with the water-stained wallpaper, but she might have been gesturing to the world itself. "Mr. Wilson's taken the children with him to the mill. He's hoping they might have some scraps what will work to fix the fence around the pigs' pen." She shook her head. "The old cart wheels we braced against the thing won't hold for long, and the pigs are smarter than people think." She tapped her temple with two fingers. "They'll figure it out sooner than you might expect, and then we'll be in real trouble." She said all of this with a half-smile as though the idea of trouble was somehow humorous.

"Your husband has taken the children to a...sawmill?" Amelia swallowed as the woman nodded vigorously.

"Ach, of course. Young Richard loves the sawmill. If we're lucky, he might get to apprentice there next spring."

"How old is Young Richard?" Amelia ventured even though she wasn't certain she wished to know the answer.

Mrs. Wilson's smile broadened. "He's ten years old." Her smile dimmed somewhat. "I know that's rather old to still have him at home, but he's a big help with the animals in the winter. And Richard, that is Mr. Wilson, wanted to keep him home another year until Tabitha is a bit older to help him in the fields for the harvesting."

"And how old is Tabitha?" Amelia really didn't wish to ask this.

Mrs. Wilson's smile brightened again. "She's five. She'll be ready for the fields this year. I must say she's quite excited for it. She's always watching her brothers go off with their father in the morning, and she's always left behind. It will be so wonderful when she can go with them."

Amelia couldn't imagine allowing her five-year-old to venture into the fields for harvesting. She'd heard of the accidents that could happen in such dangerous work and to expose a child to such a risk...

Amelia wrapped her hands around her teacup. "Are you from this part of England, Mrs. Wilson?"

Mrs. Wilson nodded. "I grew up here right on the Greyfair estate. My mum and da's place is just down this lane. We were quite fortunate to get this parcel when it opened up. Mr. Wilson had just returned from London. He was hoping to find a place in one of the tanneries there, but it wasn't as easy as we had hoped. It was only luck that got the lease here."

Amelia smiled. "I'm glad you've found a home here at Greyfair."

Mrs. Wilson was quick to nod in agreement. "I truly can't believe it at times. To have such a considerate landlord as the duke. You know his father wasn't at all as he is."

Amelia stilled, her teacup halfway raised to her lips. "Oh?" she asked.

She knew hardly anything about her husband, but she wouldn't reveal that to one of her husband's tenants. It seemed somehow a betrayal, although it shouldn't have been. Marriages such as theirs were quite common, but in the face of Mrs. Wilson's obvious enjoyment in her own marriage, Amelia suddenly found her circumstances a touch disappointing. She felt the swell of inadequacy and swallowed it down.

Mrs. Wilson nodded again, her pointed chin going up and down enthusiastically. "Ach, of course. His Grace has already done so much to improve the land for farming. It was just the other day that Mr. Wilson said to me he's looking forward to the crop this year. Should be a good one with all the improvements." Mrs. Wilson's smile faded the smallest of degrees at the end of her sentence.

Amelia leaned forward. "What is it?"

Mrs. Wilson waved off her concern. "Oh, it's nothing really. His Grace has promised he'll make it all right in the end."

"Make what right?" If she leaned forward anymore, she'd fall from her chair.

Mrs. Wilson's fingers toyed with her teacup. "It's just that it won't matter if the crop is a good one if we don't have a better way of getting it to London. We can't compete with the farmers what's on the railway. They can get their goods to the markets in London at half the cost as us." She shrugged her thin shoulders. "We just can't hope to get the price we need for our grains if we don't get the railway line."

"And the duke has promised you this railway line?"

Mrs. Wilson laughed softly and waved her hand again. "Ach, no, it's not the line itself. He says he's talking to people like him. You know." Mrs. Wilson placed a finger against her chin. "I think he said it was a merchant or a marker or something like that. He said he would be the one to allow the railroad through to the village so we can transport our harvests."

"Do you mean a marquess?" Amelia set down her tea before she dropped the cup.

Lucas was in negotiations with a marquess to allow the railroad to build a line to the village? Of what little she knew of her husband, she had determined he was a man of unusual empathy and was not afraid to act if he could help another.

So who was this marquess?

She felt the initial lick of anticipation she always felt when she thought she might be able to help. She hated herself for it, for always being eager when time and again her overtures had been met with disdain. It was clear this railway line was important to the tenants on the Greyfair estate, and should her husband have need of her help, she wished to give it.

Even if her attempts would be met with his dismissal of her.

She swallowed down the familiar disappointment. "Mrs. Wilson, do you happen to remember the name of this marquess? His title's name that is."

If she had the marquess's title, she might be able to discover which estate it was. Surely Jones or Mrs. Fairfax would know the owners of the surrounding estates.

But Mrs. Wilson shook her head. "I'm afraid I don't. His Grace only said that he would meet with the man and talk sense with him."

Amelia smiled. "I know the duke will be successful. He is most determined, and he always looks after his own." She realized she meant every word of what she said.

Mrs. Wilson smiled. "I know, Your Grace. You've made quite a catch marrying the duke."

"I know," Amelia whispered, sensing the truth in the woman's words.

Just days ago, Amelia would not have believed as much, but she did now. It didn't mean she was safe though.

She stood and extended a hand. "I thank you for your time, Mrs. Wilson. I must be going, but I hope I may visit again."

Mrs. Wilson stood and took Amelia's hand a little shyly. "Of course, Your Grace."

Amelia gathered her bonnet and made her way to the door only to pause. "I wonder if you could tell me where the great oak in the bend of the road is. I'm to meet my lady's maid there, you see. She wished to join me on my walk today but wasn't able to get away from the castle when I set off. She said she'd meet me at the oak tree."

Mrs. Wilson smiled and reached for her wrap by the door. "I'll walk with you, shan't I?" she said and opened the door to the spring sunshine. "I was just on my way out to see Mrs. Myrtle about borrowing her sifter."

Amelia hesitated on the doorstep. "Her sifter?"

A sifter seemed like a common enough item that Mrs. Wilson should have one, but then she recalled the state of the woman's teapot.

Mrs. Wilson nodded, stepping out onto the path in front of the cottage that led to the road. "I borrow Mrs. Myrtle's sifter, and she uses my grinder when she needs it. We both have our eyes set on some new things for the kitchen if the harvest is as good as it should be." Mrs. Wilson's smile was full of hope now.

Amelia's insides twisted. "You mean you can't afford to replace your sifter now?"

Amelia thought of the small contraption usually made of tin and mesh. How much could such a thing cost? She felt a stab of familiar pain for the woman's plight. After all, Amelia had been married off in order for her family to avoid the same fate.

Mrs. Wilson's gaze narrowed as she seemed to consider it. "Well, not as such really. What little we have we use to keep the stock healthy and the children fed. Makes no sense to buy something new when we can borrow from each other."

"No, of course not," Amelia mumbled, following Mrs. Wilson as the woman turned onto the road. "Mrs. Wilson, do others borrow from you as well?"

Mrs. Wilson's smile bubbled with pride. "Ach, of course, Your Grace." She pointed off into the distance to their right. "Mrs. Wheeler borrows my butter churn." To the left. "Mrs. Mathers borrows my irons, and I borrow her pastry cutter. It works out rather nicely."

"Yes, I can see that," Amelia said, but she couldn't help but feeling both sadness and pride for these people who had found a way to get by with help from each other.

These items were common household goods, and yet the Wilsons—and purportedly others on the estate—couldn't afford them. Amelia thought of the overcrowded rooms in the castle she had gone through with Mrs. Fairfax the previous day.

There was a solution in there somewhere. She only needed to find it.

CHAPTER 8

*H*e couldn't remember the last time he had taken supper in the castle's dining room. He usually took a tray in his tower room at whatever late hour when he finally finished the work for the day. But Mrs. Fairfax had informed him that his wife would be taking her meal in the dining room. She hadn't said anything other than that, but he had received the hidden meaning behind her message.

He should dine with his wife.

He was still unsettled by the events of the previous night, but if he were objective about it, he had to admit the first portion of the evening had been more than pleasant.

He quite simply enjoyed her company.

He hadn't figured that when he had first considered his scheme to catch a bride. If he were paying for one, he didn't feel as though he could be choosy about it. It was only fortune that had provided him with a wife who was not only beautiful but genuinely likable as well.

That's probably why he stood in front of the washstand in the corner of his room just then. He'd already changed his clothes, donning a coat and everything. He hadn't realized he still owned a coat, but there it was, hanging in his armoire and freshly pressed as though he were inundated with dinner invitations and required a coat at the ready.

He had splashed water on his face and washed his hands, but his eyes were caught on the washstand's mirror now. He scrubbed a hand over his jaw. He'd shaved that morning, the act cursory and hastily completed as it was every morning, but he wondered suddenly if he could stand to see to it properly.

He dropped his hand, strode forward, and seized the mirror, drawing it into position to see the entirety of his face.

It was a shock to observe his reflection, and he started, the mirror bouncing in his grip. He sucked in a fortifying breath and forced his eyes to scan the right side of his face. He was surprised to find it wasn't as terrible as he remembered.

He had first looked upon his reflection months after the fire, and his wounds must not have had proper time to heal for now his scars were little more than ruts along his cheek and around his ear. The skin was pebbled and pulled, pitted with valleys, but it was not the angry red it had been so soon after the injury. His hair had filled in more than he realized, leaving an open space immediately behind his ear with a few tufts growing awkwardly along the deep ridge there.

He closed his eyes, sudden memories rushing back at him, sending waves of pain through his body.

The heat of the flames, the roar of the fire, the splintering of wood, the thunderous crash, and then...silence.

He hadn't even felt it when the beam had hit him. He had been knocked unconscious, and he thought that was perhaps for the best. The pain had nearly been his undoing when he'd awakened days later. He didn't think he would have survived it had he been awake to feel its impact.

He forced his eyes open and reached for his razor.

He was still early, reaching the dining room before Amelia. They dined informally at Dinsmore, and Mrs. Fairfax had never rung a dinner gong. He didn't even know if they had a dinner gong. He peered about him as if noticing the castle for the first time.

He never paused long enough to reflect upon his whereabouts. He drove himself in his work to keep any thoughts at bay, but he found himself reflecting once more in the space of an hour. He didn't care for it, but again he was surprised at what he saw.

He could remember those early days when they'd first arrived at Dinsmore. The castle had been shut for some time then, and he could remember only the layer of dust that had coated everything. The doors had all screeched mercilessly, their hinges long gone rusty. He couldn't remember any other details because he'd had Stephen carry him to the tower room immediately and leave him there. It was three months before he had emerged and only when Stephen threatened the estate's entire collapse if he didn't.

He paused, his gaze catching sight of the rendering above the doorknob of the dining room door. In the brass plate surrounding the knob was an impression of the castle's lady. He reached out a single finger, tracing the silhouette. He had been brash when he'd rebuked the story the servants liked to tell of the castle's lady, and he regretted it now. Honestly, he regretted taking it from Amelia.

The fact was they didn't know who the lady was or what the castle's origins were. Who was he to deny there wasn't some grand love story attached to her?

He shifted uncomfortably, his chest tightening at any notion of love.

Footsteps behind him had him turning, and his wife appeared in the corridor. Now his chest tightened for entirely different reasons, and he stepped back, giving her space to enter the dining room.

He bowed as propriety dictated. "Good evening, Your Grace." When he straightened, he found her staring. His fingers instinctively reached for the brim of his hat before he remembered he wasn't wearing it. "Is something amiss?" He hated asking the question, but she hadn't blinked in a whole ten seconds.

She shook her head quickly, her lips parting as she clearly tried to find words. "It isn't that. It's—" She licked her lips now and pressed her hands together in front of her. "You've...shaved." She winced, nearly shutting her eyes as a grimace captured her lips. "What I'm trying to say is you look rather handsome this evening, Your Grace." Slowly her eyes slid open, and he saw an honesty there that he was coming to find quite normal for her. He swallowed, wishing to run a finger along his collar as he shifted uncomfortably at the notion.

"Thank you," he nearly whispered. He let her words wash over him, and it was as though he were falling, his stomach dropping completely. There was a beat of tense silence, and he cleared his throat, backing away to gesture to the table. "May I?" he asked, holding out a chair for her.

She slipped into it, arranging her skirts as she sat. He took the chair adjacent at the head of the table, and then he didn't know what to do. Thankfully she saved him.

"I went to meet some of the tenants today."

He stilled, his fingers curling reflexively around the arms of his chair. "You did?" Even he could tell his tone was slightly accusatory, and the way her eyes narrowed ever so much, he knew she could hear it as well.

She straightened in her chair. "Yes, I thought I should introduce myself as the new duchess."

"Of course," he said automatically, hoping to make up

for his initial skepticism. It would be her duty as duchess to the estate to introduce herself. He had no reason to question such an action. But even as he thought it, Lila's taunting laugh echoed through his mind. He swallowed and pulled his napkin into his lap. "And how did you find things?"

"Well," she said and then stopped, her teeth worrying her lower lip.

He watched her, hypnotized by her face, echoes of the night before coming back to him. Her kiss, the heat of it, the eagerness. The way her curves seemed to perfectly fit his hands. The way she writhed beneath him, uninhibited. He swallowed and looked to the door, willing a footman to enter with their dinner.

"I wonder, Your Grace—"

"Lucas," he interrupted without looking at her.

"Right, Lucas." She pulled in a breath, so worrying in its enormity, that he did look at her now. "I was wondering if you realized how poor the tenants are on this estate."

He felt the claw of dread that reminded him how precarious their position was here on the fringes of Kent. "I am aware," he said carefully.

Her eyes widened at this, and her expression relaxed. "Oh, I see. Well… I'm glad you're aware of it." She paused, her eyes scanning the table as if she were trying to find the next thing to say.

He braced himself. He hadn't considered his duchess would take an active interest in the affairs of the estate, and he couldn't stop the lick of suspicion that coursed through him. In all truth, when he had thought about marrying, he pictured a spoiled debutante, happy to waste her days in her sewing room, holding teas, and picking out gowns. He dropped his gaze, taking in the mended cuffs of his wife's dress, the careful addition of lacework along the bodice as though it were covering some mending. His wife didn't seem the least interested in gowns.

"One of the tenants, a Mrs. Wilson, said you were trying to convince the railroad to build a spur line to the village so the tenants would be able to get their crops to the London markets."

"Yes." He spoke the word swiftly, like a ball shot from a cannon, and it seemed to startle his wife into silence. He closed his eyes, drew in a measured breath. "Yes, I am in talks with a railway agent." That was little better but at least he hadn't spat the words at her. He could feel the trepidation growing inside of him. Past betrayal stoking the fire, but he tried to remind himself that she was only taking an interest in her new home. There was nothing wrong with that.

She waited as if she expected him to say more, and horribly he realized he wanted to say more. Studying her face, her captive attention, something poured over him that doused the flames of suspicion.

He wanted to tell her everything. He wanted to tell her about the impossibility of the tenants being able to compete once the railroad covered all of England, once other farmers were able to move their crops at ridiculously low costs. Even ferrying the goods down the river wouldn't be cost effective.

He wanted to tell her of the dread he suffered at the idea that soon he'd have no work for the estate's tradesmen, and he didn't know what they would do for pay to feed their families. He wanted to tell her everything, and yet his lips remained firmly shut.

"That's wonderful," she finally said when he didn't speak, but then she worried that lip again.

"What is it?" he asked, unable to bear the silence like she could.

"It's only...I imagine it takes some time to build a railway line, and the tenants are in dire need of some items. I have gone through the inventory of the castle with Mrs. Fairfax as you know, and I was wondering if perhaps—"

"No."

He wasn't sure who was more startled by the curt word. Her eyes flew to his, and he could do nothing but stare back at her. He felt his defenses like a tangible thing, stronger than the castle's thick stone walls. She was obviously trying to help the tenants and yet the idea of her going through the things in the castle, the things that had been moved from Lagameer Hall, had his skin prickling, his heart picking up speed.

He couldn't remember the move. He couldn't remember what had been salvaged from the fire. He didn't want her finding anything that might make her ask questions.

And yet he felt like the worst possible version of himself, saying no to her just then.

"You haven't heard what I was going to suggest."

"Whatever it was, it's still no." He turned back to the door, willing it to open, willing their dinner to appear so he could do something with his mouth other than make a fool of himself.

He wasn't sure how long he stared at the door, but when he finally turned back, he found Amelia slumped in her chair as though the fight had gone out of her. He slid his gaze away again only to find it drawn back to her.

She shook her head, her lips softly parted as if in wonder.

He willed himself to look away yet again, girded himself against the curiosity she stoked in him. And yet he found himself turning back to her and asking, "What is it?"

She sat up, her hands gripping the edge of the table. "You are a terribly difficult person to figure out."

It was at that moment that he knew there was a God. The doors to the kitchen finally opened, and a pair of footmen entered with their dinner.

* * *

HER EXCUSE WAS THIS: he had never heard her plan and therefore had not said no to it specifically. It would be far easier to ask for his forgiveness anyway.

It had taken much longer than she had hoped to arrange the exchange but as she stood in the castle yard, overseeing the setup of tables and carts, she couldn't have been more pleased. She tried not to think of Lucas's cold tone or abrupt manner that night at dinner when she'd first mentioned the tenants' needs. She knew his brusqueness with her was not because of his lack of concern for the tenants, and she wondered what had made him so defensive.

For a time, she worried she wouldn't make the exchange happen though.

First there was the matter of finding what she sought in the packed rooms of the upper floors of the castle. She was certain if everything that could have been salvaged from Lagameer Hall had been brought to the castle and stored in those rooms, somewhere there should have been the household items. The tea kettles, the irons, and the bellows. And if the castle already contained its own such items, there would have been extras.

Mrs. Fairfax had been hesitant at first when Amelia approached her with her request, but she soon made the housekeeper realize the simple prudence of such an endeavor.

"I suppose those things aren't doing much good sitting in crates, are they?" she had said, wiggling her way out from behind her desk, her ring of keys jangling as she did so.

Amelia had stopped her, unable to refrain from asking about the desk that so clearly did not fit in the room. Surely there was another desk somewhere on the estate that could meet the housekeeper's needs. But Mrs. Fairfax had only shrugged and said it had been her desk at Lagameer Hall, and she didn't see the point in changing it.

It had taken them three days to find the first of the crates. They had unearthed a pair of irons, a dented but serviceable tea kettle, three tea sets, all of which Mrs. Fairfax could not remember the origin of, and even a mangle.

It was on the fourth day that they had struck gold. Tucked away in a dressing room was a trunk filled with kitchen gadgets. Pastry cutters, sifters, grinders, and even a cake maker. Mrs. Fairfax had squealed when they'd uncovered that.

"I've been looking for this," she'd exclaimed, holding the tin up for inspection. "'Tis a pity I've already replaced it." She shrugged, passing off the cake maker to one of the maids enlisted to help them unpack the crates and move the items to the spacious vestibule, readying them for the exchange.

Stephen had stumbled upon their preparations and had immediately gone out to the stables to see what could be added to the pile from there.

She could admit she'd felt a lick of trepidation when Stephen had discovered them. Although it wasn't as though Amelia were attempting to hide the boxes, but she did find it curious that her husband didn't seek her out to question her about the boxes slowly appearing beside the staircase.

But then her husband had been scarce since that night at dinner. She'd seen him, of course. Sometimes they passed each other at breakfast. Occasionally she saw him out in the fields when she was visiting tenants. Once or twice she saw him at dinner. Much as that first night, she could tell he took care in dressing for the occasion. It made her stomach flip each time she saw him dressed for dinner, no matter how used to it she had grown. She couldn't help but wonder if he had dressed for her.

JESSIE CLEVER

Of course, he hadn't. He took great pains to avoid her. Why would he care what she thought of his appearance?

He had not visited her room since that first night. She wondered if this were usual behavior in a marriage. She had no one to ask and more than once she had been tempted to seek out Jones's Mrs. Mitchum. But still she refrained. She trusted Lucas to know what was normal because he'd been married before, and she had to trust that his absence was perfectly respectable.

Only it didn't feel right. Her body tingled knowing he was so close, and yet so much stood between them. She hated herself for letting her expectations get away from her. She'd received a letter from Adaline letting her know the funds had been received, and that alone should have quashed any feelings Amelia had let get out of control, but it hadn't. Even the reminder of their arrangement couldn't stop the unexpected pull she felt.

But wasn't she precisely in the same place she'd always been? Dismissed from her mother's sickbed and ignored by her husband. It was quite perfectly the same.

She focused on the bustle before her, trying to remember that the day's work was more important than anything her husband should think of her.

Standing there in the castle yard, watching weeks of hard work come together, seeing the tenants slowly filter in with their own carts and baskets as Argus trotted happily amongst them, their eagerness plain on their faces as they began sifting through the boxes for items they desperately needed, Amelia might have said she had finally done something useful.

But still she craved her husband's approval.

It shouldn't have mattered. There's was not a love match, of course, and perhaps she had assumed incorrectly that she and her husband could have been partners in the running of

126

the estate. She recalled Lucas's curt, one-word answers to her questions about estate business and knew this to be true.

Mrs. Wilson entered the castle yard then, followed by three scampering young people, a little girl whom Amelia assumed was Tabitha, a younger boy she thought might be Young Richard, and an older boy, all limbs and loping gait she assumed was the older son whose name she didn't know.

Mrs. Wilson caught her gaze and waved, a wide smile on her face. Amelia waved back, the feeling of certainty growing within her.

It had taken her and Jones two days to visit every tenant with the news of the exchange, and now she was glad they'd been so thorough. The turnout had exceeded even her expectations.

She looked up, noting the intermittent puffy clouds, and was pleased once more the weather had held. It had rained insistently while they had unpacked and sorted through the upper floor, and she'd worried the weather would delay them further. But it seemed something was finally going in her favor.

She smiled again. She simply couldn't help it. This was it. This was what she'd been searching for. With the help of Mrs. Fairfax and Jones, Stephen and a host of maids and footmen, she was finally helping. She was finally *doing* something.

"Amelia."

So wrapped up in her own elation, she missed the growl in her husband's voice and turned, her face almost hurting from smiling.

Except her husband wasn't smiling. He was glowering.

She froze.

"A word."

He didn't wait for an answer. He grabbed her by the arm and hauled her up the steps into the castle. She caught a glance of

Mrs. Wilson, frozen in horror at one of the carts, her hand over her gaping mouth. Mrs. Fairfax and Jones, standing together by a bushel of rug beaters, their eyes wide, their expressions fearful.

It was humiliating.

As soon as the door clanged shut behind them, she ripped her arm free of his grasp.

"I will not be manhandled that way." It took all her strength to keep from raising her voice, but she would not lose dignity now, no matter how her husband found fault with her.

But then she noticed his eyes. There was a fire inside of them, one he was only barely keeping contained. She shut her mouth, the old fear rising inside of her.

She'd done it again. She'd displeased another so much it caused clear displeasure to appear on his face. Why did she continue to do this? Why did she continue to try? Why did she continue to hope?

Because she had to. She couldn't live with feeling so inadequate. She knew that one day she could chase the feeling away and find her complete self. She had to.

But not here. The moments of elation she had felt so acutely had vanished, and now she only felt disappointment.

"No?" His tone was deceptively light. "Then how about this?"

He bent, putting his shoulder to her stomach and lifting her as though she were nothing more than a sack of feed.

"Put me down." The fear drove her voice up, but he wasn't listening.

He carried her like that straight up the stairs to the tower. It was as though he carried nothing at all, let alone a grown woman, and she recalled the lean muscles she had seen that day on the causeway, the ones she had felt under her fingertips for too brief a time.

She felt anger. She felt fear. But just then, strangely, wickedly, she felt anticipation.

He hadn't touched her in nearly two weeks, and she'd forgotten the power he held over her. Even now when he treated her so poorly she couldn't help but wonder what would happen next.

She thought he would stop at the door to her room, but he kept climbing. She saw nothing but worn stone, flashes of grays and browns until just as quickly as he'd picked her up, he dropped her.

She bounced. It was so unexpected she squeaked. Her hands flew to her hair, now in a tangle about her head, and shoved it from her eyes. It only took a second or two to realize where she was.

This must be his room in the tower.

She knew when he'd left her that night that the sound of his fading footsteps suggested he'd climbed upward, and she'd imagined that he'd slinked away to his own bedchamber. But the room around her was not fit for a duke. It wasn't fit for a barn animal.

He had dropped her on a cot shoved to one side, its bedclothes hanging in tatters about it, a single pillow crumpled into oblivion at one end. There was a bulky table of wood and iron shoved under the window and a single chair pulled out from it. An armoire and a washstand completed the furnishings, and the rest was cold, imposing stone. No lush carpets. No soft tapestries. Nothing to suggest a person slept here.

She peered up at him. He wore his greatcoat and hat today, and she felt a pang of loss at not being able to see his face properly. But more, she hated that he felt the need to hide himself from everyone.

She got to her feet. "You owe me an apology."

His lips parted for a moment without sound, and she knew she'd surprised him.

She pointed at the window and the yard beyond. "You humiliated me in front of the tenants. I've worked hard to earn their respect, and you treated me as nothing more than baggage. I will accept your apology now."

"I am not apologizing," he growled. He pointed to the window too. "I told you no."

"You said the word no, but you did not specify as to what. I assumed you didn't wish for me to pry into the matters with the railway." This was not at all what she thought, but she felt a glow of pride at having come up with an excuse so quickly.

He took a step back. She'd surprised him again.

"I said no to…whatever this is." The finger pointing in the direction of the yard shook now.

"This is Your Grace helping his tenants. They already speak terribly highly of you, and today's exchange will only serve to underscore those feelings."

His hand dropped. "They speak highly of me?"

"Yes." She looked him up and down as though assessing him. "They said you're considerate of their welfare, but after how you've treated me today, I can't say I see what they mean."

His lips firmed, and the scowl returned. "You had no right to arrange this…what did you call it?"

"It's an exchange. The tenants bring items they no longer need, and Mrs. Fairfax helped me to pare down the castle's inventory, ridding it of the unnecessary items to increase the efficiency with which the household is run, and in so doing, you also help your tenants. It seemed like a mutually advantageous endeavor."

He blinked. Two seconds of silence passed before he

ripped off his hat, tossing it into a dark corner as a growl erupted from his throat.

"You disobeyed me."

"Disobeyed you? What am I, your dog?"

His lips snapped shut at this, whatever rebuke he'd been about to voice effectively silenced.

She crossed her arms over her chest. "If I am to fulfill my duties as duchess, you need to learn to trust me to perform them. I will not have you hovering over my every decision."

"I didn't ask you to perform any duties as my duchess."

"Then why am I here?" she fired back.

"For this," he growled and grabbed her.

CHAPTER 9

inally.

She didn't know how much she wanted him to touch her until he finally did. Then like setting flame to a fuse, she ignited. She grabbed the lapels of his greatcoat in both fists, pulling him closer as his mouth devoured hers.

His kiss was possessive and full, as if to remind her who she belonged to, as if she didn't already know. Her mind could tell her one thing. Tell her to stand up for herself. Tell her to force him to respect her.

But her body couldn't be denied. This attraction that crackled between them couldn't be ignored, and she didn't wish to. She wanted it. All of it. And she wanted it now.

She wanted him to touch her like he had done that first time. It wasn't what he did to her. It was how he did it. His touch made her feel precious, wanted, and desired. It made her feel alive. For the first time in her sheltered existence, she sparked with life, and it was heady and exhilarating. Only he could make her feel that way.

His hands went to her back, making quick work of the buttons of her gown. She felt the bodice loosen, and she plunged her hands beneath the lapels of his greatcoat, shoving it from his shoulders. He let go of her long enough to let it drop to the floor, and then he was on her, pushing her back until her legs collided with the cot behind her.

She tumbled down, her arms wrapped around his neck as she did, and he fell atop her. The weight of him crushed her, and she reveled in it, the feel of him pressing into her, her legs caught in his as though they were tangled into one.

Her heart soared at the thought, and she quickly pushed the feeling down. This wasn't about that. But even as she told herself this, she couldn't help but wonder if someday, someday there might something more between them, and would she want that?

He pulled her gown down, and she was forced to let go of him long enough to pull her arms from the sleeves. With a quick tug, he had it off and tossed it carelessly over his head.

He leaned over her, his uneven hair framing his face, and she reached up, heedless of his scars, and cupped his face in both of her hands.

"Aren't you supposed to be scolding me?" she whispered.

"Who says I'm not?" he said right before capturing her mouth again.

His kiss had a way of enveloping her, tricking her into believing there was nothing else but them in the whole of the world. The sensation was exquisite, and she let him torture her, his lips nibbling one corner of hers and then the other before tracing a hot line along her jaw.

She let her head fall back, giving him access to her neck. He shifted, pressing his lips to the very spot where her pulse throbbed, and she shuddered, her hands raking down his back.

"Lucas," she moaned, her knees coming up, her legs wrapping around his waist so she could press the part of her that ached against him.

She found him already hard, and she moved her hips, circling until her core rubbed against him.

"Jesus," he moaned, pulling back, pulling away from her.

"No," she mewled, her eyes flying open, afraid he would run away again.

But there was a mischievous smile on his face, and he bent, pressing a soft kiss to her lips.

"Don't worry, darling. I'm not done with you." He shifted, his hands going behind her, lifting her.

He pivoted, bringing her atop him so she straddled him as he sat on the edge of the cot. He pushed the hair from her face, cupping her cheeks as she'd done to him.

"I thought debutantes were supposed to be innocent," he murmured against her lips.

"I'm no debutante," she said, nibbling his lower lip.

He growled, deep in his throat, and his hands moved to her back. She wasn't surprised when her corset loosened seconds later, and he yanked, pulling it from her. She had only her chemise and pantalets left to her and yet he was still fully clothed.

"Lucas." She couldn't stop the plea in her voice, but he only laughed against the spot behind her ear where his lips had traveled.

"So impatient." He licked her, sending a bolt of fire through her.

Her fingers curled into his shoulders, and her hips lifted of their own according, grinding against him. He groaned, his hands going to her hips, pinning her in place.

"I want to see how wet I make you," he whispered.

She didn't know what his words meant, but his tone made her shiver. She relaxed against him, her body opening, trusting, wanting.

He slipped his hand between them, and she thought he would find the slit in her pantalets but instead he pressed the rough fabric against her. She jerked at the sensation, pleasure and pain rippling through her.

"Lucas?"

"Do you like it when I touch you, Amelia?" he whispered. "Do you?"

She couldn't respond. Her head had fallen back, and she was unable to hold it up as his fingers toyed with her. The rough fabric rubbed against her sensitive nub, stroke after sensual stroke, and she trembled, her body coiling. She tried to stop it. She tried to wait, to prolong the pleasure, but she couldn't.

"Lucas, I—" The air caught in her throat as the tension built.

"Do you feel that? Do you feel how ready you are for me?"

She did feel it then, the dampness between her legs as though her body yearned for his, wished for his sensual assault.

"Yes," she moaned, burying her face against his neck as she tried to withstand the building tension.

But his fingers kept moving, slow deliberate circles made intolerable by the rough brush of the linen. He slipped a hand under her chin, brought her head up until her forehead rested against his.

"Tell me what you want, Amelia. Tell me what you want, and I'll give it to you."

She didn't know what she wanted. She didn't know... anything about this. She only knew how he made her feel. So she said, "My breasts. They're heavy. They ache for..."

"They ache for this?" He moved his free hand so slowly, such a small movement, she didn't think he'd done anything at all, but then pleasure spiked through her where his fingers had brushed her nipple.

"Ah, Lucas." Her fingers flexed involuntarily, and her hips jerked, straining against his patient hand.

The fire built, the tension grew, her body coiling, readying, just one more—

His hand stopped, his fingers pressed against her.

"No," she moaned. "Lucas, I want—"

"Not yet, sweetheart. Not yet." He held his hand there as he dipped his head.

She thought he would push the strap of her chemise from her shoulder, expose her to his greedy mouth, but he didn't. Instead he placed his mouth on her, and using his tongue, rubbed the rough linen against her painful nipple. She arched, her hips going forward, and a pleasure so acute rocked through her she knew she needed more of it. She needed it now.

But he was still torturing her, his tongue stroking circles around her pebbled nipple, and still the hand he held against her hot core didn't move. She ached. She ached...for something, but he only continued to torture her.

"Lucas, please." She lifted her hips as far as she was able and came down against his inert hand. Pleasure. Intense, focused pleasure at the place where she'd rubbed against his hand.

She did it again, but this time she thought he let her rise up a little farther, come down a little harder against him. Again, the pleasure. Again, she lifted herself, grinding her nub until the pleasure grew and grew and finally—

The climax rocked her, both for its intensity and for the fact that she'd done it to herself. She had given herself that pleasure, and he had shown her how.

"Lucas. You...I..." But she couldn't put it into words. There was too much. Between the physical pleasure and what he had shown her, it was too much.

Vaguely she became aware of rustling. Both of his hands were between them now, and she realized he was undoing his trousers. She shifted onto her knees, giving him room to free himself. Finally he gripped her hips and only then did he find the slit in her pantalets to ease her down on his hard shaft.

She had thought the pleasure she had given herself could never be matched, but she was wrong. Feeling him inside of her bordered on pain, and her sheath tightened as if holding on to him.

He moaned, burying his face against her breasts. But then he was moving, slamming up into her even as he lifted her hips, bringing her down as he raised himself up. He was so deep inside of her she thought he might touch a part of her no one had ever seen. The part she never let anyone see, the last part of her that was still whole and undamaged. She wrapped her arms around his neck, held on to him, hoping for something different this time. Something that felt right.

Something that didn't leave her empty.

"Amelia, I can't. You feel too good."

She knew what he meant, but she couldn't make herself speak. The words were caught in her throat as desire overtook her. She wanted him. All of him. She wanted to feel complete.

He thrust into her, holding her hips in place now as he lifted himself, controlling how it felt, taking his own desire. But his desire was hers too, and she felt herself coiling again, felt the climax coming.

"Amelia, I want to watch you touch yourself." His words confused her, and she leaned back, met his gaze.

"Touch yourself, Amelia. Like you did using my hand. I want you to do it with yours. Please." The desire in his eyes was stark, and she was filled with an urgency to do what he asked if only to feel the power she held just then. This ability to drive him mad.

She leaned back, reaching between them until she found her nub through her pantalets as he had done. Her touch was tentative at first, not knowing how to touch herself to draw pleasure, but she was already so sensitive the barest of touches sent electricity crackling through her.

She lurched forward, her free hand going to his shoulder to hold herself upright.

"Oh, God, Lucas. That...that was..." But she didn't have any energy left for her voice.

She'd found a rhythm now, circling her nub in small, deliberate strokes. It was different, not as deep or biting, but then she looked up and found him watching her. Watching what she did to herself.

She exploded, her body convulsing with pleasure as he thrust into her one more time. She collapsed against him, and he fell back against the cot, pulling her with him.

He stroked her hair, her back, murmured soothing words against her forehead, but none of it mattered. She thought her heart would rip from her chest it beat so furiously. Her body radiated spent passion as if her climax had an echo, and she bathed in it, this glow that filled her body.

Slumber waited at the periphery, but she didn't want to answer its siren call. There was something that wasn't quite right. Something was wrong. She eased to the side, slipping into the crook of her husband's shoulder, her head falling there as though it were meant for her.

Only then could she reach between them, her hand sliding down her chest, finding the damp spot where his mouth had sucked her, moving farther, finding the hem of her chemise.

For one blissful moment, she thought she was wrong. She thought maybe this time he had given all of himself to her.

But then her fingers found it. The sticky dampness that had been there the first night, the evidence of the ghosts that haunted her husband left to dry on her belly.

CHAPTER 10

"**A**nd then I think we should send a parade of elephants down his drive and stampede them through his portrait galleries."

"Yes, that seems right," Lucas mumbled.

Stephen sighed. "Cousin. You're not paying attention."

Lucas looked up sharply, his hands full of the maps they had been sorting through in the duke's study. He held the maps up like a shield, knowing perfectly well why he was distracted but not wishing to discuss it.

Just the sight of the maps had his mind wandering away. What was the point in studying them one more time? What was the point in building any of this if there was no heir onto whom to pass it?

That day in his tower room still haunted him. It was clear now that all his effort, all his scheming to negotiate for a bride was fruitless. Because even with a passion so great it still rattled him, Lila was able to penetrate it, cutting her claws into his future from her grave.

He couldn't produce an heir.

He closed his eyes briefly, blocking out the maps that

tormented him with their meaning. When he had first arrived at Dinsmore, he had found in the estate a reason to live on, a reason to wake every morning and go forth, doing his best to build the estate back to its grandeur, yes, but it was more than that. He was creating something new, something better, for his tenants and the villagers.

Something he would one day pass on to his heir.

But it didn't matter any longer. He couldn't do it. He lusted after his wife, even now when he resolutely avoided her. He could still taste her on his lips, still hear her moans echoing in his ears. Could still feel the way her hands gripped him as though she would float away on a wave of desire if she let go.

None of it matter because Lila was stronger than all of it.

She had destroyed his past, and she would stop his future.

"You're right, and I apologize." He shifted the maps, pushing aside some ledgers that were stacked on the desk to make room for the sheets of paper he held.

Finally there was enough room to lie them flat, and he did so, spreading his hands over them to work out the wrinkles. The valley was displayed in full then, stretching from one end of the map to the other with the village of Dinsmore perched on the most southeastern edge. He leaned against the display, perching over the map. "There must be something here with which to persuade Aylesford to at least grant an audience to the railway agent."

Stephen wedged one hip against the desk, a pen pressed between his fingers. "That's just what I was saying. If we can find another way into Aylesford's good graces, we may be able to convince him to lease the land." Stephen pointed to a stretch of the river along the eastern edge of the marquess's estate. "Do you know if he's leased rights to the waterway here? Perhaps if he's already engaged in a fruitful leasing venture, we can convince him to hear out the merits on the railway proposal."

Lucas heard each of Stephen's words clearly, but for some unknown reason he couldn't put the words into context. His mind was muddled with the futility of it all. He rubbed his face with his hands and collapsed in the cavernous chair behind the desk. He had to remember there were still people who were counting on him even if his greatest achievement of all was now out of his reach.

Stephen didn't speak for a solid ten seconds, and he was grateful for that.

"I take it marriage is not the answer you thought it would be," his cousin finally said.

Lucas shut his eyes and leaned his head back, picturing his wife as she had looked in his arms, her head thrown back as the intensity of her passion gripped her. He had been so close. His own desire gripping him by the throat until he thought he couldn't breathe and yet—

He hadn't been able to do it. He'd pulled out at the last possible moment, spilling his seed against her stomach. She could still be with child. He knew that, and perhaps that would be enough. But he couldn't help shake the sense that he was letting Lila win. *Still.*

"I am finding the wife I thought I would get is not the one I actually got," Lucas finally managed between gritted teeth. "I thought she would be a spoiled debutante, happy to spend her hours on gowns and social calls." He met Stephen's gaze. "But it appears Amelia is far more dangerous."

"Do you mean the exchange she orchestrated? I thought it was rather brilliant." Stephen's mouth lifted on one side in a grin of admiration.

Lucas frowned. "Don't you find the woman's interest in the estate concerning?"

Stephen's grin disappeared. "I find it to be expected. She is the duchess after all. She has responsibilities here."

Lucas pushed to his feet and paced to the windows, his frustration demanding he move. "I find it rather annoying," he grumbled.

Stephen didn't say anything for several seconds and then, "I think you've had the run of this place for a long time. It's an adjustment to have assistance in the management of your tenants."

Lucas swung around. "My tenants. Precisely. Who is she to be meddling in their care?"

Stephen's expression cleared for the briefest of moments, and then the man looked away as though composing himself. Lucas straightened, flexing his fingers as he prepared for his cousin's response.

Finally the man looked back up. "I think this has nothing to do with your wife, cousin."

"What does?"

Stephen straightened, picking up his crutch from where he'd placed it against the desk. "I think you need to ask yourself that."

Lucas pondered his cousin's words for a moment, but it was as though he were repeatedly hitting his head against the stone wall of the castle.

"Are you suggesting this is my fault?"

"I'm suggesting you are giving power to those who should never have held it."

Lucas swallowed and looked back out the window. Stephen was right. He was giving power to ghosts, but he couldn't stop it. He was haunted by what had happened to him, and he wanted nothing more than to stop it from happening again. But that would mean he would be forced to deny Amelia her rightful place as duchess.

He flexed his hands into fists again, hating himself and hating Lila more.

"You didn't tell her of your fondness for black pudding, did you?" Stephen finally asked, and Lucas knew it for the olive branch it was.

He turned around, forcing his features to relax. "I did not, and black pudding is a perfectly acceptable dish."

Stephen wrinkled his nose as if to disagree.

But seeing his cousin standing there was too much. It was a reminder of how many people depended on him. He turned back to the window. The duke's study overlooked the estuary, and though the day was bright, a wind had sprung up that sent waves crashing against the rocks below. He braced his hands against the window frame and leaned his forehead against the cool glass.

"She was asking too many questions," he grumbled. "She wanted to know why I had sought out a wife."

"What was that, cousin?" Stephen asked. "Your wife was showing an interest in your person by asking you about your intentions for her? How dreadful."

Lucas snapped upright, sending a glare in his cousin's direction. "She was prying."

"She was engaging in conversation."

"She was being nosy."

Stephen folded his arms over his chest. "And you are being childish."

Though the accusation was accurate, Lucas couldn't help but feel slighted.

"She's your wife now, Lucas," Stephen said softly, and the word *wife* slithered over Lucas like it never had before.

Amelia didn't deserve that. It was someone else who had made him wary of the word.

But Stephen was right. Amelia was his wife now. That she

should ask of his intentions only seemed natural, but his past was anything but natural, and he wished to keep it from her. Did he mean to protect her from it? Or keep her from knowing it?

Stephen shifted on his feet. "You should go bathe and change."

Lucas halted abruptly as he'd been about to engage in some pointless yet gratifying pacing when Stephen's suggestion hit him.

"I beg your pardon?"

"You should bathe and change," Stephen repeated, nodding in the direction of the clock above the mantel of the fireplace. "It will be time for supper soon, and you can join your wife for the meal. Take the opportunity to apologize for whatever it is you did and make amends." Stephen gestured at Lucas's person. "But you can't do it like that. The smell will put her off her beef."

Lucas looked down at his mud-splattered trousers and soiled shirt. There was a drainage issue in the east fields they'd been attempting to sort out that afternoon, and it had become a slimy affair rather quickly.

"You know I don't have time to dine this evening. There's work to be done," he said, gesturing to the pile of maps. His cousin didn't need to know he hadn't dined with his wife in nearly a week. Not since that afternoon.

"You're married, cousin." He spoke the words in a ponderous, slightly exhausted tone. "You must make time for these things."

He must make time for Amelia was what his cousin meant to say.

"No," Lucas said simply.

"Yes," Stephen shot back and took a step toward him. "You know as well as I do that the Aylesford situation will not improve unless you decide to meet with the man personally. You cannot keep sending me, a mere mister, to do your work, Lucas." He gestured to the maps now. "You know how important this is to Dinsmore, and yet you do not act as though you do. The railway agent said we had until the first of May to convince Aylesford. That's mere weeks away now. I only hope you realize what you must do before it's too late."

He deserved the reprimand. He knew that and yet it stung. Not because someone below him in title should scold him but rather because Stephen meant so damned much to him. He could see the frustration in his cousin's eyes, but it didn't compare to the frustration Lucas felt. He knew what he must do but...

"You know I can't show my face," he said, the words plain, his tone neutral.

But Stephen shook his head. "I'm not sure it's your face that's stopping you, cousin." He moved to the door then, calling over his shoulder. "I'll have Mrs. Fairfax send up a bath." He paused, casting a glance back at Lucas that was filled with genuine concern. "I mean it, cousin. Amelia seems like a fine lady. Treat her with some care."

Lucas feared it was too late for that.

SHE ONLY ARRANGED to meet Mrs. Mitchum at Jones's cottage when it became clear it was her only choice.

Lucas was once more avoiding her. This shouldn't have concerned her. In fact, she should be exalting in her freedom. Alice had written to say they were able to hire a footman, and Adaline had ordered a new gown and would be able to attend some balls that season. It was all exactly as Amelia had hoped, but she couldn't seem to accept it.

Something haunted Lucas, and she hated seeing him when the ghosts of his past resurfaced. It was in the clipped, one-word answers he gave when she asked about estate business and in the clothes he chose to wear, hiding himself from the world. Her husband was not a vain man, and she thought his scars were not cause for his agitation. Not as great as it was. Not something that would stop him from getting her with child.

For the first time, she missed her mother. Her mother would have been able to tell her if what Lucas was doing did indeed prevent a baby. For some reason, she had to know for certain. She couldn't rid her mind of the soot-blackened cradle, and she knew the key to unlocking Lucas's past lay in getting an answer to why he always aborted their lovemaking.

She didn't wish for the servants to know what was happening, which left her with only Mrs. Mitchum.

She emerged from the castle, the late spring sun warming her shoulders immediately. Jones stepped up behind her.

"Are you sure you wish to walk, Your Grace? The village is nearly two miles from here."

Amelia smiled, the sea air already bolstering her courage. "Yes, I'm quite sure."

She'd not taken two more steps when they were suddenly surrounded by a cloud of dust. She raised her hands as if to shield herself from it, but the situation was quite obviously hopeless. The layer of dust on the sleeves of her gown was visible within seconds, and she peered down at her skirts, knowing what she would find there only to be forced to close her eyes against the grit that still hung in the air.

When she finally opened them, she found a pair of workmen beside a cart of stones having been emptied on the ground not far from them. At least the workers had the notion to appear sheepish.

"Begging your pardon, Your Grace," one of them said.

Amelia nodded with a smile of reassurance, but Jones

said, "Ach, it's good they didn't try this on the day of the exchange. What a sight that would have been."

At the reminder of the exchange, Amelia's stomach tightened. The day had been a success, regardless of what might have occurred otherwise. There wasn't a single item left when the tenants finished making their way through it. At least that was what she had found by the time she managed to make her way back to it.

Mrs. Fairfax and Jones had immediately showered her with stories of satisfied tenants, pulling overloaded carts with found treasures, their arms carrying what their carts couldn't hold.

Amelia had expected to feel a measure of pride, but the success of that day was overshadowed by her other troubles.

What had Lucas meant about the reason she was there at Dinsmore? If she took his meaning literally it was as though she were to serve as some kind of concubine, but that didn't seem to fit with Lucas. Especially with the way he seemed to avoid her.

No, there was something else at work here. Something she hadn't known, and she suspected her father had not been told. The Duke of Greyfair had sought out a wife for a purpose, but she had the horrible sense his plan was not going how he wished it to. She wanted to speak to him, to get him to talk to her, but she knew it would be futile. She needed Mrs. Mitchum.

The walk into the village was more pleasant than Jones had intimated. It was hardly more than a couple of miles on flat coastal land. There was a smattering of tenants along the road, but none had been out in their yards as she passed. Eyeing the parcels of land, another thought occurred to her.

"Jones," she began. "Do you know how large the Greyfair estate is?"

Jones shook her head, pulling Amelia around a puddle in

the road. "Not as such. Greyfair lands stretch all the way up the valley, nearly to the northern ridge what's runs along the river."

None of those geographical markers meant anything to her, but she nodded anyway.

"I see. So Greyfair holdings are vast?" she asked.

Jones nodded. "They're even bigger than that Aylesford chap's, although you'd never think it for the way he acts."

"Aylesford?" The name rang a note in her mind, distant and foggy.

Jones nodded in a northerly direction off the road, and Amelia got the sense she was referring to land that bordered the Greyfair holding.

"The Marquess of Aylesford. Old, stuffy fellow, Mrs. Fairfax says. He's not like the duke. Doesn't like anything changing the way things have been, you see. Too happy and fat to like things mussed up for hisself. He's not at all like the duke," she said again, her voice trailing off.

Amelia couldn't help but smile at the servant's obvious respect for her employer, but the name still bothered her. "Do you happen to know the marquess's family name? I seem to remember mention of a Marquess of Aylesford, but I can't recall from where."

Jones shrugged. "I haven't the slightest idea of his lordship's family name. I've only ever heard His Grace refer to the gentleman by his title."

Amelia tried to let it go, but the name still lingered, unsettled in her mind.

The road soon grew narrower, and a small lane of cottages popped up on either side. Jones took the one on the right, and Amelia followed. The maid stopped at the third cottage in, opening the worn wooden gate that led into the front yard. Although it was worn, it made no sound as Jones pushed it back, suggesting it was well-cared for if old and faded.

Amelia's gaze traveled over the cottage and again she noted age, but there was equal evidence of repair. Like the piece of sash, mended with a differently sized board to hold the shutter in place or the stones placed carefully in the depressions left by years of rainwater pooling along the walkway to the front door.

Jones opened the front door and led Amelia inside. The cool interior of the cottage was a welcomed relief from the hot spring sun, and peering about her, she gathered the same cared-for if worn sense of the place she had gathered from the exterior.

"Mum?" Jones called out from the bottom of the stairs that ran up the center hallway where they stood.

"Ethel?" came the startled reply, only it came from the back of the cottage.

This was followed by some scurrying noises, and Jones called out, "Tis nothing to worry over. I've come with the new mistress from the castle."

The scurrying stopped almost at once, and Jones beckoned for Amelia to follow her down the hallway. Before they could reach the doorway at the end, a woman stepped out into the corridor, her hands worrying an apron tied at her waist.

"Ethel, dear. We weren't expecting you." The woman's tone was pleasant and matched the careful lines of her face. "Your mother is quite worried."

Amelia felt a pang of guilt. She'd only decided that morning to call on Mrs. Mitchum. The woman looked nothing like a witch, and Amelia wondered once again why the villagers might call her as much. She looked like a kind, older woman with her graying hair neatly pulled back and pinned at the nape of her neck. Her clothes were serviceable and plain, but somehow Amelia knew the woman didn't care much for her appearance. She was too far away for Amelia to discern any more details.

"Your Grace." The woman curtsied now with a bow of her head.

"I'm terribly sorry if we've inconvenienced you or Mrs. Jones. I didn't mean to arrive unannounced. It's only—"

But Mrs. Mitchum had already waved off Amelia's explanation while Jones disappeared through the door into the back of the house.

"Tisn't anything at all, Your Grace. Ethel's mum will love seeing her for a bit." She nodded in the direction Jones had disappeared. "Come now. I'm sure you'll be wanting a cuppa after your walk."

Amelia followed the woman and found herself in a small but clean kitchen filled with the scent of herbs and fresh bread. A woman, bent and pale, sat by the cook stove in a rigid wooden chair, a series of shawls tied tightly about herself. Amelia went over to her, taking her hands into her own.

"I'm Amelia Bennett, the new Duchess of Greyfair. It's an honor to meet you, Mrs. Jones," she said, squeezing the woman's hands.

The woman blinked, her eyes cloudy as though her sight were not clear, but her face was unlined, and Amelia realized the woman was a great deal younger than Amelia would have guessed from how she huddled against the warm cook fire.

"Your Grace," Mrs. Jones said, her words ragged as though she struggled to draw a full breath. "It's so good of you to come for a visit. My Ethel has done nothing but talk about you since you arrived."

Amelia felt uncomfortable with such praise. She was simply unused to the attention, so she diverted it away from her. "You've raised a remarkable young woman, Mrs. Jones."

The older woman smiled, and Amelia noted she was missing some teeth. "I have, have I not? It's the one thing I did right in this life."

Amelia squeezed the woman's hands again. "I wouldn't be so quick to judge. You've still a lot of life left." She spoke the words with a hint of humor, and the other woman rocked back with a laugh.

"Oh, I'm not so sure about that, Your Grace, but I thank you for the kindness."

Amelia squeezed the woman's hands a final time and released them. "It isn't kindness at all. Just a simple fact."

"Mum, it's a beautiful day. What do you say to a cuppa in the garden?" Jones moved, resting her hands on her mother's shoulder as if to draw her attention. "I'll help you, and you can sit in the sun for a spot. What do you say to that?"

Mrs. Jones's eyes widened at her daughter's suggestion. "Is it truly warm today?"

"The warmest it's been in ages. It might even dry out your old bones."

Mrs. Jones laughed as her daughter helped her to stand. Jones had her mother to the door before turning and casting a wink in Amelia's direction. How it was that Amelia had acquired an ally so quickly upon her arrival at Dinsmore she'd never know, but again she felt that shifting inside of her, the sense that something was different now.

"It's difficult," Mrs. Mitchum said from her place at the stove where she was setting a dented copper kettle to boil. She looked up, meeting Amelia's eyes directly. "Being a new bride. And I can't imagine what it must be like for you. I would assume you haven't lived in a castle on an island before." A playful smile teased at Mrs. Mitchum's lips, softening her words.

Amelia felt her own smile coming, felt herself leaning into Mrs. Mitchum. "No, I haven't had the pleasure of saying

I've lived in a castle before. Although I'm finding Dinsmore to my liking."

"And the duke?" Mrs. Mitchum's voice was pleasant and warm. Once Amelia might have thought such a question would be asked in order to pry some dark secret from the bride of the Ghoul of Greyfair, but not anymore. "The duke is kind and caring. He works hard to better the lives of his tenants," she said, never letting her eyes wander from Mrs. Mitchum's.

It was a moment before the woman smiled broadly, moving to fill a chipped teapot painted in florals with an aromatic spoonful of tea leaves.

"I'm glad to hear as much. We think highly of our duke, you know."

Amelia swallowed and reached for the back of the wooden chair Mrs. Jones had so recently vacated, feeling the need to occupy her hands.

"Mrs. Mitchum, Jones—Ethel, that is—suggested you might be knowledgeable in an area where I'm afraid I'm rather unschooled."

Mrs. Mitchum gave no reaction to Amelia's statement. She pulled several teacups from a cupboard and placed them next to the teapot.

"I should think there are many such areas for you. I find young ladies such as yourself are left unprepared for what marriage will entail."

Amelia couldn't help but notice the woman's hands as she worked and the glaring absence of a wedding ring. Did Mrs. Mitchum speak from experience? Was she really unmarried? Did she use the title of missus to protect herself? Or perhaps a widow?

"My mother passed away a few months ago," Amelia said, and it drew a startled look from Mrs. Mitchum.

"I'm terribly sorry. I didn't realize." She turned, facing

Amelia directly now and abandoning the tea things. "How terrible it must have been for you then."

Amelia felt a pang of guilt but didn't speak.

Mrs. Mitchum gestured to the scrubbed wooden table in the middle of the kitchen. "Please. Sit." She wiped her hands on her apron as she had done when Amelia first caught sight of her and offered a chair to Amelia.

She took it, pressing her hands in her lap to keep her nerves at bay.

Mrs. Mitchum took a chair opposite and placed her hands flat on the table. The woman exuded a calm that was catching. Although her mind still flittered from one thought to another, Amelia felt herself relaxing.

"Mrs. Mitchum, I must know how it is one begets a child." The sentence was clunky, but it was the only way she could think of to ask the question without blushing.

Mrs. Mitchum's lips tightened ever so subtly. "I see," she said, but there was no note of censure in her voice. "I take it marital relations were a surprise to you."

Amelia shook her head. "It was not a surprise, no. It was rather…confusing." She picked up her hands, laying them flat on the tabletop like Mrs. Mitchum had and leaned forward. "To be honest, I'm not sure he—" She licked her lips. "I'm not sure we did what was necessary to produce a child."

Mrs. Mitchum's eyes were understanding. "In order for you to grow a child in your womb, your husband must plant his seed there. Tell me. When the act was completed, was there a dampness between your legs?"

Only weeks ago such a question would have had Amelia blushing, but she needed answers now.

"No. It was on my belly." She gestured to herself where she had wiped away the wetness from her stomach that night and again that afternoon in the tower room.

Mrs. Mitchum's lips tightened again. "I thought as much.

No, Your Grace. Your husband must empty his seed inside of you. Do you know what I mean by that?"

She was asking about the part where Lucas had entered Amelia. She nodded, her determination not quite strong enough to speak of such intimate details.

Mrs. Mitchum nodded. "Good. Then you must see that he does so if you wish for a child."

The woman's words struck like a physical blow, and Amelia pressed a hand instinctually to her belly. She hadn't thought of being a mother. Her own had been so awful it wasn't something Amelia had aspired to. But when Mrs. Mitchum said it out loud it sparked something inside of her, something wondering and curious. What would it be like to have Lucas's child? The need for answers shifted, and instead of the urge to help, it coalesced into something more personal.

Amelia shook her head. "Then why would my husband have not done so? Why would he leave his seed as he did?" Her throat tightened on the words, both out of embarrassment and concern.

Mrs. Mitchum's eyes had taken on a concerned light that sent a wave of unease over Amelia's skin. "A man will empty his seed in such a way so as to prevent the making of a child." The woman shook her head. "But why would your husband not wish for a child? You are properly wed, no? The child would be his heir?"

Amelia's fingers curled into the fabric of her gown, but she didn't feel it. She could only think of the small wooden cradle, blackened from the fire that had killed Lucas's wife and nearly killed him.

CHAPTER 11

*H*e didn't realize how dark it had grown until the knock at the door roused him from his work. He was in his tower room, hunched over the same maps he had been studying for months now, the same ones he'd all but memorized, and he was no closer to finding an answer to his problems.

Which only made Stephen's words ring truer.

Lucas must meet with the marquess himself.

Perhaps gentleman to gentleman, Aylesford would see the benefit of a lease to the railway. If Lucas could couch his argument in the correct strand, maybe the marquess wouldn't see it as trade but rather as a mere piece of estate management, a duty any titled gentleman would carry out.

After all the arguments Stephen had presented the marquess with so far, this seemed the weakest, and yet that was likely why it would work.

Because Aylesford wouldn't sink to the depth of trade. He was too good for it, and Lucas would need to appeal to the man's ego. Even if it meant he would need to use his position as duke to do so.

The knock came again, and he shook his head as he pushed back from the rutted table he used as a desk.

"Enter," he called at the same time every muscle in his body clenched.

He had been so absorbed in his thoughts he hadn't remembered who it was that would be knocking at his door at this hour. He was so used to his life containing only Mrs. Fairfax or Stephen that his memory hadn't yet expanded to include his wife.

She came through the door in neat, certain steps and paused, her hand on the doorknob. He watched her scan the room, her motions slow and deliberate, and he realized she likely couldn't see him all that well in the near dark.

He was hit with the sudden, insane urge to hide. This was rapidly followed by the even stronger urge to stand, go to her, sweep her into his arms, and—

Take her to his cot?

He closed his eyes against the ridiculousness the image suggested and for the first time hated himself for still being like this.

Still hiding. Even now.

He knew what it was he was doing. Avoiding a proper trim from a skilled barber, eschewing the latest fashions in favor of the greatcoat and hat that concealed him, refusing even the simplest furnishings that would suggest a human lived in this room.

For he didn't feel human.

Not anymore.

"Amelia," he called softly through the darkness after far too many seconds but before her gaze had reached his side of the room.

He might not feel human, but he still remembered what good manners were. He stood as was proper and bowed slightly. It was overly formal, but just then, in the dark, his wife's open face silhouetted in the light of the single candle he had lit, he felt the need to do something a gentleman would.

"Your Grace. Lucas." She stumbled on his name, and even in the dimness, he could see her lick her lips.

He turned about, trying not to think of the instinct overtaking him, trying not to feel the desire simmering just under the surface as he reached for the tin of matches under the window. He shook one free and used it to light the lamp on the table, raising the wick until light flooded the room. He took longer than was necessary to replace the globe and turn, and even then, he closed his eyes.

He wanted to see Amelia in the lamplight, and worse, he wanted to enjoy it. He wanted that first glimpse of her to be as magical as he knew it would be, and he wanted nothing more than to feel the simple pleasure of looking at her.

Only weeks ago he wouldn't have allowed himself such a thing, but now he allowed himself to indulge.

Was it because she had never balked at his touch? Was it because she had always met his gaze directly? Was it because she was her and only she had the power to transfix him like this?

He thought suddenly of the last time they were in this room, and his throat closed. He looked away, forcing himself to draw a steady breath.

"I had hoped to have a word with you," Amelia said, and he wasn't sure if it was her words or the tremulous tone of her voice that had him looking quickly back.

"What is it?" A cool fear gripped him suddenly, and he understood not for the first time how tenuous his hopes for the future were. He hadn't even been able to—

He swallowed, pushing his fears down.

She opened her mouth, closed it, and stepped fully inside the room, shutting the door quietly behind her. She had that way of moving, as though she didn't wish anyone to hear her. She had the same way in her speech, choosing her words carefully as though she were taking up as little air as possible. He wasn't sure when he had first noticed it, but here in the close confines of the tower room, the dark pressing in all around them, it was more pronounced.

She took a step forward and said, "I wish to know why you do not want me to have your child."

He wasn't sure what sliced through him first, the shock or the pain. The shock was understandable. He had been wrong in assuming she did not know the mechanics of the marriage act it would seem, and she had certainly ascertained that he was not doing what was necessary to get her with child.

But the pain was unexpected. He wasn't sure if it were the words themselves or the way in which she said them that stoked the worst of it. For it sounded as though he didn't *wish* her to have his child. It was as though he found something distasteful and unworthy about her that would suggest she was the last person with whom he would want to produce his child.

It was like a dagger directly to his heart. Had he made her feel that way? Had he made her believe he found her lacking in some way?

But underneath these fears hummed a nearly fatal one.

For suddenly he realized he very much wished for her to have his child.

He pictured her, her belly swollen, her face aglow with the expectation of new life, and he knew—*he knew*—he wanted nothing more than to see it. He wanted to have a child with her.

But even though he knew, it did not mean his body would go along with it.

"I apologize if I've misled you. I had thought to prevent a pregnancy until you had settled in here." The lie rolled off his lips, and he hated how comfortable he had gotten in hiding his shame behind manufactured words.

Her gaze twitched as though assessing his statement, and finally she looked away, her head turning to the door. He watched as time seemed to splinter around her, as the decision to turn back took hold of her.

"You're lying to me. I would like to know why." Again her words were efficient, and the directness of her gaze slammed right into his chest.

"I'm not—" But he stopped.

Silence pulsed between them, his lie dangling like a specter, the thing that would forever haunt their marriage if he denied it now.

She took another step closer. "If you find there is something...wrong with me—" She choked on the word as if it were too difficult to speak, and the pain in his chest grew. "If you find me lacking, I should like to know. I can make amends or at the very least try to improve. I swear it." Her eyes had grown wider, and the sincerity and determination in them slayed him.

It hit him then. *Her* pain. He had been so consumed by his own that he had never seen hers. He waded back through her words. He hadn't been thinking clearly, readying the defense he would need to give, and he couldn't remember the nuances, the words she had selected.

He shifted his thoughts. "Amelia, it's nothing to do—"

She spun away before he could finish, and she hunched her shoulders as if to hide her face from him, but he caught the low noise she made. It was a curious noise, not one of self-pity or anguish, but more of...despair.

But somehow that made it worse. It filled him with a sense of loneliness, a loneliness he didn't understand.

He reached for her, but his hand stopped before he touched her.

Just as quickly as she had turned, she spun back around, her shoulders straight and unyielding now, her chin up.

"It never does have anything to do with me," she nearly whispered, the quiet heat in her voice stinging. "And yet it does."

The words were perplexing, and he sensed they came from a place far away and deep within her, a place in her past he wasn't privy to, and something inside of himself shifted again.

She had spoken of her sisters; she had seemed bereft merely speaking of her late father. He had assumed she came from a cozy and close family. But her words then were confusing and suggested a history much darker than the one he had fabricated for her.

Uneasiness gripped him, and his stomach dropped as though he had forgotten something. But then all at once, he saw it. She'd never once mentioned her mother.

"What do you mean?" he asked carefully.

Her lips parted, but she closed them as if changing her mind. He waited, bracing himself involuntarily, but then horribly, she smiled. It was a beautiful smile, taking up the whole of her face and lighting as though from within. The fabricated gloss of it broke his heart.

"Nothing," she said, her voice firm now. "I don't mean anything." She shook her head and turned to the door. "I'm sorry to have disturbed you, Your Grace."

Terror gripped him. Her body was taut, poised, and unyielding, and yet her words were those of someone lost.

What did she mean?

I don't mean anything.

Did she not mean to speak to him or was it worse than that? Did she think she didn't mean anything to him?

"Lila." It came out of him like a shot from a pistol, the

name firing from his lips as though it could reach out and physically stop her from leaving.

It worked. She froze two steps in front of the door.

He licked his lips, willed his heart to stop racing. "My first wife. Her name was Lila." He suddenly seemed unable to speak in more than three or four words at a time. He took a deep breath, filling his lungs with air as though it would ease the panic and pain in his chest. "She died." Two words. It was only getting worse.

But then Amelia turned, and even that was careful and precise, her feet shuffling a small circle on the floor as she turned back to him. Her expression was clear, her brow smooth, and she watched him carefully as if weighing his every word.

Only something was different now. She didn't judge his words the way she had seconds before. It was as though she anticipated them. As though she were marking what he said against something she already knew.

Not for the first time, he thought of the rumors, the ones he had worked so carefully to spread, and he knew what she was thinking.

The Ghoul of Greyfair had murdered his wife.

And yet, she didn't flee. She didn't back away. She stood there, ready, and waiting.

And for once, the words seemed to tumble out of him.

"She was carrying a child when she died in the fire. The same fire that gave me these scars." He stopped, drew a breath, but he wasn't done. "I tried to save her. I went back for her. And this happened." He gestured to the side of his face. "Part of the ceiling fell on me, and Stephen pulled me to safety." The next words, the last words, didn't wish to come, but he couldn't pull his eyes from Amelia. She stood there, silent and still, and suddenly his future rushed before him. A future without a child. A future without an heir to continue his work at Dinsmore. A future without her. And suddenly the words sprang free. "I wasn't able to save her."

But even as the words left his lips, he knew there were other ones, other words left unspoken, other words that were far more dangerous.

* * *

SHE HAD SUSPECTED the truth all along, but to hear him speak it rattled her.

He hadn't become a ghoul trying to murder his wife. He had become a ghoul trying to save her.

The sudden sense of loss took her breath away, and she found herself unmoving, her gaze never wavering from him. Guilt followed, the kind of guilt that was all-consuming, and this had her pulling in a breath again.

She had practically thrown herself at him. That first night when he'd come to her, she had foolishly thought he wanted her, but really he was grieving, reminded every day by his scars of all that he had lost.

His wife.

His child.

And what had she done? She'd made it worse, just like she always did. Her mother had been right. There was no place for her.

"I'm so sorry," she finally said, but her voice was little more than a whisper. She blinked, forced herself to swallow, and met his gaze again. "I am very sorry for your loss. I shouldn't have —" But the words and the pain they carried stuck in her throat.

She'd tried to force him to get her with child. She'd confronted him about it like he'd lost a significant sum at cards. When he had watched his wife and child die in a fire, unable to save them.

How could she do this? How could she always seem to make things worse when she was simply trying to help?

She backed to the door, slowly, one foot and then the next, focusing all of her attention on not giving in to the urge to flee. She wouldn't do that. She wouldn't embarrass herself like that. She'd already done enough.

"I shouldn't—" she tried again, but all the words stopped in her throat now.

She had been right. It was safer being alone.

"I'm sorry I bothered you. Good night," she said instead, the words tripping so easily from her lips, and she reached for the door.

"Please don't go."

At first, she didn't think she'd heard him correctly, his voice was so low and steady. She paused, her hand reaching for the doorknob, but she turned her head back to look at him.

He looked lost, much as he had that first night. It seemed like yesterday, but it was weeks ago now. How had so much time passed?

"I don't wish to further burden you. I'm sorry I—"

"You're not a burden."

It wasn't what she had said, but somehow, he'd routed out her truth. She was a burden, whether he said it or not.

But then her memory flashed back on that afternoon, here, in this very room when he'd taken her. She had asked him why she was there, and he had said only two words. *For this.* What had he meant by that? Was he attempting to produce an heir when he knew he could never love again?

She had known all along she was a bought bride, but when everything fell together in her mind with stunning, cold clarity, she realized the truth of it.

Lucas grieved for his dead wife and child. She was there

to serve as nothing more than a means to an end. He would never love her.

And when had she started to hope he might?

Probably when she started to fall in love with him.

She raised her chin. Such circular thoughts would do her no good. If he wished for her to stay, she had no right to refuse him. She was there for a practical reason after all.

"If you wish," she said, but she didn't move away from the door.

The instinct to protect herself was too strong, especially now that she knew the entire truth. But somehow it was strangely comforting, knowing the real reason the duke had sought out her father. It was all far less confusing when it was a simple arrangement.

She pushed her hands down her skirts to relax her fingers, not realizing how tense she had been.

"Can I get you something to drink?" He gestured to the table in the corner that held a decanter and some glasses.

"I've never had anything strong."

His smile was soft as if her admission amused him. "Then perhaps a small one to start."

She suddenly felt awkward standing there in front of the door, which was absurd considering all that she had done in this man's presence. Heat flooded her cheeks as the memory of that afternoon came rushing back to her, and she looked away, moving to the fire as if studying the flames, anything to ease the worry that she didn't belong there.

Moments later he stood beside her, offering her one of the glasses he held. "Drink slowly."

She took the glass, careful not to let her fingers touch his. There was nowhere to sit in the room except the chair by the table or the cot, and neither of those seemed like a good idea. So she stood, holding the glass in her hands as he watched her. She took a small sip and immediately coughed as the burning liquid hit the back of her throat.

He reached out a hand, steadying her, and she hated how good it felt to have him touch her, even if it was her shoulder.

"What is it?" Her voice had gone gravely and tortured, and she swallowed, clearing her throat.

"Whiskey."

She took another sip and was surprised to find only a mild sting instead of the crippling burning. She let the liquid roll on her tongue, attempting to discover a taste now that her mouth wasn't being assaulted by it, and she was surprised to find woody tones with notes of...

"Cinnamon?" She spoke the word as soon as it formed in her mind.

His smile was slow, appreciative. "That's the oak casks. It can give the whiskey a spicy flavor."

She eyed the amber liquid still in the glass, rolling it slowly around. "Interesting."

Silence filled the space between them then, and she felt the usual need to fill it. She looked around for inspiration, but the room was literally barren.

"You should sit."

She couldn't help the swift glance she gave him, her eyes wide. "I'm fine. Really, I am."

He gestured to the cot. "Please. I'm sorry it's not..." He scratched the back of his neck before giving her a sidelong glance. "Real furniture. I've been meaning to get around to that one day."

She couldn't help but smile, and the tightness in her stomach eased somewhat. She made her way to the cot and sat, careful to perch on its edge as if this would mean she weren't truly sitting on it. She held her glass between her palms, letting the smoothness of it distract her.

He took the chair by the table, and she was grateful for it. When she glanced at him, she noticed the pile of papers on the table for the first time.

"Did I interrupt you?" she asked.

He was quick to shake his head. "I was trying to think, but I wasn't making much headway. Your knock was a welcomed distraction."

Tension radiated from him as he sat upright in the chair, his shoulders and spine never touching the back of it. It was as though he were waiting for something. He probably thought she would ask questions about his wife and child, but she had learned long ago that no one appreciated her interest in their personal business, and it was better not to ask those kinds of questions.

And really she didn't want to hear about how much he had loved his wife.

"Is it anything I can help you with?" she asked instead, nodding in the direction of the papers.

He glanced briefly behind him but soon shook his head. "It's really rather boring. I'm trying to negotiate a railway lease to get a spur line to the village."

She remembered back to what Mrs. Wilson had said, and she sat up straighter. "You're trying to get a way for the tenants to transport their crops to the London markets without the expense of traveling by road."

He had been about to take a sip of his drink when he stopped, his lips parted, the glass suspended before him. "That's right. How did you…"

"The tenants. They all speak rather highly of you."

If the light had been better, she might have thought he blushed at the compliment. As it was, he set his glass down quickly on the table, but she didn't miss the way it shook slightly as he did so.

"I am only trying to do what is best for them."

"I'm afraid that can be more than what most landlords do for their tenants."

He studied her for a moment, and again, she felt that niggling sense to fill the void.

"Do you often bring ladies up here to sample some whiskey?" She made her tone light and gave him a half smile to let him know she kid.

But his laugh came quick, if fleeting. "Does Stephen count?"

She shook her head. "No family relations do, I'm afraid."

"Then no, I must say you're the first."

She gestured with her glass. "In that case, I would recommend you giving the decor some attention. Other ladies might find your sense of style rather lacking." She gestured to the corner where a washstand was held up by an overturned crate. "Although I must give you credit for ingenuity."

He laughed again, longer this time, and she realized she liked the sound of it. He didn't laugh often, and she wondered if she had ever heard him laugh before then. The thought tripped her, making her mind stumble into blankness, and the room grew silent again.

"You said you had sisters, but you've never mentioned your mother."

She looked at him, her fingers suddenly seizing on her glass. "Yes, two sisters. Why?" she said as if she hadn't heard the last bit.

His mouth lifted on one side. "I was hoping you might tell me about her."

"Oh." She wondered if she could pretend to have misunderstood, and she moved the glass to her knee as she considered it. "I'm not sure there's much to say really. My mother preferred to leave our care to nannies and our governess." She watched his face, wondering if that were enough. "Adaline is the eldest. She's two years older than me, and it was just enough of a gap that she often chose her friends over us little sisters." She said this with a smile, hoping he knew she didn't mean it harshly. "She's always looked out for us though. Alice, the youngest sister, is rather absorbed in her studies as I mentioned. She needs a lot of looking after sometimes."

She glanced at him, but then looked again at the concerned expression on his face. Had she said too much or not the things he wished to hear?

"What is it?" she finally asked when his pensive look became too much.

"I was just wondering where you were in there. If your older sister was with her friends and your youngest was studying, where were you?"

She pressed her lips together and looked down at her palms wrapped around the whiskey glass. Her heart was racing, and she willed it to slow. Her emotions didn't matter. She could simply tell him the facts. "I had to care for our mother and take care of household matters when she got sick." She looked up sharply. "Not that I cared for her. Not in that sense. She—" The words stuck in her throat again, and she willed the muscles of her mouth to move. "She hired a nurse, of course. It was the best course of action. She had a particular way she wished for things to be done, and I didn't always meet her expectations." She spoke each word carefully, and she was glad when they were finally out.

She refused to lie over such mundane matters, but she also didn't wish to speak of it. Of her mother's disappointment. Of her father's neglect. Of the loneliness that had dogged her. What was she to say? She was surrounded by family and yet utterly alone. The man had lost his wife and child. Her loneliness was laughable.

But he was still watching her, his eyes unmoving as he seemed to drink her in.

"Were you happy, Amelia?"

That was not a question anyone had asked her, and she looked away sharply, poking at a piece of hair that had escaped her braids to cover the hasty movement.

"Of course, I was," she said, but she heard how bright her tone was. "I wished for nothing." Out of the corner of her eye, she caught the frayed edge of the cuff of her dress and closed her fingers over it as if to hide it. She smiled, the movement hurting her face, and she held up her glass. "Is it time for another?"

CHAPTER 12

*H*e woke with her in his arms.

He blinked, the worn linen of the pillow scratching his cheek, and even though he knew he was lying down, the room seemed to tilt and spin around him. He shut his eyes.

She was warm and soft and curled so perfectly against him, and as reality dawned, a shock spiraled through him.

How long had it been since he'd held someone like this? Just held her? In their two brief encounters, there hadn't been much afterward. He'd been in too much of a hurry to flee, overwhelmed and haunted by his memories and the pain that radiated through him after each failure.

But this?

This was something else.

There was no pressure here. There were no demons. There was just comfort and closeness that could only come from a connection with another person.

Only…how had they gotten into this position?

If he moved at all, he would fall off the cot and directly to the floor. He realized how tightly he held her, his leg wrapped over both of hers, his arm pinning her to his chest. Was it to hold on or to keep her away from the cold and damp stone wall on the other side of the cot?

He remembered her coming to his room so late the night before, her soft knock echoing through his memories. She had confronted him about something, but he wasn't quite there yet, and his recollection was splintered with a vision of her silhouetted by the fire, her face soft and reflective as though she were seeing something else. He had thought his revelation would have spooked her or maybe just upset her. But her reaction had been something else.

It had been inward instead of outward.

He'd watched it happen. Her eyes closing, her lips pressing together, and then turning to run.

He knew about running away too well, and he understood the instinct that drove it.

Something about what he had said hurt her. But it wasn't because she had thought the rumors were true, and that he had murdered his wife. He could tell it wasn't that simple by the fact of what she had said next.

I don't wish to further burden you.

If she had thought him a murderer, she would have done anything to placate him and leave. But she hadn't done that. Instead, she'd apologized.

For what?

Asking him a question the answer to which directly affected her future?

He didn't know what had compelled him to ask her to stay, but there was something vulnerable and heartbreaking about the bend in her shoulders, and he couldn't let her go.

So he'd poured her a drink. And then another. And then—

They'd fallen asleep.

His eyes flew open, focusing almost immediately, and he

took in the outlines of the room, softened by the sun peeking through the shuttered window. She had fallen asleep, her second drink unfinished on the floor by the cot. It came back to him in a rush, and he could see it as if it were happening again. Her eyes fluttering as if she couldn't keep them open, her long fingers setting the glass on the stone floor as she picked up her knees, curling her body into itself as she lay back on the cot.

He hadn't been able to resist. She was right there, all softness and beauty, and the strains of the day had made him weary. He'd set down his own glass and carefully, gritting his teeth in hope that she wouldn't wake up, slid onto the cot beside her.

But her breathing had never changed, and she made not a single motion to suggest he'd disturbed her. And he had fallen asleep, sleeping the sleep of the dead like he hadn't in years.

Her hair smelled of wildflowers, something like lavender and honeysuckle. He wanted to stay there forever. But vaguely he heard the sounds of the yard below and knew the castle was already awake for the day. He needed to be there, for the tradesmen and his tenants. He knew Stephen could handle things, but it wasn't how Lucas preferred it.

He eased himself from the cot although he had been correct. One subtle movement and he slipped off the edge of the damned thing. He really must see about a proper bed. He stood and looked down at his sleeping wife, her hands curled under her cheek as though she were a child, and another memory came back to him.

Her mother hadn't wished for her as her nurse. Why? Was Amelia too young? Did her mother wish to protect Amelia from the vagaries of chronic illness?

But that didn't sit right with him. Amelia had said she didn't always meet her mother's expectations. Was the woman too high minded? Did she demand too much of her daughters? Or was she simply a loving mother wishing the best of her offspring?

He didn't think so. He pieced together the Amelia he had come to know, and in her he saw a determined woman bent on helping where she could. Last night she had come to him because she wished to know the truth, and yet he'd only told her part of it, and the guilt of that burned inside of him.

She had revealed so much about herself, but he continued to hide from her. He felt more like a monster than ever.

He picked up his greatcoat and hat, not bothering to tend to his toilette for fear of waking his wife, and slipped out the door.

Instead of going to the castle yard, however, he detoured, descending the steps to the kitchen. He found Mrs. Fairfax in the room she used to conduct business. She stood, her eyes wide at his sudden appearance.

"Your Grace, you didn't ring. I would—"

"Mrs. Fairfax, I should like to hold a dinner." He stopped. Looked around. "Where is your desk?"

The room was much smaller than the one the house-keeper had occupied at Lagameer Hall, and yet she had insisted on keeping the same desk for her business even though it made the room uncomfortably small. But that desk was gone and in its place was a fine rosewood writing desk, correctly proportioned for the quaint quarters, so much so that the room appeared to have grown. There was even a small chair for visitors in one corner and a potted plant in another.

Mrs. Fairfax blinked. "Her Grace found this one in the rooms upstairs. She suggested it would work perfectly here, and I must say she was right."

Mrs. Fairfax had nearly lain upon the desk when Lucas

had suggested she find another, and yet Amelia had convinced her to accept this substitute?

The housekeeper reached out and stroked the delicate wood. "I must say the tones truly brighten the room. Wouldn't you agree?" Not only accept the desk but love it as well. She looked back at him, her hand falling away from the desk. "What was it you were saying about a dinner, Your Grace?"

But before he could answer, Stephen appeared in the doorway.

"Lucas." His tone was brisk. "A word."

Apprehension crawled its way up his neck. He nodded to Mrs. Fairfax and slipped from the room.

"What is it?" he asked softly as they reached the corridor, but Stephen only shook his head and indicated Lucas should follow.

When he stepped into the castle yard several minutes later it was to find two of his tenants, a Mr. Burrows and a Mr. Waterstone, waiting at the base of the steps. Their parcels lay side by side on the east end of the Greyfair estate.

"Your Grace," Stephen said with a nod as they reached the two men. "Burrows and Waterstone have come with some interesting news."

"What is it?" he asked without preamble.

Burrows was tall and round while Waterstone was short and angular. It was Burrows who spoke first, turning his worn but clean felt hat in his hands.

"It's the missus, Your Grace. She came back from her weekly shopping in the village all a'flustered by something she'd heard down at the milliner's."

Waterstone held up an index finger. "My wife's heard the same thing, you see, Your Grace. That's why I's come with Burrows here. I wanted you to know it's more than a rumor."

"What is?" Lucas wanted to wring the news from the men

but instead tugged on the cuffs of his greatcoat to will himself to be patient.

"It's the marquess, Your Grace. That Aylesford chap. He's dead, Your Grace."

It was as though the very air itself ceased to move around him. He blinked once, twice, thrice, before he could find the ability to speak.

"The Marquess of Aylesford is dead? How do you know this?"

Waterstone held up the index finger again. "It's the milliner, Your Grace. The housekeeper herself from the Aylesford estate come to see him about black ribbon. She wanted a length of it for the laurel wreath for the door at the estate."

"The laurel wreath?" Lucas breathed, the muscles along his neck tightening. A laurel wreath was usually only hung for a single reason, especially with black ribbon.

Burrows nodded emphatically. "It's just as I's said, Your Grace. Aylesford is dead, and the housekeeper was looking to place a laurel wreath on the door."

Lucas slid a glance at Stephen, but his cousin's expression remained neutral. He looked back at the tenants. "Did she say when the marquess's son would be coming to the estate to attend matters?"

Waterstone's thin lips parted in a jittering grimace that revealed his missing teeth. "That's the worst of it, Your Grace. His son's not coming."

"His son isn't coming? Surely the man will wish to take over his estate now that he's the marquess."

Burrows was already shaking his head. "That's just it, You Grace. The son's not the new marquess."

Lucas crossed his arms over his chest, feeling his patience wane. "Then who is?"

Waterstone and Burrows shrugged together as if they were some kind of cut-rate pantomime.

"Dunno," Burrows said. "The marquess and his son killed each other, you see. They were dueling over the same mistress. The one didn't know the other was having her too." Both men's eyes had grown round and wondrous at the idea that a father and son would both have the same mistress, not know of the other's treachery, and kill each other over her.

"They killed each other in a duel?"

Burrows and Waterstone nodded solemnly.

"It's said the son turned first but the father didn't trust him. They shot at the same time, and now well—" Waterstone shrugged as if that were all the story.

Burrows leaned in. "The housekeeper says the solicitors are looking for the heir now. Some gentleman in London. A cousin or something."

Lucas nodded, forcing his face to stay relaxed even as his thoughts raced. "Thank you for coming to us with the news. You're both good men." He gestured to the stables. "See that you stop at the stables on your way out for some bags of oats."

Both men's gazes darted in the direction of the stables, their eyes widening at the prospect of free feed.

"Why, thank you, Your Grace." Burrows and Waterstone nodded profusely.

He waved the gentlemen away with a smile and a nod of thanks. When they were a good distance away, he turned to Stephen. "We're back at the start, aren't we?"

"With the clock ticking. The first of May is coming fast, and we need to make the contract before the railroad starts allocating its resources for the next spur lines."

May was only five weeks away. It wasn't enough time. And that was assuming these solicitors found the heir before then.

"If the heir is a gentleman in London, he shouldn't be too hard to find."

Stephen laughed. "But if he's anything like the Aylesford son..."

"He'll be shot in a duel with his own father?"

Stephen grimaced. "There isn't a chance that could repeat itself."

Lucas stared off in the distance, his mind swirling as he muttered, "I didn't expect it to happen at all."

Stephen scratched at his chin. "I don't suppose the new marquess will be a good chap and listen to reason?"

For the second time in a matter of minutes everything about him seemed to come to a standstill. "What did you just say?" he asked, turning back to Stephen.

The man blinked, his eyebrows going up as he seemed to think back on his words. "I said do you think he'll be a good chap?"

Lucas shook his head. "No, the other part."

"That he'll listen to reason?"

"That." Lucas nodded, the events of the past several weeks swirling around him. The exchange. The desk. His own admission. "That's it."

Stephen's sigh sounded as though he carried the weight of the world on his shoulders. "Of course. That's been it from the start. But these titled gentlemen—present company excluded, of course—never are ones to listen to sense."

But Lucas's gaze had already drifted away from Stephen, up the stone walls of the castle that had gone speckled in greens and browns in the blast of sea air until his eyes settled on the window high in the east tower.

"We can't control whether or not he'll listen to reason. But we can make sure he hears it from someone who can convince a housekeeper to give up her desk."

"What?"

He felt Stephen's curious gaze on him, but he didn't answer the man. Because just then he had other things to consider. He needed his wife. He needed her talent at negotiation. He needed so much from her. Yet he had given her only half-truths. It was far less than she deserved, and now he would ask for even more.

He swallowed and looked away, the past knotting his stomach. He couldn't get her involved in this. He couldn't force her to help him with this mad scheme he had found himself in, the one that drove him to chase away the darkness that haunted him. And yet, he couldn't think of another way out.

If they only had one chance at speaking with the new marquess, of convincing him to lease his land to the railroad, they needed the best possible person for the task.

And for that, she deserved the truth.

All of it.

* * *

SHE EYED HIM, tension building in her stomach.

He stood before her in the yard, the reins of two horses in his hands. She recognized Hercules, the stallion she had learned had saved her that first night from the causeway. The other was a gray mare, soft in color with brilliant lines and posture. But while the horses were magnificent examples of the quality of horseflesh of the Greyfair stables, there were other more concerning things about the tableau before her.

Lucas had never sought her out before.

It was always her seeking him, usually as he was running away from her.

The fact that he should request her company now alarmed her, but that he should do so after she had so blatantly trod over his painful past terrified her.

"You wish for me to accompany you on a ride?" she asked, her voice tentative if not slightly tremulous.

In the past weeks, she had grown used to his occasional dark moods, the way he seemed to vanish like a ghost at times, but she had also seen him caring and compassionate, and she knew what his touch alone could do to her. It was a tumult of emotion that rivaled her own inner confusion.

But she was his wife, and somehow the bargain still didn't feel sure in her place there at Dinsmore.

"There's something I'd like to show you," he said, avoiding her question as he handed the reins of the gray mare to her.

She'd ridden very little. They had kept only a matched set for their carriage, but even then, in the end, they'd had to sell off the horses and the carriage for that matter. As she took the reins from her husband, she hoped she didn't embarrass herself.

She wasn't feeling quite so certain on her feet that morning. She'd woken on the cot in his tower room, alone and cold and confused. The events of the previous night came back to her in a rush like a blast of cold water from the estuary, but still, they didn't help to clarify her present situation. She recalled the whiskey, her bold request for a second glass, but then...

Well, she was fairly certain she had fallen asleep, the second glass still in her hand. She wasn't used to the bewitching effects of alcohol, and it was apparent the more celebrated effects she had heard of didn't work on her, but rather it simply lulled her to sleep.

How embarrassing.

She'd barged into his room and demanded an explanation for why he wouldn't get her with child, and she'd not only ripped open his painful past but then she'd fallen asleep on him.

He'd probably happily left her there on his cot and

wandered the halls of the castle in the dark of the night like the ghoul he was purported to be.

She knew that wasn't true, but she drew comfort from the idea of it.

He wore his hat, but she noted it wasn't pulled as low as it usually was, and he'd left his greatcoat off. The day was warm, late spring melting into early summer, and the idea of some fresh air was alluring.

She took the reins from him, moving to put her foot in the stirrup when his hands seized her waist. A small gasp flew from her lips as he lifted her into the saddle. The move was perfunctory, and she hated how her heart raced from his touch. She swallowed, willing herself to have some sense.

This was not a love match. Danger lay that way regardless.

He mounted Hercules and turned in the direction of the causeway.

She followed, pleased to find the horse well trained and calm, trotting behind Hercules as though she were used to it. The sun was hot on her shoulders as they crossed the open space of the causeway, but soon they were in the dappled shadows on the opposite shore. She looked back at the castle, wondering what the view was like atop a horse. She'd crossed the causeway numerous times to visit tenants, but from up here, the castle looked entirely different.

It was grander for one, the stone reflecting the early morning light like a beacon, the craggy shore of the island highlighted from bright morning sun. The ocean waves washed against it, water spraying in beautiful arcs. It should have seemed intense and brutal, but from this distance, it was only powerful with the grace of it. She was hit again with that stunning sense of rightness, of the feeling that she was home, and she rubbed at her chest, willing the sensation to pass.

They climbed the gentle hill that led away from the shoreline. The trees were denser here, almost a forest, but the horses seemed to know the way, and she needed to do very little to stay on course behind her husband.

She hadn't been this way on the Greyfair estate. The village and the tenants were in the opposite direction, and she'd never had reason to venture up the hillside. She found like much of the rest of the estate it was beautiful and just a bit wild. The canopy was filled with the call and response of birds, and the air was thick with the scent of wildflowers, moss, and pine. That pang of pride came back to her, but this time she didn't try to push it away. She held on to it, contained it, and hoped it wouldn't hurt her.

Lucas slowed in front of her, his horse dancing impatiently as he sidled to the right, giving her space to come up beside him. They had reached a clearing of sorts. She hadn't been able to see it before because her husband's large frame had blocked her view, but now she drank it in.

The clearing rimmed a cliff that broke away down into a valley, sweeping out for miles in every direction. The sun shone on the far side of the valley, leaving the space closest to them shrouded in shadow, but the starkness of it left her breathless. It was a moment before she realized Lucas had dismounted and moved to her side, waiting to help her down.

A jolt of anticipation went through her, and she pressed her lips together, controlling her features as he reached up for her. His touch sent a flame whispering through her, but he set her on the ground much too quickly, dropping his hands and stepping away from her. She was watching the horses, their noses already investigating the ground, so when he took her hand, she jumped.

She wasn't wearing gloves, and neither was he, and the touch of his skin against hers sent her heart galloping. She hated it, how her body responded to him, and again, she kept her features schooled. Her most recent blunder was still too fresh, and she wasn't ready yet to forgive herself for it.

He brought her to the edge of the clearing, almost to the edge where the land dropped away to the valley below. There was a spot of sunshine where the canopy overhead broke away, and he pushed down a bed of grass for them to sit on. It was soft and spongy, and she was surprised by how comfortable it was, both sitting there on the grass and being there with him.

She waited for him to speak, but the silence stretched between them. The wind weaving through the grass and the occasional chirp of a bird the only sounds. She glanced at him only to find his gaze far off toward the valley, a twitch in his cheek.

She wrapped her arms around her bent knees. "It's beautiful." She kept her tone light so as not to jar him from whatever thoughts churned in his mind.

Still, he started slightly at her words and glanced quickly at her before looking away.

"It is," he said. His tone, though neutral, had a weight to it that had her stomach tightening.

She knew what was coming. She'd heard this tone before, and she wrapped her arms around her knees more tightly, bracing herself physically for what she knew she couldn't brace herself for emotionally or mentally.

She'd stepped too far, and he was sending her away.

Over time she had gotten used to this kind of rejection, and it no longer held the sting it once did. Now it was so common, she'd almost missed it.

"This is where the railroad would go."

It was a second before she realized of what he spoke. The railroad. The spur line he was hoping to convince the railway to build that would give the tenants access to cheap transportation for their crops.

She swallowed, her mind racing to reset itself. She followed his gaze out over the valley now. Had he brought her here to show her this? Why?

"The valley, though, belongs to the Marquess of Aylesford. Stephen and I have been trying to negotiate with the man for nearly a year. The railroad needs to have a lease signed by the first of May." He plucked a long piece of grass from where it stuck up between his booted feet and ran the blade between his fingers. "I received word this morning that that Marquess of Aylesford has died."

She sucked in a breath. "Oh, that's awful. But..." She hated voicing the words. They seemed so callused. "But perhaps the new marquess will be more open to speaking with you."

Lucas was already nodding as she spoke. "I had thought the same. The marquess's son has a reputation for being a dandy. Stephen and I wagered he would have been a more agreeable sort."

Her skin prickled. "Would have been?"

Lucas finally met her gaze. "The marquess and his son killed each other in a duel over a shared mistress."

She did not have the fortitude to school her features then. "That's...awful."

Lucas laughed softly. "You mustn't control your emotions for my sake."

"That's disgusting," she amended.

His laugh was louder now, and he lifted his head, so the sun made its way under the brim of his hat. He looked almost youthful then, and her heart squeezed.

"What's to happen now?" she asked.

Lucas drew a deep steady breath before replying, and even though his face remained relaxed, she couldn't stop the ripple of apprehension that coursed through her.

"The solicitors are looking for the heir. Even if they should find him before the first of May, there will be little time to negotiate with the man."

She reached out a hand, unable to stop herself, and gripped the arm he had propped on one knee. "I'm sure you'll be able to see it through in time."

He dropped his gaze to her hand, and she snatched it back. But before she could press it against her chest, he caught it, drawing her hand between both of his. They sat there like that, her hand in his. She wasn't used to such attention, and she wanted to squirm, pull her hand back, but his touch was too much, and she didn't want it to end.

"Amelia." He didn't look up at her as he spoke, and again his tone changed, sending her stomach rolling. "There's something I need to tell you. I wasn't entirely truthful with you last night." He looked up, and the intensity of his blue eyes struck her. "I owe you more than that."

She tugged at her hand then, the closeness, both physically and emotionally, were too much, and she felt the danger crawling along her skin. The physical part of their relationship she could manage but not this. No one had claimed to owe her anything, and the weight of such an idea nearly suffocated her.

"No, Lucas, you mustn't." She shook her head and yanked at her hand again, but he didn't let go.

Instead, he pulled her hand until she fell against him, and he held her there, forcing her to meet his gaze.

"Amelia, my wife died in the fire, and she was carrying a child. That much is true. But—" He stopped, licked his lips, his eyes searching her face as though the words he needed to say were there.

But she was no longer listening to his words. She was hypnotized by the stark fear in his eyes, the raw pain still reflected there even though years separated him from it. She reached up her free hand, unable to stop herself. The need to place her hand against him, to absorb the pain into herself was too great.

"Lucas, you mustn't torture yourself. You did everything you could—"

He shook his head, cutting her off. "Amelia, no." He repeated her name, and she wondered if he needed to speak it to keep himself here, away from the torturous memories. "Amelia, the baby she carried wasn't mine."

CHAPTER 13

*T*he words left a painful burning in his throat. He'd never spoken them aloud. Ever. Not to Stephen or Mrs. Fairfax. They knew the truth, of course, but not from him.

They had heard Lila's bitter accusations, screamed at a level that had shaken the very plaster on the ceilings of Lagameer Hall.

He kept his gaze focused on Amelia, kept his arms wrapped around her as though the physical contact would keep him from getting trapped in the images and sounds that haunted his mind.

"Lila, my first wife, didn't wish to marry me, but her father arranged the match. She was bitter and spiteful. She took a lover almost as soon as we were wed, and he got her with child." He swallowed as his throat closed, but he pulled in a breath, determined to continue. "She enjoyed parading in front of me, showing off her rounded stomach as the child grew. She took pleasure in taunting me, knowing I would be forced to claim the child that wasn't mine as my heir."

Now his throat did close, and he let it. He had gotten

enough out for now. He wished to close his eyes. He didn't want to see Amelia's reaction. He didn't want to see it because she had been forced to marry him too.

But she wouldn't let him hide. Of course, she wouldn't. Her hand cupped his cheek, caressed the scars on his face before sliding up to push his hat off his head. It tumbled into the grass behind him, and she leaned forward, her forehead pressed to his.

"I'm so sorry, Lucas," she said, and she could have said anything at all if only she spoke his name like that, again and again, as though it were the most precious thing to her.

The muscles in his throat relaxed, and the words came spilling out.

"That child didn't deserve to die." His voice shook, the image of his wife turning away from him, running into the flames. "That baby didn't deserve to have its life ended that way. Ended because Lila hated me." He reached up, gripped the back of Amelia's neck as if to emphasize his words or perhaps to hold her closer, unwilling to release her, needing her as an anchor as he spoke the part that hurt him most. "I would have claimed him as my heir. I would have." He growled the words, the push of emotion forcing his teeth to grind. "I would have claimed him no matter what. All of this, this life, the things we do in it, what is the point unless we are leaving it to pass on to someone else?" He leaned back to look her in the eye, but he didn't release his grip on her. He had to see her face when he said it. It was the respectful thing to do. "That's why you're here." The words trembled, and he swallowed. "I need an heir to pass all of this on to." Here he nodded at the land around them, and she turned her head in his grip, taking in the rolling hills, the towering pines. "That's why I approached your father. I knew he had three daughters and a need for funds. I knew he would agree to it."

"You wish for me to give you an heir?" She whispered the

words, a line appearing between her brows as she turned back to him. "But you…"

She didn't need to finish the sentence. He had been carrying the burning guilt since that first night when he'd been unable to leave his seed in her.

His jaw clenched though, and he had to look away from her. From the understanding so clearly written across her face, from the pain that reflected in her eyes, the pain he knew she felt for him.

"I can't…I can't…" He couldn't say it. He couldn't. Sitting there in the grass, surrounded by the sheer innocence of nature, his wife cradled in his arms, her hands clinging to him as if she feared he would float away. He couldn't admit the truth, and yet he couldn't keep it from her. "I can't trust again." The words were so simple while their meaning was perilous. "I can't trust another, and if I don't, I'll never have the heir I desire. When Stephen brought me here, I was incoherent with pain, both physical and mental, and I made him put me in the tower to die." She jerked in his arms, but he only tightened his grip on her. "And then one day I realized I wasn't going to die, and when I stepped into the castle yard, I saw the work that must be done." He looked back at her now, needing her to understand. "It gave me a reason to keep going. Helping these people. Bringing Dinsmore back to the flourishing estate it once was, but I can't finish what I started without the railroad." He shook his head, feeling the finality of his word. "But it won't matter at all. Not if I don't have a son to leave it to."

She didn't speak. She studied him, unblinking, as her fingers curled into his hair. He didn't know if she could understand what any of it felt like to him. This overwhelming sense to continue what he had started, to leave the safekeeping of the people of Dinsmore to the next Duke of Greyfair, his son. To know how he battled the war of memories in his head, the child lost in the fire, the child that wasn't his but didn't deserve the fate that awaited him, the burn of shame and betrayal his wife had cast upon him, the same guilt that shrouded him still.

But just like that night when she'd seen his scars for the first time, she didn't use words to convey her feelings. She used action, and now she kissed him.

She wrapped her fingers in his hair and pulled his head down to hers, her lips setting off a spark that traveled straight to his center. And in a single touch, he was gone.

He had given everything of himself, and she hadn't run away. Not from his scars, not from his past, and not from the thing that caused him the most shame. That he had allowed himself to be betrayed. That he hadn't known of his wife's duplicity until she had used it like a banner to proclaim her sordid triumph over him.

But it all fell away as he laid Amelia back into the softness of the grass, the springy blades cushioning them both. She may have started the kiss, but soon he took it over, unable to keep himself from touching her, consuming her. It was the same every time she touched him, every time he was close to her. It was as though having gotten close weren't enough, and he needed to have more. All of her. He needed all of her, and finally he thought he could give her all of himself.

He kissed her, savoring only her lips for what seemed like an eternity, but he couldn't get enough of her kiss. Only when the need to explore more of her grew too great did he shift, drawing her under him as his hand traveled down the length of her, finding every curve and valley he knew now. He knew her body in a way he'd never expected to, and yet he didn't know her entirely.

Because he had let the past stand between them.

The thought jolted through him, and anger rushed to fill the space that desire had only seconds earlier. He backed up, lifting his head, and peered down at her. She lay there, her eyes closed, the reeds of grass creating a halo about them that kept the world at bay. It was just them, here on the cliff overlooking what would be the salvation of Dinsmore, of what would be the future of the Greyfair title. The weight of it all pressed in on him, but it was nothing compared to the urgency that roared through him at the sight of her.

Suddenly he needed to make her his, all of her. He needed to give himself to her in a way he never thought he would give himself to another again.

Her eyelids began to flutter, but he captured her mouth before she could open them, and a groan slipped from her lips. It spiraled through him, burrowing into the parts of him that still lingered in uncertainty. But once his lips touched hers again, it vanished, and his desire overwhelmed him.

Her fingers bit into his shoulders, pulling him closer as his own hands explored, cupping her breast, filling his palm with the curve of her hip. It wasn't enough. His fingers found the buttons that marched down the front of her gown, and he groaned, thanking a god he didn't believe in that the gown buttoned in the front. He had her bodice off her shoulders in seconds as she pulled her arms free, hardly letting him go long enough to do so.

Her fingers trailed down his back, and in a flash, he realized he wanted her to touch him. All of him. He sat up, yanking his shirt over his head before he realized the sun would show all of him. The scars that pebbled his chest, the deep, red lines that marked his back. He froze, kneeling between her spread legs, feeling the stomach-dropping sensation of exposure. At least that first night, there was only the murky light of candles. But now he knew she could see everything.

But then she smiled, the expression slow and languid as her eyes lit with pleasure. She liked what she saw, and it rattled him. He dropped to his elbows above her, capturing her mouth with utter devastation. When her fingers touched him, so tentatively as though he were some kind of precious work of art, he shuddered, his muscles rippling in involuntary response to the feel of her skin against his.

"Amelia," he groaned against her mouth, but that was all.

Every thought fled; every emotion shattered as she continued to run her hands down his back, her fingers skimming over his scars as if they were nothing more than a part of him. She shifted, opening her legs to him, and he flinched with the spike of arousal it sent through him. He throbbed for her, but he wanted this moment to last.

He shifted again, bringing up one hand to loosen the ties of her corset. He loosened it enough to slip his hand under the back of it and lifted her, holding her up with one arm as he used his other hand to pull the garment free. It was only her chemise now, and as he gazed down at her, he could see the dusky rose of her nipples through the thin fabric. His gaze traveled to her face to find her studying him, her eyes so watchful as he now understood she always was.

He reached up a hand, and with a single finger traced the line of her brow.

"You're so beautiful," he whispered.

She reached up, and again, pulled him down for a kiss. They tumbled into the grass again, and soon he had her chemise pushed down to her waist along with her bodice, and she was exposed to him. He cupped her breast, his fingers finding her nipple, teasing it into a hard peak before sucking it into his mouth. She arched in his arms, her hands pinning him to her as she writhed.

"Lucas." There was a pleading in her voice as she was trying to get her leg over his but it was trapped in her skirts.

Reluctantly he let go of her long enough to sit up and pull her skirts free of her legs, shoving them to her waist. He realized only too late the mistake he'd made. She was bared before him. She wore no pantalets, and the creamy smooth skin of her thighs shown in the full light, and he wanted to stop himself. He wanted to savor the moment, but his gaze was drawn to the very center of her.

The other two times they had made love had been rushed, and he'd never taken the chance to enjoy studying her. But now he did. His heart beat so loudly it echoed in his ears, and his hand trembled as he reached out, followed the line of her thigh up to the thatch of curls that hid her sensitive nub from him.

"Lucas." His name was nearly breathless on her lips, and his heart pounded faster.

He pulled his hand back, scrambling to free himself of his trousers.

He couldn't wait. Next time. He swore next time he would make it last.

When he touched her, she was already wet, and his body throbbed in response to her readiness. She lifted her knees, opening herself further to him. But then she lifted her arms, her hands reaching for him, but he was too far away. It undid him, seeing how desperately she wanted to touch him. He fell forward, bracing himself above her as her arms closed around him, and a rush of feeling roared through him, so complex and complicated he couldn't have named an individual feeling. He only knew this was right. This was where he was meant to be.

He pressed his lips to her neck as his hand found her sensitive nub, stroking and circling it as she lifted her hips, pressing into his teasing fingers. He didn't speak and neither did she as he slid into her, as she tilted her hips to accept him, as he felt the shame of his past vanish if only for a moment.

And then he was pounding into her, unable to hold

himself back. She arched, pressing her hard nipples into his chest, writhing against his fingers, seeking her pleasure as she gave him his. He couldn't hold on; desire gripped him in a stranglehold, and he stroked her, flicking his finger against her nub, but she reached down, pulled his hand away.

"Just you," she groaned, and that was it.

The last of his resolve melted away, and he thrust into her completely. She cried out, her body tensing around his, and the intensity of her pleasure cut through him, setting off his own. He came, hard, and he held on to her. He cradled her as he spent himself inside of her, and as she wrapped her arms around him, the voices that haunted him were finally silent.

* * *

AFTER THAT IT was like a dream. A dream from which she didn't wish to wake.

After that day on the cliff, her husband stopped running away from her.

He still tended to his estate business with Stephen during the day, but he attended meals with her, asked her about her work in running the household, and her conversations with the tenants. And every night he came to her room...and stayed.

He held her through the night, and he let her hold him, and it was something entirely different from what she had imagined her marriage would be to the Ghoul of Greyfair.

Lucas Bennett was no ghoul. She knew that now, just as she had sensed all along. But the truth was far worse than any rumors society could conjure, and she knew every night she held him that his memories weren't far away. That was what she feared now. That the moment on the cliff had opened some kind of dam inside of him. He had told the truth of his past, but he still hadn't dealt with it himself. She knew that even if their relationship had improved.

His past still lingered like a third person in their marriage, and it frightened her. But it wasn't the only thing that frightened her.

She'd fallen in love with him.

She felt it before she could understand what it was. It was a sensation deep within her bones that swept over her at the mere sight of him. It was a calming rightness that gripped her when she saw him striding across the yard, speaking animatedly to Stephen about one of the improvements, Argus trotting behind them both. The way he shucked his coat to join in when the tradesmen were faced with a daunting task. The way he studied her when he made love to her, like she was still a wonder to him.

She dropped the book she had been leafing through in the library, her hands shaking with the memory of making love to her husband, and she chided herself for being so ridiculously romantic. If she didn't know herself better, she would say she was sick with love for her husband, and the thought only served to increase her fear.

She tried to think otherwise. She tried to understand that her past encounters did not indicate how her marriage should be, but it was hard when the wounds inflicted upon her by others were still so fresh, and she had nothing to refute it.

She had discovered the library not long after the exchange. She had been inventorying the castle's linens and silver when she'd come upon the room on the same floor as the family rooms in the newer part of the castle. She was struck by the room's brilliance, the windows facing south so it captured the sunlight on a good day, and the towering shelves of books shone with anticipation.

Today, though, was cloudy and gray, the windows struck

with intermittent raindrops, but it suited her work, creating a closeness suggestive of study.

She picked up the book and rubbed the dust off of it with her skirt. The few gowns she had brought with her were grievously starting to show the wear of her arduous endeavors at Dinsmore. She fingered her faded skirt, knowing she would soon need to ask Jones to make an appointment for her with the modiste in the village as she had said she would.

She set the book back on the shelf and moved to the table where she had laid out a fresh notebook and pen. She wasn't sure when she had started cataloging the library. It was only that the idea had occurred to her when they had finished emptying the rooms of the items brought to Dinsmore from Lagameer Hall. It seemed only right to know which books were a part of the duke's collection, and it wasn't as though she minded the task. The only dangerous part about it was she had a tendency to get lost in the pages of one book or another and the task was taking far longer than she had imagined.

She picked up the pen and dipped it in ink to make the next notation.

"I'm not surprised to find you in a library."

She jumped, sending ink splattering across the table at the sound of the voice in the doorway. She looked up, her eyes widening, her brain scrambling. She knew the voice, but it was impossible that it should be here at Dinsmore.

"Ash," she breathed, her eyes taking in the man silhouetted by the light from the doorway. It was in that moment that memory connected with the present, and she suddenly understood.

The man in the doorway smiled, slow and one-sided, and she felt a rush of homesickness. Quickly she set down the pen, absently rubbing her hands on her already ruined skirts.

"Ash," she breathed again, shaking her head. "You're the new Marquess of Aylesford." That was why she knew the title of Aylesford. Somewhere deep in her memories was the image of Ash's uncle, a gentleman with a stomach more robust than his mustaches.

Mr. Ashfield Riggs was Adaline's oldest and dearest friend. Amelia liked to think Ash was friend to all the Atwood sisters, but she knew he liked Adaline best. They were of a similar age and had entered society at roughly the same time. It had a way of bonding people that Amelia would never understand, never having had a season herself. She could admit she had been envious of her sister's easy friendship with Ash, but Amelia wasn't surprised to find that envy had vanished.

He gave a neat bow. "Your Grace, I hope you do not think I mean to intrude. A very lovely woman at the door said I would find you here."

Amelia smiled. "That would be Mrs. Fairfax." She stilled, perhaps finally realizing Ash stood in her library. "What are you doing here though? Is it my sisters? Are they well?" She picked up her skirts and made her way to him even as his smile grew at her rapid questions.

"Your sisters are all well. Adaline told me I might find you here."

She stilled, sorting through his words, connecting pieces of her life that should never have been brought together. She shook her head, saying once more, "You're the new Marquess of Aylesford."

That smile again, the sadness still in his eyes. "It would seem so." He cocked his head, that boyish glint to his eye. "Were you expecting me?"

She was momentarily confused because in fact, she had been expecting him, but he didn't know that. She wanted to blurt it out right then. She wanted to tell him why it was so important that he was there, that he was in fact the new marquess they had been waiting for, but she stopped herself.

It wasn't her place, and her past experience kept her mouth shut. She shouldn't speak where it wasn't her place. Not like this. There were places where she felt comfortable testing her boundaries, but here she knew when to stop. Lucas wouldn't wish for her intrusion.

She smiled, trying to cover the momentary awkwardness. "Actually, my husband was expecting you. He had been speaking to the previous marquess about some estate business," she said instead.

Ash's eyes widened. "Terrific. Where can I find the man?" He looked about him playfully as though the duke might be on the shelves with the books.

She touched his shoulder, not able to stop a laugh. "I believe he's seeing to a fencing problem one of the tenants is having."

Ash raised both eyebrows. "Fencing. I probably should know more about such things now that I'm a marquess. Don't you think?" His tone changed ever so slightly, and Amelia understood it was only because she knew him so well that she had heard it at all.

But what did the tone suggest? Was he unhappy with his new fortune? Did he not wish to be a titled gentleman?

Ashfield Riggs was the son of a gentleman of good family, if not titled. She searched her memory but was hard-pressed to root out the specifics. She had known Ash for so long, she had forgotten the details of him. His father had been a judge and was well respected, but that along with the vague memory of his uncle was all Amelia could recall. It wasn't as though Ash weren't used to a comfortable life. That much wouldn't have changed. Was it the demands the title would require of him that had given him this sarcastic edge?

"I don't know," she said with a shrug. "I think anyone's life is what they make of it."

He studied her quietly for a moment before moving into the room, stopping at the table where her notebook lay. He tapped it with one finger. "Lost in books again, Amelia?" He laughed softly and shaking his head, lifted his gaze to her. "I thought you might have outgrown such things upon your marriage."

She straightened her shoulders at the suggestion. "One does not outgrow books, Ash. Do not say such things."

His laugh was whole and musical, and for a moment, he was the childhood friend she remembered and the pain in her chest loosened its hold on her.

She made her way over to him, taking the spot beside him to look down at the progress she had made in her notebook. He tapped it again with a single finger.

"At least your penmanship is decipherable. Adaline might as well be writing in ancient script."

She laughed again, feeling a lightness she hadn't felt in weeks. "I'm afraid you speak the truth." She shook her head. "I never could understand how Adaline's writing could be so abysmal. We had the same governess."

Ash picked up the pen she had been using, twirling it between his fingers. "You forget, little sister. Our dear Adaline is not the best at exercises which require an extended amount of attention."

She smiled. "I'm afraid you're right. You remember how she was at her French lessons."

Ash grimaced and dropped the pen. "No worse than at her dancing lessons. Do you recall how she trod on my toes?"

"Your toes? I'm lucky I still have any left foot from when she decided to practice with me."

He turned to her then, the playful expression she knew so

well on his features. "Did you know I'm to have a ball? You must come."

She wrinkled her brow. "I have no plans to be in London though—"

He waved off her statement. "I'm having the ball here at my new estate. I thought I would introduce myself to the local gentry."

She felt the usual trepidation at the thought of a social gathering, but she squared her shoulders. A country assembly would be good for the Duke of Greyfair. Perhaps it would work in furthering his cause with the railway lease.

"How lovely. When is it?"

Ash bowed then, his manner exaggerated, and she remembered now just how playful he always had been. That was likely why Adaline liked him so much. He could make the dullest drawing room seem lively.

"May I have this dance?" he asked.

Amelia gave an equally exaggerated curtsy. "Of course, my lord."

He pulled her into a dizzying whirl then that matched no steps she had ever learned. Her heart sang with the familiarity of him, of this friend who knew her and her sisters. It was as though he were a glimpse of the home she had left and didn't realize until now how badly she missed.

He twirled her about the room, barely missing tables and sofas, making her laugh until she thought she might lose her breath.

And then suddenly he was gone.

She didn't know what was happening. She saw it. She saw every single moment of what happened next, but her mind couldn't put the images together. It didn't make sense. Any of it.

Lucas was there. He had grabbed Ash away from her, and he was—

She lunged forward, putting her body between Lucas and Ash. "Stop!" she screamed, but Lucas shoved her aside, his fists flying at Ash's face.

She tumbled backward, crashing into the table where her notebook lay. She heard a crack as she fell to the floor and didn't know if it were her or the table.

"Lucas!"

Stephen's voice. Thank God, Stephen was there somewhere. Hands were on her then. Mrs. Fairfax. Jones. They were pulling her to her feet. Mrs. Fairfax was asking if she were all right, but Amelia couldn't answer her. Stephen was on Lucas now, pulling him away from Ash. Ash stumbled backward to the door, his hand on his face, blood dripping through his fingers.

He crashed into the doorframe and stopped, dropped the hand from his face and she saw the damage Lucas had wrought.

"Oh God," she whispered.

But Ash smiled his playful smile, and the sadness in his eyes grew thicker. "It appears as though I'll need to save that dance for another day, Your Grace," he said. "I don't think your husband approves."

"Keep your hands off my wife," Lucas growled, and Amelia realized it was the first time he had spoken.

But with his words she felt the last of her fear give way, and finally, *finally*, she understood the thing that she had suspected all along. The thing that had kept her from fully believing in the safety of her love for her husband.

She saw him then, saw the fury in his eyes, saw the way Stephen held him.

Saw the way he hid his face from Ash.

Ash gave her a nod and slipped through the door and with him went the last of her hope that this time things would be different for her.

She straightened, pulling her shoulders free from Jones and Mrs. Fairfax. She didn't rush. She didn't march. She simply walked to where Ash had stood. Then she turned to her husband.

She saw the fury that tightened his features, saw the twitch in his cheek, his taut jaw. Stephen had released him now, backing away slowly as though from a wounded animal.

She understood then the defensiveness when she asked about the estate. She understood what he had said that day on the cliff about trusting again.

"Who the hell was that?" her husband growled, his voice low and unyielding.

She hated herself then. Hated herself for the satisfaction she took from her next words.

She raised her chin. "Ashfield Riggs, my childhood friend." She paused to make sure he was listening before she said, "And the new Marquess of Aylesford."

This time it was she who walked away.

CHAPTER 14

The worst of it was he didn't remember what happened.

Most of all he didn't remember pummeling the Marquess of Aylesford.

It was as though a veil had been thrown over his eyes and only now that the moment had passed could he see clearly.

His hands throbbed, and he peered down at them as though they were alien to his body. Two of his knuckles bled, and all had already begun to swell. His shirt was ripped and hung awkwardly from one shoulder.

Where was Amelia?

He blinked, trying to figure out where he was. He never came into this room. Never had reason to but he'd heard voices. He remembered that much. When he had returned from the stables, he had heard voices. One distinctly belonging to his wife and the other was…

The Marquess of Aylesford.

Amelia.

He had to find Amelia.

Someone touched his arm, and he jerked, sending up a

fist before he could stop himself. He dropped his hand immediately, his heart racing as Stephen cowered behind him, both hands raised in defense.

"Easy, cousin," he said, his tone light and gentle.

He scanned Stephen's person, stricken with the thought he may have hurt him in his confusion, but his cousin appeared unharmed. A noise behind him drew his attention, and he whirled, finding Mrs. Fairfax and Amelia's lady's maid—he couldn't think of her name just then—righting a table. The maid picked up a leather-bound book from the floor. It dripped blue ink, and the expression on the girl's face was one of heart-wrenching sorrow. He could afford a new notebook. The girl shouldn't appear so devastated.

Mrs. Fairfax caught his eye and looked away as though she couldn't bear to see him. He turned back to Stephen.

"Where is she?"

Stephen only pointed, his gaze wary. Lucas followed the line of the man's finger. The door. She'd left. Had she gone with the marquess?

That unholy fury swept within him, and he sucked in a breath, willing it to calm. What was it? What was that strange power that had engulfed him?

He didn't say another word. He nearly ran through the door, and finding the corridor empty, sprinted in the direction of the vestibule.

He found the space quiet and empty, the doors firmly shut. There was the scrape of stone above him, and he looked up. He knew that sound. Someone had just gone into the tower.

He took the stairs two at a time, reaching the tower in seconds. But she had already reached her room and bolted the door by the time he got there. He knew because when he tried to open it moments later, he found it locked to him.

"Go away." Her voice was clear through the thick door.

"No." He said it to the door more than to her, as though the thing was what stopped him. "Amelia, I must—"

The door flew open, and there stood his wife. He reached both hands toward her as though he could hold her in his grasp and ensure she was safe, but he froze at the sight of her.

She was crying. She didn't make a sound and yet tears ran down her cheeks. He reached for her again, and she shifted, putting the door between them, and it was then he noticed the open trunk behind her.

A coldness swept over him, and he dropped his hand.

"There is nothing more you need to say. I understand," she said.

He moved his gaze back to her, and now he noticed how carefully she held herself. It was as though she feared she might fall apart at any moment and was doing her best to keep track of herself.

"Understand?" He shook his head, but he never moved his eyes from her.

"I thought you mourned for the lost child. That you mourned for the life that you should have had, but that wasn't it at all." She shook her head, her voice strained with tears.

"What are you talking about?" He thought she would rail at him. That she would scold and belittle him for what he had done to the marquess.

Her *friend*. Dear God, he had done that to her friend. What had the man been doing here? Why had he been dancing with his wife in the library?

It was like he was reliving it, the scene he had interrupted suddenly appearing in his head. His wife. In that man's arms. He was making her laugh. He was dancing with her. Lucas would never dance with her. Lucas had never made her laugh. Once again, the spark of flames roared through him, and his fists curled, his jaw tightening and then—

It wasn't jealousy.

He blinked, the memory settling within him, and he was left dazed and confused. He had thought he had attacked the man out of jealousy, but that wasn't it at all.

Amelia stepped forward, her entire body rigid, the tears still flowing unbidden down her cheeks, and she met his gaze directly.

"You are not afraid of your future because you're afraid of losing another child. You do not hide in this castle because you're ashamed of the scars on your face. You hide because those scars are the *mark* of your shame." She pointed at his face now, at the place where the fire had scarred him. "Those scars are a reminder of betrayal. Of how Lila *betrayed* you." She dropped her hand, her mouth opening and closing without sound.

But she needn't speak further. Her words had hit the wound still open inside of him.

She was right.

When he had seen her with the marquess, it wasn't jealousy that filled him. It was rage and anger.

At someone else. At Lila.

"There is no reason for me to be here," she said now. "Not while her ghost is standing in my place."

Her words penetrated the fog that realization had cast over him, and he blinked as if coming awake again. He shoved his fingers through his hair, trying to will sensation back to his muddled brain.

"Amelia, what are you saying—"

She moved away from the door, and now he saw it fully.

She was packing.

Her trunk lay open, and she'd begun to toss gowns into it,

skirts and stockings hanging over the edge of it. Books tipped haphazardly into it.

"Amelia." He could only say her name; all other words had left him.

The sight of the opened trunk had stricken him mute.

She turned on him again, the tears still coming, her body just as tense and strong.

"No." She said the word softly, succinctly. "I will not stand for it. Not now."

He touched her then, just her arm, even as he ached to pull her close to him, to wrap his arms around her, to let her comfort him now that he realized the truth.

She was right. Lila still haunted him. Now, here, in the present, she was still controlling him. He hadn't realized. Not like this. He thought her just a painful memory, but she had become more than that.

He didn't give a damn about his appearance. Let people stare. But his shame. His shame he couldn't stand. And there it was. On his face for all to see. To remind him every day of how stupid he had been.

She jerked her arm away from him, backing up until her legs struck the open trunk.

"Amelia, please. I'm sorry. I know those words don't mean much right now, but if you give me a chance..." His throat closed as he took in her face. Her beautiful face streaked with tears he'd put there. "I can't bear to see you cry. I can't—" He swallowed, willed the words to come out. "I can't have done this to you," he whispered, feeling the words shake him to his core.

Her lips parted but in shock this time, her eyes going wide, her hands pressed to her stomach.

"I'm not crying for you. I'm crying for me." Her voice broke on the words, and once more he felt his body go still with a truth he hadn't seen.

She raised one hand to her chest, holding it just above her heart. "I'm crying for the little girl who didn't deserve her mother's scorn. I'm crying for the young woman who didn't deserve to be pushed to the edge and forgotten. I'm crying for the damage it did to me. That I accepted this without question." She flung out her hands as if to encompass whatever it was that stood between them.

He had thought it an arrangement, a marriage of equal opportunity for both of them, but now he saw it through her eyes. She had been married to the Ghoul of Greyfair without her consent, banished to a cold castle on the uneasy coast.

She had been neglected, discarded, and made to feel worthless, and then her future had been taken away from her.

He stepped back, his hands going weak at his sides.

"I'm not going to stand for it any longer. I'm not going to let other people decide what I'm worth." She advanced as he retreated, that hand against her chest turning to a single finger tapping at her breastbone. "You do not get to make me feel this way. You do not get to make me feel like there is no place for me here, no future here, because you've given my place to your dead wife."

She whirled away from him before he could form words, and he felt her accusations fall over him like a heavy, cold rain. He searched for words, something to say to stop her as she continued to fling things into the trunk.

"Amelia." Again, he could only find her name. "Amelia, you're right."

She stilled her hand outstretched for a bonnet as his words seemed to wash against her like the ocean against the shore. Slowly, so painfully slowly, she lowered her hand, turned only her head to him.

"You're right," he said more clearly now. "You're right about everything. I have let Lila control me even now. I have let what she did to me determine how I've lived my life. There is no excuse for it." He took a step back, his boots shuffling against the stone as he was unable to even pick up his feet properly. "But the worst of it is that I allowed her to hurt you. I let what she did ruin your life too, and I cannot forgive myself for that." His chest tightened to a point of pain that was greater than any pain he had ever suffered.

He knew it for what it was.

It was his heart breaking.

Standing there, looking at his wife, the tears drying on her cheeks, the bleakness, the hopelessness that surrounded her. Standing there in the room they had shared. The room where he had thought he could begin a new life.

But he hadn't gotten rid of the old one yet.

He backed up again and now he was standing in the doorway, his boots both in the room and out of it. He met his wife's quiet gaze, her words seemingly run out.

"I will have the carriage brought round to take you to London." The words rang through the quiet of the room. "To take you back to your family."

It was too much. Those last words had taken everything from him. The very words he had hoped to use about them.

Family.

His family. The one he had meant to create with her.

But how could he when he still lingered in two places? A tentative grasp on the future while the past continued to strangle him?

He had to let her go. He had to let her go because he loved her.

He took a final step back, and now he was standing on the tower landing, watching his wife through the door, her body poised for flight.

But her eyes had gone soft and wondering, her lips

slightly parted as if wishing to ask a question they couldn't form. Perhaps she was changing her mind. Perhaps she wished to stay.

He couldn't let her make that mistake.

"Goodbye, Amelia," he said and left her.

* * *

SHE STEPPED DOWN into the vestibule, her hand caressing the balustrade. She peered back at where her fingers lingered, her eyes dropping to the lion's head etched into the iron spindle. Her heart squeezed at the sight of it. She looked around her, at this place that had so frightened her that first night.

Yellow sunshine filled the room now, the golden hues interrupted by greens and reds where the light came through the stained glass at the top of the stairs. She turned to take in the knight, his sword raised as he prepared to march into battle.

She was done battling though. Again, her heart squeezed, and she had to look away.

She had been filled with such hope when she arrived here. She had thought things would be different. That she would be a duchess. That her title and her role as wife would give her reason and respect.

But it couldn't when that role had never been hers to begin with.

She adjusted the cloak she held over her arms and started for the door. She had stupidly thought she would change when she became a duchess. She thought somehow that would erase her mother's opinion of her. That it would undo all the hurt. That it would fix what her mother's death had prevented her from fixing.

Instead it had only made it worse.

Her husband, the man she loved, didn't love her in return, but that wasn't even the worst of it. He'd disrespected her. He'd insulted her place by—

Her throat closed, images of Lucas punching poor Ash.

Ash.

How was she going to tell Adaline what had happened? She couldn't go to the Aylesford estate to see if he was all right. It wasn't proper. She had to get to London. Surely Ash had sent word to Adaline.

She stilled, her fingers curling into her familiar worn cloak.

What would Ash say? Would he tell her sisters that she had married a brute? That the rumors of the Ghoul of Greyfair were true?

How would that make her feel? She felt a twinge of guilt that she even cared what her sisters would think, but she did. She still craved their approval, even now.

But she should crave their approval. They had stood by her when their mother hadn't. They had looked out for her even if their interests differed so wildly that sometimes Amelia was forgotten.

With the distance of time, she had gained a new perspective on her relationship with her sisters, and she knew it for what it was.

Three very different women growing up in the same space and trying to find their places in the world with a less than helpful mother and a rather absent father who did his best.

The hard edges of her memories had worn away now that she had seen what true sorrow looked like.

She looked over her shoulder and up the stairs as though she could see his tower room that was more like a stone prison than any place a human should inhabit. Once she had drawn him out of that room and into hers, and she had believed she had saved him.

But that had been a painful lesson to learn. She couldn't save anyone. One could only save oneself, and that was what she was doing.

She turned to the door just as she heard footsteps behind her.

"Amelia?"

She pivoted, her eyes finding Stephen in the shadows. She squared her shoulders.

"Stephen, I'm sure you mean well but—"

"I'm not here to defend him," he said, coming toward her, one hand raised in peace. "I love the man, but sometimes he's a bloody arse."

Amelia's lips twitched on a smile, and she bit her cheek to keep the expression at bay.

"I was hoping you might come with me. Just for a moment. There's something I'd like you to see."

She looked over her shoulder at the doors. "The carriage is probably waiting—"

"Yes, I know. I heard you're leaving." He bowed his head, shuffled his feet. "I was very sorry to hear it. I had hoped you wouldn't let my cousin's poor behavior spoil your home here."

Home.

She had thought it was home for a while, and even now her heart broke to think she was leaving it.

She looked again at the doors. The need to be gone was strong, but Stephen was right. If she fled now, she was allowing Lucas to ruin this place where she had felt she belonged. What was waiting for her in London? Would she be destined to care for Uncle Herman while her sisters married and left?

Suddenly running away didn't seem like the noble and strong decision she had thought it to be.

She forced a soft smile as she turned back to Stephen. "I believe I have a moment to spare."

Stephen smiled and turned back the way he had come, disappearing into the shadows under the stairs. She followed him, surprised to see he was heading for the servants' stairs at the back of the house. She remained silent, curiosity capturing her tongue as she descended to the kitchen below.

The silence was the first indication that something wasn't quite right. She peered around Stephen down the corridor, hoping to catch a glimpse of the kitchen beyond, but they were still too far away.

Stephen stepped into the kitchen first, moving to the side, and she could finally see what lay before her.

Mrs. Wilson.

Amelia stopped, her feet suddenly frozen to the stones beneath them.

"Mrs. Wilson." She shook her head, a sudden urgency gripping her. "Whatever is…"

But she didn't finish the sentence. The kitchen was full. Of people. Of tenants and villagers and servants. Mrs. Mitchum and Jones's mother, wrapped tightly in a shawl by the cook stove. The milliner and the blacksmith who had saved the carriage she was to take back to London.

Mrs. Fairfax and Jones stood before all of them, expectant smiles on their faces. Stephen had taken a stool to the side, his gaze sheepish as though he had been caught in a deception.

Amelia stepped forward, dropping her cloak on a chair to take Mrs. Wilson's hands into hers.

"Whatever is the matter?" She squeezed the woman's hands even as she studied the rest of the occupants of the kitchen.

Mrs. Wilson looked to everyone else before she cleared her throat. "We want you to speak to the marquess about the railway lease."

Amelia blinked, the woman's words not making sense. "I'm sorry?"

Mrs. Wilson nodded as if to emphasize her point. "We—" She nodded at the others in the room. "We wish for you to negotiate with the marquess. Get him to see reason about the railway line."

Amelia looked about her, at the smiling, encouraging faces, at the nods of agreement.

"You wish for me to speak with the Marquess of Aylesford about the railway lease. But that's—" Her words trailed off on a nervous laugh, and she looked about to find Stephen. "Surely His Grace would prefer—"

"He wished for you to speak to the new marquess," Stephen said quietly, his face folding into a look of consternation. "He mentioned something about a desk."

Mrs. Fairfax made a mumbling noise but seemed unable to stop her smile.

"He never said anything to me," she replied.

Stephen raised an eyebrow. "He was supposed to. The day we learned there was to be a new marquess he said he was going to speak with you."

Heat flooded through her, and she looked away as if to hide the color that was surely in her cheeks now. She remembered the day they had learned there was to be a new marquess. Only she and Lucas had been preoccupied. He probably hadn't remembered that he meant to speak to her on that topic.

Amelia let go of Mrs. Wilson's hands to press her own to her stomach. "I don't know the first thing about railway leases."

"I can tell you what you need to know," Stephen said with a nod.

The others nodded enthusiastically.

"He's right, you know," Mrs. Fairfax said. "If anyone can do this, it's you."

"I wouldn't be a lady's maid if it hadn't been for you," Jones said softly, her eyes shining with unshed tears, her smile tremulous in gratitude.

Amelia's chest tightened.

Mrs. Wilson was nodding now. "I wouldn't have a proper pastry cutter of me own without you." She pointed at a tall, slender woman in the crowd. "I'd still be walking over to Patsy's every time I needed to make a pie if it weren't for you."

A pastry cutter seemed so insignificant, but the bright, relieved expression on Mrs. Wilson's face told her it wasn't. Not to her.

Mrs. Fairfax took a step forward. "Those rooms would still be filled with the stuff brought from Lagameer Hall if it weren't for you. This castle, this home"—she held up her hands, her eyes traveling to the ceiling as if to take in the whole of the structure—"would still just be for storage, a life paused, if it weren't for you." She gestured to the servants standing behind her. "We would still be waiting if it weren't for you."

The enormity of what she had accomplished struck her then as her eyes moved around the room. Because there it was. All of it. Everything she had done in the few short months she had been duchess at Dinsmore. She could see it now. The lives she had made a little easier. The darkness she had pushed away. The good she had done. It was all there.

And she had been the one to do it.

All by herself.

No one had told her she was worthy of it. No one had

told her she was good enough for it. She had simply seen a need and stepped in because she was capable of making change.

Something swept over her then, standing there in the kitchen, surrounded by these people who had come to mean so much to her in so little time. It was as though she had passed through a waterfall to find the hidden cove of splendor on the other side. Everything was more colorful here, brighter, and best of all, filled with possibility.

She stepped to the chair where her cloak lay, her fingers burying themselves in the plush fabric.

"I shall need to know exactly what the Aylesford estate stands to gain from the railway lease." She looked to Stephen who nodded directly.

"I can give you all the specifics."

She looked to Mrs. Wilson. "I'll need an understanding from the tenants of what they hope to gain. Personal stories. Not numbers and facts. I want to know how this railway will change everyone's life. Just like the pastry cutter has changed yours."

Mrs. Wilson's smile was broad, her eyes shining. "I can do that, Your Grace."

She looked to the milliner and the blacksmith. "I need to know about the transportation of goods to the village. How it is done now and how long does it take for goods to reach the shelves. I want to know how the availability of goods is affected by the time saved shipping them on a railway."

The two men nodded in understanding.

Finally she turned to her lady's maid.

"Jones, I'll need a gown."

Jones's eyes widened as she squeaked in surprise. "A gown, Your Grace?"

Amelia nodded. "A stunning one." She shook her head as

she thought better of it. "An unforgettable one," she said, strength bubbling inside of her.

"Your Grace?" Mrs. Fairfax said, one eyebrow lifted in question.

Amelia gathered her cloak, raised her chin. "I'm going to a ball," she said.

CHAPTER 15

*H*e didn't know what day it was.

He'd gone into his tower room the day Amelia left and hadn't bothered to emerge. What was the point? Once the draw of estate matters was enough to give him purpose, to pull him from his cot, but that no longer held the appeal it once did.

Not because he would never have an heir to pass it to, but because he would no longer share it with her.

He was alone. Finally and completely. It was as though once acknowledging Lila's ghost it had vanquished her. He no longer felt that unnatural haze that had sometimes clouded his view. It was as though he had been dazed since that night of the fire, seeing a world tainted by his first wife's deceit and only now realized that he had painted his reality with his pain.

And he'd lost everything.

He'd lost the future he had hoped for and the wife he loved.

He rolled over, facing the cold, unyielding stone wall of

his tower room and ignored the sunshine that now squeezed through the cracks along the shuttered window.

It was another day apparently. A new dawn. The time of morning he had looked forward to the most because it held such promise.

Hang it. Hang it all.

A knock sounded at the door, but he didn't even flinch at the noise now. Mrs. Fairfax had been bringing trays of food that sat mostly untouched where she left them on the table. He didn't open his eyes. He didn't acknowledge as he heard the scrape of the door against stone.

Let her bring food if it made her feel better. He didn't want it.

Just as he hadn't wanted a drink since the first one he had knocked back...how many days ago was it?

He couldn't even get lost in a bottle of whiskey. The whiskey reminded him of her.

Another sound reached his ears, one that had him reluctantly turning over.

The sharp staccato of Stephen's crutch against the stone floor.

"If you've come to tell me some rubbish about life worth living, I'll save you the trouble. It isn't, and I'd rather be left here to die if it's all the same to you," he mumbled, not opening his eyes.

The footsteps stopped, and he heard the chair being pulled back from the table.

"I'd let you die if it were an option, but as I've already gone to so much trouble saving your arse, I'd rather my efforts not be in vain."

Lucas opened a single eye a mere slit to take in his cousin. The man lounged in the chair, picking at the tray of food Mrs. Fairfax had left earlier.

"Really? I would think you'd rather not put more energy into something that's already cost so much."

Stephen barked a laugh and pulled a chunk of bread loose from the loaf that sat on the tray, scooping up some apple butter on a knife at the same time.

"That would probably be wise, but I have the sense you'll be angry at me later if I let you lie here."

"And why is that?"

Stephen took a generous bite of the bread and apple butter, chewing ponderously. Lucas's stomach growled in response, and he put a hand to it in admonishment. He didn't want food. He didn't want anything. He only wanted her.

Instead of answering him, Stephen finished his morsel and stood, shuffling against the table to grasp the knobs of the shutters above it and yanked them open. Glorious sunshine poured into the small space, and Lucas snapped his eyes shut, putting his arm over his face for good measure.

"You're not helping," he grumbled.

"Did you know I worry sometimes that you're beyond help?"

He moved his arm and opened both eyes at this. Stephen was an eternal optimist. Even when Lucas feared he wouldn't walk again, when the wounds on his back had started to heal, the skin tightening so uncomfortably he couldn't stand up straight, Stephen had told him to give his body time. The human body could work miracles if only given the patience in which to do it.

To hear Stephen suggest there was no help left for Lucas had him sitting up, leaning back against the stone wall he had stared at for days.

"Why do you say that?"

Stephen had taken another bite of bread, and Lucas waited for him to finish it. Finally his cousin gestured to the window with the remaining chunk of food in his hand.

"Do you know it's been almost two years since the fire?"

Lucas blinked, searching back in his memory. It had been spring, nearly summer like it was now. The horses in the stables had begun to foal, and he had been spending an unusual amount of time there. That was why he wasn't in the house the night the fire started. Why he had been going in to find Lila instead of being trapped inside himself. Why he had probably lived when she hadn't.

"I found her that night," he heard himself say, and Stephen's sharp look matched Lucas's own surprise that he had said those words. "I found her," he said again, his mind going back to that night. The same images had played through his mind like a sick pantomime for two years, but for some strange reason, they no longer held the bite they once did. The images were no longer haunting. They were filled with a stark sadness that overwhelmed him. "I found her in the upstairs corridor. Not far from where you found me most likely. She was right there. Barefoot. In her night-dress. I reached out for her. I think I called her name. Told her to follow me. There was still a way out." He stopped as that night played back in his head, as he watched her turn away from him, as the roundness of her belly became silhou-etted by the flames. "She ran from me. Back into the fire."

Stephen watched him as he spoke. It was the first time Lucas had talked about what he saw that night. Stephen had told him—weeks? Maybe months? He couldn't be sure—after they had come to Dinsmore, as Lucas lay on this very cot wondering if he would live or die that they had found Lila the next morning. She was in her room, what was left of it, lying on the floor as if she had fallen asleep. The flames had never touched her, and she had likely died from inhaling the smoke.

At the time he had taken it as Lila's final stab at him, her last chance to hurt him. But now he didn't see it that way. He saw it for what it was. A desperate woman's means of escape, the only one she thought she had open to her.

Amelia had done that. Amelia had cleared his mind of the anger of betrayal, had shown him the truth of his shame.

And he had lost her.

"I'm so sorry, Lucas," Stephen finally said, his voice faint with old pain.

Lucas turned his gaze to his cousin, studied his worn features. So much sadness had happened in the briefness of their lives, and he hated it. He hated how it touched everything, how it shaped everything, and how it still affected everything.

From when Stephen's own father had disowned him, when Stephen had come to live with Lucas and his father so many years ago, when they had come here to start over when everything had been destroyed, when Lucas had bargained for a bride to give him what he believed was the last decent thing in this world.

He hadn't realized at the time what good surrounded him. The closeness of his cousin. The loyalty of his servants. The riches of the land that belonged to the Greyfair title. It was strange how sometimes all one needed was a different mindset.

"I'm done being sorry," Lucas finally said, propping his arms on his bent knees.

"It's exhausting," Stephen mumbled, and Lucas couldn't help a smile at how true his cousin's words were.

"I appreciate that you've come to save me again, but I think you're too late. I've already been saved, and I must get on with it."

Stephen raised an eyebrow but took another bite of bread without speaking.

"It seems I was letting Lila's betrayal control me. Even now." He could see Amelia standing before him, tears running down her cheeks. Not for just the pain he had caused her but for an old pain too.

"Is that why you tried to murder the new Marquess of Aylesford with only your hands?"

Lucas cringed. "Was it bad?"

Stephen barked a laugh. "The poor man barely left with his life."

Lucas closed his eyes. "I've ruined everything, haven't I?"

When Stephen didn't answer right away, Lucas peeked at his cousin.

The man wiped crumbs from his fingers as he said, "That remains to be seen."

He opened his eyes again. "How's that?"

Stephen stood, shaking the rest of the crumbs from his coat. "Amelia is going to the marquess tonight to negotiate his agreement to the railway lease."

Lucas dropped his feet to the floor, his hands gripping the edge of the cot. "She...what?" He couldn't make the words go together to form coherent sentences.

"Amelia is going to the Marquess of Aylesford's estate to try to get him to agree to the railway lease." He brushed his hands together again. "I've told her everything she needs to know about the lease. She's gathered personal stories from the tenants on how the railway will improve their lives, and she even interviewed several of the tradesmen in the village to see how this will make getting goods on shelves in the village more efficient, benefiting Aylesford's tenants as well as Greyfair's. Hopefully this knowledge coupled with the fact that the new marquess is apparently an old friend of the family—" Here Stephen stopped to give him a knowing glare, and Lucas felt a new shame crawl over him for having pounded the poor bloke. "She will be successful in negotiating the lease."

"But—" He stopped, trying to figure out which question to ask first. But there was only one that burned inside of him. "She left for London."

Stephen watched him for a moment, and he knew his cousin understood what he was really asking, and that was the question he answered.

"She didn't leave, cousin. She stayed. For the tenants, the villagers, the servants, and probably against all reason…you."

A warmth started in the center of his torso and began to spread, melting into his legs and arms until his skin tingled with it.

She had stayed.

She hadn't left. She hadn't turned away from him.

But—

He looked up, met Stephen's gaze. "Why tonight?"

Stephen made his way around the chair in the direction of the door. "The new marquess is having an assembly tonight to meet some of the local gentry. Amelia was invited before you decided to ring the poor man's bell."

"An assembly? My wife is attending a ball tonight?"

Stephen nodded as he placed one hand on the doorknob. "Yes, she is. Heard she's had a pretty gown made for her and everything. She's not leaving anything to chance."

Lucas stood abruptly, and the room swam around him. He hadn't been on his feet for extended periods of time in days, and it took him a moment to get his bearings.

"Stephen, I need you to go to the village."

Stephen frowned. "What for?"

"I need you to find someone who can properly cut my hair."

* * *

SHE STEPPED FROM THE CARRIAGE, the skirts of her gown carefully held up in her hands. The Georgian facade of the Marquess of Aylesford's country home loomed up before her. The sky above it was painted in tones of pink, orange, and purple as it settled into night.

She shouldn't be here alone. Her husband should be standing beside her.

Pain radiated through her, and she closed her eyes briefly before reminding herself why she was there.

This wasn't about Lucas. This was about her. This was about finding the strength she didn't know was inside of her and finally—*finally*—letting others see it.

She only wished she believed her own thoughts.

The door opened before her, and a servant was outlined by a soft glow.

"Lady Amelia?"

She started at the sound of her old name, and it felt somehow wrong. Her eyes adjusted to the light, and the servant took a small step forward at the same time.

"Alfred." She smiled for what felt like the first time in days at the sight of the Riggs' faithful butler. "You came with Ash?"

Alfred gave a small bow. "Of course, my lady."

She climbed the stairs, the smile still on her face. When she reached the door she dropped her skirts, letting them fall in a delicate cascade, the finery of which she still wasn't used to. Jones had outdone herself. It was she who had suggested the color and style that would best fit Amelia, and the maid was not wrong. In fact, she was terribly right, and Amelia had never felt so beautiful.

The gown was pure gold and fell away from her hips in a decadent waterfall of draped tiers tied off with tiny pearls stitched into the shape of roses. The bodice was fitted with a patterned satin that made her appear taller and accentuated what little feminine curve she thought she had. The ensemble was completed by straps of billowing silk that lay against her upper arms, leaving her shoulders and collar bare. She had never felt so exposed, and yet she had never felt so confident either.

It was no wonder there was a note of question in Alfred's voice.

"I'm afraid I've gone and become a duchess now, Alfred," she said, the smile not leaving her lips.

Alfred had been with the Riggs family since Amelia could remember, and more than once the quiet, stern man had picked her up from a fall or surreptitiously passed her a book when she had been forgotten at the outskirts of a gathering.

Alfred smiled now, and there were new lines framing his eyes and mouth. He had grown old while she had grown up, and somehow seeing the passage of time on his face comforted her. Alfred was still here even if so much had changed.

"I was hoping to see the marquess before the rest of his guests arrived."

Alfred gave a nod and stepped back through the door. "I shall see if he is at home."

He gestured for her to enter, and picking up her skirts, she made her way carefully inside.

She had grown used to the old regal air of Dinsmore Castle, but a country estate like this was something foreign to her, and she proceeded with caution. She found herself in a cavernous space lit by an extravagant chandelier that floated above her. Everywhere the light touched there was gilt and marble and polished wood. The air itself was ripe with flowers and citrus, and at once, she felt as though she had drifted into a fairy tale.

She didn't realize Alfred had left her alone there until she heard Ash's voice echoing as if from a distance.

"Old Dobson had elegant tastes, didn't he?"

She looked up and found Ash leaning on the balustrade of the floor above. She sucked in a breath as the bruises on his face were evident even from this distance. She felt the weight of what she was about to attempt crash down on her for the hundredth time in the past week and once again she wished her husband was there. As soon as the thought came, she shoved it away.

He had no room for her in his life, and she didn't need him in hers.

She must have made an outward indication that she had seen his bruises because he waggled his eyebrows at her now.

"I plan to tell my guests that I won the fight with the Ghoul of Greyfair. I hope you'll go along with it." He moved to the stairs and came down them at an easy lope.

He was still the Ash of her childhood, happy and carefree, even if he were a marquess now. But as he drew closer, she saw a seriousness in his eyes she didn't remember.

"Amelia, I know I make light, but I want you to under-stand that if you should have need of my protection you only must ask." His voice was grave, and if she hadn't been staring at him, she would have thought it came from someone else.

She didn't know at first of what he spoke but slowly real-ization dawned.

"Oh God, no," she stammered, shaking her head furiously. "He's not—that is he's not to me—really he's—" She stopped and drew in a breath, licked her lips, and refocused. "Lucas is not like that. He's actually kind and compassionate. It's only he has scars from events which occurred in his past, and I'm afraid you trod on one of them."

Ash's forehead wrinkled in speculation. "Compassionate? The Ghoul of Greyfair is compassionate?"

"I promise to agree with you when you tell people you won the fight that caused those bruises if you promise not to tell anyone that the Ghoul of Greyfair is no ghoul at all. He's actually rather extraordinary."

Something flashed across his face then that she couldn't have guessed at, but he seemed to draw some kind of conclusion that satisfied him. He motioned behind them, and she understood he wished to walk with her. They began making their way down the marble and gilt corridor to one of the wings of the sprawling house.

"When your sister told me you had wed, I couldn't really believe it. I suppose you'll always be Adaline's little sister to me and never a wife."

His words were truer than he knew, and they stabbed at her until she had to look away as though admiring the portraits they passed.

"You'll be surprised then to hear I've come early to speak with you because of a matter pertaining to my husband's estate."

Ash slowed and gestured to an open set of doors on their left. She shifted, following him inside the room only to find herself in a ballroom that was impossibly more resplendent than the foyer had been. Six chandeliers suspended from the ceiling gave the room the feeling of daylight. The opened terrace doors that lined the opposite wall were painted with the deepening night sky and allowed the warm early summer breeze to drift into the room, carrying with it the heavy scent of blossoms.

She paused, feeling the grandeur of the room overtake her much as her task already had.

She faced Ash. "My husband had been negotiating with the previous marquess about allowing the railway to lease a portion of your estate to build a spur line into the village. I've come to ask you as the new marquess to consider my husband's request."

Ash blinked. "You've come here to negotiate a railway lease. For your husband."

She shook her head. "Certainly not for my husband. The railway lease is to benefit the tenants of both the Aylesford and Greyfair land and the residents and tradespeople of the village."

Ash took a step back and crossed his arms over his chest. "What do I have to gain from such a lease?"

"Your tenants will have access to a cheaper means of transportation for their goods to market. That means they stand a chance to make a greater profit, which in turn could lead you to increase your rents. That is in addition to the revenue from the lease itself, which I understand from similar leases can be quite reasonable."

"Why should I allow a railroad to invade my land?" He raised an eyebrow, and she knew he was testing her.

"Because without it your tenants will be unable to compete with other producers already on railway lines, and they will be forced to leave. You'll lose the rents and be faced with the trouble of finding new tenants on less than desirable land." She raised her chin. "You must come to terms with the fact that the old way of doing business is changing, and access to a railway line is the only way of competing."

"You speak as though I were a merchant." She saw the glint in his eye and felt the game shift. Ash had no prejudices against anyone, let alone merchants, but he was attempting to see what she knew.

She flexed her hands and tried to keep the smile from her lips. "I speak as though you were a prudent and strategic landowner concerned with the future profits your estate should bring you." She held up a finger. "One thing though. Should you consider the lease, I recommend you withhold the mineral rights to the land. I've heard there can be some excellent deposits found in coastal areas."

The smile he had so obviously been trying to hold back came free now, slowly spreading across his face.

"Amelia Atwood, I fear you've grown up."

She returned his smile. "It's Amelia Bennett actually."

Ash laughed. "I would ask for a place on your dance card, Your Grace, but I fear your husband might come back to finish what he started."

Her throat closed suddenly, but she smiled through it. "You have nothing to fear, my lord. My husband is not one for social gatherings."

Something dark and perhaps sad passed over his eyes then, and she tried to catch it to understand what it was that had changed about her old friend, but it was too fleeting.

"You know I will need to find a wife when I return to London. I can only hope she is half as strong as you."

Amelia's smile came easily now. "You know there are two more Atwood sisters on the market. Perhaps one of them will be to your liking."

Ash stilled, his smile somewhat out of place, and she wondered what it was that she'd said that had struck him so. The moment was shattered by the appearance of Alfred announcing the arrival of the first guests.

Ash waved in acknowledgement before turning back to her. "I'm afraid duty calls," he said, gesturing to the side of the dance floor where a refreshment table had been set up. "Do make yourself comfortable." He started for the doorway but stopped and turned back to her with a quizzical bent to his head. "I suppose your husband is in touch with a railway agent who would like to arrange this lease."

She gave a quick nod, her heart skipping in her chest.

Ash smiled and gave a satisfied nod. "Tell your husband to send your railway agent over in the next few days. I'll need to leave for London next week, and I should like to have the lease settled before I do."

She tried hard to keep the glee from her voice as she said, "I shall do that."

The room was soon filled with the ladies and gentlemen of the estates along this stretch of the coast, and Amelia was soon lost amongst them. She sipped at lemonade and gave gracious replies to curious interludes from neighboring landowners who had the occasion to meet Stephen but not Greyfair himself. She cringed inwardly every time she heard as much, knowing the true reason now for her husband's seclusion.

The music started shortly after, and the dance floor was packed with both young and old enjoying the rare occasion for a country assembly so late in the spring when most of the countryside had returned to London for the season.

There was a pleasant monotony to it as one song slipped into the next, the dancers exchanging places, the low buzz of conversation ongoing.

Until a splintered quiet ruptured the pleasant haze, and she realized something had changed. The buzz of conversation had turned to startled whispers, some even hushed gasps. The lemonade shook in her hand before she knew her body had started to respond to the agitation sweeping through the room because there was only one thing that could cause such a stir.

She moved, pushing her way through the crowd until she could see the door.

He was there.

At least, she thought it was him. It was his beloved face, that familiar scowl and impatient eyes, his broad shoulders and—

He'd cut his hair. His beautiful, thick, uneven hair was trimmed close about his head now, and she regretted its loss.

But oh lord, what it did to him.

Gone was the husband she had found hiding in the tower,

the Ghoul of Greyfair the rumors suggested. Before her stood the Duke of Greyfair, a gentleman of society and a man among men.

She realized with a jolt that he had found her through the crowd, and his eyes burned into her even from this distance. As though sensing his intent, guests parted to give him room, and he made his way easily to her.

"I'm sorry to be so late," he said when he finally reached her. "Stephen and I had a devil of a time finding my evening wear."

His tone was so light, so open, so...*normal* when so much pressed down on her she thought she might suffocate. But then she reached up, her hand moving instinctually, and her palm found its place along his cheek.

Atop his scars.

"Lucas," she breathed and just like that, the spell was broken.

The silence that rang around them returned to the low buzz of conversation, and the orchestra started the next dance. They were no longer a spectacle but just another couple in the ballroom. The Ghoul of Greyfair had vanished when he was discovered to be just a man. They would still be watched. Of that, Amelia was certain, but they would no longer be scrutinized the way the rumors would warrant. And with that knowledge, something shifted inside of her. Something that felt dangerously like hope.

She pulled her hand back, remembering where she was.

"Lucas, it's...that is...Aylesford has agreed to see the railway agent about the lease. He was hoping you might arrange it." She watched his eyes as she spoke the words, hoping to see a glimmer of something in them, something that would tell her what he was thinking.

"I don't give a damn about the railway lease," he whispered, his eyes alit with a fire she'd not seen in them before.

"What?" The word was tremulous as she leaned her head back, as Lucas gripped her arms with righteous intent.

"I don't care about a railway lease, Amelia. That's not why I'm here."

She searched his eyes. Searched and searched and hoped. "Then why are you here?"

A single line appeared between his brows as he seemed to drink her in. "I'm here for you, Amelia. You're all that matters."

She didn't want to believe him. She knew that way was perilous, to open her heart to the idea that this might be different. That finally she would be seen as worthy and enough. She had only just discovered she didn't need another's approval. That she didn't need someone to tell her she belonged. The strength had been inside of her all along.

But he was here, before her, and he had cut his hair and found a suit and—

Stepped into a ball for the whole of the countryside to see his scars. The mark of betrayal. The evidence of his shame.

And he'd done it for her.

She swayed with the weight of it, this idea that he would face his greatest demons because she mattered more than the fear that controlled him.

"Lucas—"

"Greyfair." Ash appeared then, smiling like the congenial host he was. "I didn't think you were going to make it this evening, but I'm so glad you have. I wish to speak to you about this railway lease your wife mentioned."

Lucas let go of her only long enough to slip her arm through his. "Aylesford, I owe you an apology, but I'm rather busy right now. Might we discuss this later?"

Ash slid his gaze to her, a knowing smile on his lips. "I'll accept that apology over a glass of whiskey. Seek me out when you've had a chance to catch up with your wife, will you?"

She watched the exchange as though she were seeing a pantomime in French for all she knew what was happening.

Lucas and Ash shook hands then, of all things, and as Lucas turned her in the direction of the terrace doors, she caught a look of stark regret on Ash's face that left her wondering.

CHAPTER 16

*E*veryone was staring.

Lucas could feel the heat of their stares burning into him, and his hand flexed, wishing to pull the brim of his hat down. But his hat wasn't there, and his head felt bare and cold. The damned barber had nearly cut off all of his hair. He wondered absurdly if Amelia would even know it was him. He could see his ears for the first time in more than two years, and they looked as though they didn't quite belong on his head.

But she had recognized him.

Through every stare that had pinned him when he'd first stepped into Aylesford's ballroom, he could feel hers above the rest. It was as though they were connected in a way that wasn't seen or understood but was only felt, and it pulled them to each other.

He didn't understand why she went on about the railway lease when there were such more important matters to discuss until he remembered what Stephen had said. She had come there tonight to negotiate the lease.

And she'd done it. Despite what Lucas had done to end all

hope of seeing the railroad spur line connecting the village to London, she had overcome it.

Of course she had.

Wasn't the fact that he was standing there proof of her powers?

As he pulled her through the terrace doors and out into the falling twilight, he couldn't help but wonder how else he could harness her powers for good. But even as he thought it, he dismissed it. He could never harness her. Not ever and not a single part of her. It wouldn't be fair.

The terrace was quiet, and he suspected his entrance was to blame for that. Everyone had rushed inside to get a glimpse of the Ghoul of Greyfair. But he didn't feel like a ghoul any longer. He only felt like a man, lost without his wife.

He didn't stop on the terrace once his eyes lit on the stone steps that led down into the gardens, and keeping her arm tucked into his, he led her out into the shadows. He didn't know the estate, but he kept his back to the manor house and plunged ahead until the lights of the house had faded enough to allow them to see the stars.

He paused suddenly, letting her trip into his embrace. He knew it was cheating, to catch her off guard like that, but he suddenly needed to feel her, to hold her and touch her and convince himself that she was real, that she was real and that she hadn't left him.

He owed her an apology too. He knew that and yet it seemed so insignificant. It wasn't enough to tell her he was sorry, and standing there under the stars, the scent of gardenias thick in the air, he felt the inadequacy of words well up inside of him, and it robbed him of speech.

They stood like that, Amelia's face turned up to his, her golden gown radiant in the starlight, and he suddenly couldn't tell her what she meant to him.

"Are you going to say something?" she whispered.

"Yes. I had planned to. I'm just not sure how." He stuttered each sentence as though it took all his effort to piece them together, and it had.

"May I start?"

He frowned, nestling her closer against him. "What do you have to say?"

"I miss your hair. You don't look yourself without it."

He laughed, the sound coming so unexpectedly it almost seemed broken. But it broke the dam inside of him, and he realized there was something more important than an apology.

"You were right," he said, keeping his voice firm and steady so she understood the sincerity of his words. "I was letting Lila control my present and my future, but worse than that, I wasn't giving her her peace."

Her brow furrowed in concern, and he went on, trying to explain.

"The night of the fire I wasn't in Lagameer Hall. I had been attending the birth of a foal in the stables. I had been there all night when the shouts of fire came from the yard." He swallowed, waiting for the images to come out of the deepest recesses of his mind, but they never did. He still saw that night as though it were still happening, but the clarity of the memories had been lost as he'd finally released his grip on them. "Stephen tried to stop me, but I had to get Lila out of there. I had to save the child. He didn't deserve to die even if he wasn't mine." His throat closed again, and as if sensing his pain, her hands pressed into his back, holding him tight. "I found her. I had almost reached her when—" The images in his mind vanished with a starkness that pierced him, and his words jammed in his throat.

"You don't need to talk about this, Lucas. It's all right. I don't need to—"

"I need to." There was a determination in his voice that had been missing, and he wondered what other changes she had wrought on him. "She ran away from me, Amelia. She turned back into the flames and disappeared. They found her the next morning, but I didn't know any of that. I only know what they told me when I woke up at Dinsmore. There's nothing else that I remember of that night, and it's haunted me ever since. Not knowing what happened to her. Only being able to guess what it was like for her in the end, but I realize something now. Something that you made me see. By marrying me she had had her choices taken from her, but in the end, she thought she only had one choice left to her, and she took it, no matter the devastating consequence."

Pain poured from him now as if it were a tangible thing, and he was letting it go. It ebbed and flowed with each word, with each memory, and when in his last words, he *felt* what Lila must have felt, the desperation stole his breath.

"Lucas." Amelia wrapped her arms fully around him, tucking her head beneath his chin as she held him.

They stayed like that, locked together with only the stars to see them for a long time. It was only when he caught sight of the gooseflesh on her bare shoulders that he realized she grew chilled. He eased away from her long enough to shuck his jacket and wrap her in it, pulling her back into his arms.

"This jacket smells like dust," she mumbled against his chest.

"It would be best if you don't ask where we found it."

She laughed softly. "Would you like me to put it in the exchange next year?"

He leaned back and with a single finger under her chin, lifted her face to his. "Does that mean you're staying?"

Her face sobered, and she closed her eyes as if gathering herself to speak.

"Lucas, I shouldn't have acted the way I did, and I'm sorry.

I had thought it was your responsibility to make me feel like I had a place at Dinsmore when really I should have seen it for myself. I should have trusted myself, been compassionate with myself, and above all I should have respected myself enough to know my strengths, and instead I let the animosity of others cloud my judgment. I'm so truly sorry for that. I know I will be stronger in the future, but I know I won't always be perfect. I hope you'll understand."

"Amelia, I—" He stopped, studying her face as she watched him, and it was like each of them understood the other perfectly in that moment. He could feel it, vibrating between, the words left unsaid.

They were each afraid to say it. He understood that now. They were words each had spoken once that had caused them pain, and now they were afraid to say them again.

He let go of her long enough to cup her face in his hands. "Amelia, I love you. I want all of you, and I hope you can take all of me."

Her eyes searched him, and for the first time, he realized he had grown used to her gaze, and he never wanted to hide his face from her again.

"I love you, Lucas," she said just as sure, just as strong. "And I will take all of you forever."

He kissed her then, finally and completely, and there in the starlight, he felt his past let go.

CHAPTER 17

ome years later...

"Prepare to be boarded!"

Amelia stopped just inside the door to the nursery, pressing the bundle in her arms closer to her chest instinctively as she observed the chaos.

She couldn't see Lucas although she had heard his voice seconds before she had come through the door, so he must have been in there somewhere.

The girls' cots had been pushed together to form a barricade, and Annabelle stood in front of it, her wooden sword held high, her pirate hat lopsided on her dark curls.

"You have to help me up, Annie," Ava reminded her older sister. "I'm too tiny to climb up there on my own."

Amelia couldn't help but smile at Ava's practical tone. At four years old, the cot was a struggle for her, but Annie was only too eager to help her sister over it.

Lucas had taken great pleasure in choosing the girls'

names. He had spent weeks making lists of names that started with the letter *A* for both a girl and a boy each time. She had asked him why he hadn't just used the list from when she was pregnant with Annie when she was carrying Ava, but he said that just wasn't the same. So he'd started a new list.

Mrs. Fairfax, Jones, and Stephen were only too happy to provide their own input.

Speaking of Stephen...

She cast her gaze to the side where Stephen sat on a stool behind the bookcase one of the girls had pushed away from the wall to form a sort of prison, she realized. Lucas's cousin wore a pink sash tied about his chest and a tiara composed of paste jewels in riotous tones of yellow, purple, and blue.

"What happened to you?" She tried very hard to keep the sound of laughter from her voice.

"I was boarded. They made me walk the plank. Now I have to play the part of the captured princess." He nodded at the bundle in her arms. "You couldn't have made a third one to play the princess, could you?"

She peered down at the baby nestled in her arms, pushing aside the blanket to see his sleeping face. "I'm afraid not," she whispered.

Stephen stood, retrieving his crutch from where it was braced against the bookcase. It was now festooned in strings of purple beads. "Girls, do you smell that?"

Annie loosened her grip on her sword, twirling to the door as Ava peered over her shoulder, her eyes rounder than Amelia had ever seen them. Amelia sniffed the air and caught the scent of fresh baked bread.

"Mrs. Fairfax's apple butter," Ava whispered like a prayer.

"Race you," Stephen called over his shoulder as he scurried through the door.

Annie dropped her sword, her hat falling from her head

as she bolted for the door. Ava sauntered, never in a hurry to get anywhere, and she stopped at Amelia's side and looked up.

"I do so love Mrs. Fairfax's apple butter. I think I love it more than playing pirates with Annie." On that solemn note, she left.

Amelia looked back at the carnage of the nursery to find Lucas had popped up on the other side of the cots.

"Am I to believe I've been saved by a girl?" He wrinkled his nose at her.

She nodded to the sleeping baby in her arms. "Let's say Ash saved you."

Lucas's eyes fell on the bundle, and he scrambled over the cots to get to her side, his fingers already reaching.

"Is he awake?"

"No, but he just finished feeding so he might let you hold him for a while."

Ash had proven a mighty eater, and he didn't like to be too far from food for too long. She passed him over to his father who sat on Stephen's vacated stool.

"I almost had to walk the plank," he murmured, staring down at his son. "I hope Ash enjoys something less lethal. Like chess."

"You hate chess."

"I know, but at least a loss wouldn't mean I had to prance about in that tiara and sash." He grimaced, and Amelia couldn't help but laugh.

She moved over to her husband, resting against his shoulder to peer down at their son. Lucas had let his hair grow back, and it hung in thick curtains about his face. She reached down and pushed it back around his ear, so she could see him, and the light caught her wedding band still nestled on her index finger where she had placed it on that stormy night so many years ago. She hadn't relinquished it even when Lucas had tried to have it fixed. It reminded her of all they had overcome, together, and it gave her hope for the future, no matter what it would bring.

"You have your heir," she whispered, still not quite believing Ash was there.

Lucas snorted a laugh. "I had my heir years ago."

She straightened to look at him. "What do you mean?"

He looked up, his eyes curious. "Annie."

"Annie? The sword-wielding pirate?"

Her husband nodded. "I'd leave everything I could to her. You've seen how she gives orders. She's just like her mother." He said this last bit with a mischievous glint in his eye, and her heart warmed at the look of happiness splashed over his face.

"I love you," she said, surprised yet again at how easily the words came now.

"I love you too," he said and put one arm around her waist, pulling her close as he cradled their son in his other arm.

"Do you think he knows? About his sisters, I mean?" she asked after a moment.

"I think he can sense it," Lucas said gravely. "Look at him. He's already bracing himself."

Amelia laughed softly. "Sisters aren't always that bad."

Lucas looked up, love obvious in his eyes. "Not if you pick the right one," he said and pulled her down for a kiss.

ABOUT THE AUTHOR

Jessie decided to be a writer because there were too many lives she wanted to live to just pick one.

Taking her history degree dangerously, Jessie tells the stories of courageous heroines, the men who dared to love them, and the world that tried to defeat them.

Jessie makes her home in New Hampshire where she lives with her husband and two very opinionated Basset hounds. For more, visit her website at jessieclever.com.

Made in the USA
Monee, IL
02 November 2022

16998766R00146